AN INVISIBLE BETRAYAL

By Sam Burnell

Sam Burnell

For Mumm-Ra

CONTENTS

CHAPTER ONE 5
CHAPTER TWO 25
CHAPTER THREE 47
CHAPTER FOUR 71
CHAPTER FIVE 91
CHAPTER SIX 116
CHAPTER SEVEN 147
CHAPTER EIGHT 171
CHAPTER NINE 194
CHAPTER TEN 217
CHAPTER ELEVEN 234
CHAPTER TWELVE 246
CHAPTER THIRTEEN 280
CHAPTER FOURTEEN 300
CHAPTER FIFTEEN 322
CHAPTER SIXTEEN 352
CHAPTER SEVENTEEN 371
CHAPTER EIGHTEEN 400
CHAPTER NINETEEN 424
CHAPTER TWENTY 452
CHAPTER TWENTY-ONE 475
CHAPTER TWENTY-TWO 500

CHAPTER TWENTY-THREE 514

CHAPTER TWENTY-FOUR 532

CHAPTER TWENTY-FIVE 551

CHAPTER TWENTY-SIX 570

CHAPTER TWENTY-SEVEN 606

CHAPTER ONE

London – April 1553

It was late, the weather cold, and London was waiting for the hours to pass until the sun dragged the wet city into another day. All the print shops in the street were shuttered and silent except for one. Weak light leaked around the edges of the closed shutters and from under the bottom of the door. Thin lines of illumination marked the shop as in use. The press was silent, the repetitive narrative of thump and grumble absent.

"Are you finished yet?" Preston called from his workshop at the back of the print shop. He was a short, squat man with wiry grey hair sprouting from his ears, nose and escaping from around the edge of his closely fitting cap. Threads from the fraying cuffs and collar added to his scarecrow-like image. Any neatness he once possessed had forsaken him when his wife succumbed to the sweating sickness taking with her their only child.

"Yes, it's ready," Hester replied, indicating the banked plate with the tightly set lines of leaded dye letters. Hester, younger and attired in a dark leather jerkin, woollen hose and sturdy boots, was an image of precision in contrast to Preston's chaotic appearance. The only slight imperfection being a thin white scar that severed his right eyebrow into two halves.

Preston crossed the print room, collecting a candle. He stooped over the plate, examining it. Furrowed lines appeared between his spouting brows as he ran his eyes over the work. "Run a print from it and bring it to my desk. I'll check it to the original. When you've done that, there's another sheet that needs setting up; you can collect it when you bring me this print."

"But we agreed I could use the press once I'd finished!" Hester exclaimed in dismay, flinging his arms wide as he spoke.

"Well, you haven't finished yet, have you?" Preston grumbled, turning to leave the front of the print shop.

"If it's the same as the one I've just done, it will take me half the night to complete. I'll have no time left," Hester persisted, following the printer.

"That's not my fault, is it? I pay you to set letters, so set them," Preston threw back over his shoulder as he shuffled towards his workshop.

"You pay me half what it would cost to employ an apprentice, and our agreement was I could use the press at night," Hester's temper was rising. The blue eyes that laid upon Preston's back were burning with fury.

"Get this last sheet set, and this is all yours," Preston waved an arm airily around the print shop.

"No. We had an agreement," Heston leapt forward to stop Preston's departure. The corner of a banked tray of letters was intent on stopping his advance, catching in his sleeve. Hester lurched forward, his balance lost; he fell, and the tray, still snagged by the linen, was wrenched from the top of the bench. Each of the small compartments began to empty. The lead dyes, ink-stained and dull, drummed on the floor like hail.

"Look what you've done!" Preston's eyes were wide. His arms outstretched uselessly towards the falling letters. "Stop them!"

On his hands and knees, Hester crawled across the floor, away from the cascade. Letters had caught in the creases in his clothes, in the fold at the top of his boots, were captured by the linen cuffs of his shirt and were rolling from his back. Empty, the wooden rack, unbalanced now, tumbled to join the printer's letters on the floor.

"You fool!" Preston grabbed the tray. Turning it, he gave an audible moan of despair when his eyes met the dozens of empty sockets where the dyes should have rested. "This is your doing. I don't care if it takes you all night. This tray will be set to rights, and if any of them are damaged, you'll be paying for new ones. Do you hear me?"

Hester, rising from the floor, shedding letters, glared at Preston. "We had an agreement."

"I don't care what you think we had. You are responsible for this …."

Hester waded through the lead, like nails on a smith's floor.

"Don't stand on them, you fool!" Preston had his hands in front of him to stop Hester's progress.

Hester didn't stop. His boots on the angular lead, they cut into the boards as he trod on them. A fist took hold of Preston's apron, pulling him close. "You'll get to your knees. God's words will not be stilted."

Preston tried to pull from the hold. Hester's other hand fastened around his hairy throat, the nails digging hard into the skin. "We had an agreement. One made before God."

"Please .... stop .... you're hurting me?" Preston whimpered, his fingers trying to break Hester's hold, and failing.

Hester ignored him, tightening his grip he added his left hand to reinforce the pressure. "We had an agreement, old man."

"I'll help, please .... stop ...." Preston pleaded; Hester slackened his hold. "What do you want me to do?"

Another hour, and he'd be done. Galveston sat back in his chair, stretched out his aching spine and watched the ink on the completed ledger page dry. The last entry was from a doleful little man called Hal Cooper, who paid a weekly pittance to reduce the debt he owed. Galveston was pretty sure the debt would never be paid in full, Cooper, bent-backed and shuffling with age, was unlikely to live long enough. Why his employer had agreed to such terms, he couldn't understand. Myles Devereux was not noted for his acts of kindness. He was sure there would be more to it; there had to be. It could be that Cooper was supplying Devereux with information, he was loosely attached to Norfolk's household, and that might provide the answer.

Galveston blew on the page, satisfied it was completely dry, he dipped his pen back into the ink and inscribed the date in the book.

'15th April 1553'

Beneath it, he wrote the name Anne Hesketh and the carried forward balance next to it. It was a lot of money. The poor woman had borrowed from Devereux to extricate her idiot son from Marshalsea, not that it had done her a lot of good. The boy had been free of debtor's gaol for less than a month before incautious gambling had seen him back inside there again. Anne Hesketh had then been forced to borrow more to extricate him for a second time.

Galveston had been there when she'd dropped to her knees before Devereux and begged him to take her son on. Devereux had done it before, paid for men's release from Marshalsea, and they were now in his employ. But they were men like Drew Bent and Haddy Marlow, hard men with souls as cold as river ice at Michaelmas. Anne's son was a useless lanky lad who the farrier in Brinkton Street had turned off for idling, and it wasn't likely Devereux would have a use for him, and he had told her as much. But he had loaned her the money to pay off her son's debt.

Hal Cooper was the next entry, a small debt owed by a broke-back man who tended the graves at St Bride's church. Then Alun White, a man Galveston disliked. He was the landlord of the King's Head in Wall Street, a dire inn with a reputation for poor food, terrible accommodation and watery ale. It was, however, near the pig market, and White made his money from those trading there who needed housing and food and didn't know any better. The pig market was notorious for brawls, fights, and pickpockets, and the King's Head Tavern, the closest alehouse to the market, was the scene of many such incidents. White paid Devereux to ensure his staff weren't knifed, his property wasn't ransacked, and his customers paid their bills. Amongst his clientele when the markets ran were a good quantity of Devereux's men ensuring a relative degree of harmony at the King's Head and removing those who sought to disrupt it. As such, he wasn't a debtor but paid his dues monthly to Devereux to ensure the smooth running of the tavern.

The following three entries were for small debts on money loans Devereux had made; there were hundreds of similar loans made during the year. Small amounts needed to pay off a debt, cover the cost of a burial, a wedding, to buy tools or much-needed clothes. Devereux would supply the money required, they would foolishly agree to his terms, and then their names would be added to the ledgers, and they would find themselves paying Devereux more than they wanted to for longer than they had imagined. The delight men took in loans was as short-lived as a spark from an anvil.

Galveston laid his pen down; he could feel the familiar pain beginning to gather behind his eyes. He knew it was working by candlelight that made his eyes ache, the lighter summer evenings seemed a long and distant memory. It was time to get his clerk, Peter, to start completing the ledgers for him. The lad's hand was steady and neat enough, and he was quick, and if Galveston was honest with himself, he probably made fewer mistakes than he did.

But change was the issue.

Devereux was no fool, he'd recognise that there was a change in the penmanship in the ledgers, and he would know it was likely to be Peter. If Devereux had the slightest doubt in his abilities and thought for a moment that Galveston was getting too old for the job, he knew that he'd be replaced in a moment. Devereux didn't tolerate weakness in anyone.

And, of course, there was the other problem. Galveston looked at the remaining unused pages in the ledger, he was about two-thirds of the way through. Perhaps he'd get Peter to complete the entries when this one was filled. If he began at the start of a new volume, Devereux may not notice the change in writing.

Galveston rubbed his eyes, and stretched out the tight muscles in his neck before opening them again and lifting the pen from the table. A few more lines and he would be finished.

In the morning, two of Devereux's men would arrive as they did every Friday, and he'd take the ledgers and spend the day in the White Hart Tavern, recording those who came to pay their debts and those who wished to take out new loans.

Galveston frowned.

Outside the door, he heard the unmistakable noise of the tread of footsteps on the stairs rising towards his office. Peter had left hours ago; he'd closed the door on the boy when he'd gone, and he was sure he'd dropped the latch into place.

The footsteps continued to rise up the stairs. Slowly.

Maybe Peter had come back?

Or one of Devereux's men?

Devereux had no respect for the time of day or privacy when it came to his business.

The footsteps continued.

Who was it?

It certainly wasn't Peter. He bounced up the stairs, taking them two at a time; it was not him.

There was nobody else in the building apart from himself. Downstairs was a cobbler's shop, closed now, and it had its own entrance, and they had no direct access to the rooms above occupied by Galveston. Above his office was the room that he occupied when he wasn't working in his office. Nobody else was in the building, and he was sure he'd locked the door when Peter had left earlier that evening.

The footsteps stopped.

It seemed like a long time before there was a knock on the door.

Devereux's men wouldn't knock on the door; they'd haul it open, armed with their master's arrogance and place their demands.

The knock repeated.

Galveston partly rose from behind the desk.

"Hello," Galveston said in a voice that shook slightly.

There was no reply.

"Hello, Peter, is that you?" Galveston said, a little firmer, needing to say something and not wanting to sound afraid.

The knock came again for the third time.

Oh, for God's sake. Stop acting like a fool!

"Come in. Who is it?" Galveston said, his voice a little firmer.

The handle dipped, and the door opened.

Galveston's shoulders relaxed, and he let out a tense breath. "What are you doing here? I thought you were coming on Saturday?"

"I just wanted to have a quick word in private," his visitor said, not closing the door behind him

A movement in the open doorway caught Galveston's eye, his brow furrowed. "Who's with you?"

"A friend," the man said, stepping towards Galveston.

Galveston tilted his head to look past him at the man in the doorway. He was armed with a long knife, bare thick veined forearms showed in the dim light, his head was shaved, and an ugly scar twisted the corner of his left eye towards his mouth. And the mouth .... it was set into a chilling leer that bore nothing of welcome or friendship.

Galveston felt a sudden chill run down his back, swallowing hard he returned his gaze to the man standing before him. "What do you want?"

"I need more, I told you that," the man said, banging a fist down on the desk.

"I don't know what you mean, I've been helping you. Like I said I would," Galveston replied, the tremor returning to his voice.

The man let out a long breath. "All I want is for God's true word to be heard, but so much lies in the way …. like you."

CHAPTER TWO

Myles Devereux, ignoring his tailor, who was fussing and smoothing the fabric of his sleeves, stared from his window over the rooftops of London. Devereux was known to be a distant cousin of the Earl of Devon, Edward Courtenay. The link might be distant, but Myles ensured that the fact remained in the forefront of the men's minds, and he dressed accordingly.

He wasn't a man who had a liking for anyone to be too close to him, and the ministrations of Master Drew, his tailor, were beginning to gnaw at the edges of his nerves.

One of his clients once described Devereux as 'angular' in appearance and demeanour. Unfortunately, the statement had been made within his hearing, and the opinion had been one the client had deeply regretted.

But it was one Myles secretly liked. Angular!

His tongue was sharp, his mind agile, his justice swift and his rules amongst his men were unbroken. If that was angular, then so be it. His face was delicate, pale and defined, with high cheekbones below dark eyes and narrow severe brows and could very well be described as angular. He didn't care; he'd been called a lot worse.

His clothing matched, luxurious, crisp, and always neat. Myles Devereux was as well preened as cats' fur. There was nothing careless about Myles Devereux, and if angular was the opposite of slovenly, then he was happy.

"There, Master Devereux, I think the doublet is a perfect fit after the adjustments you so rightly pointed out that needed attending to," Master Drew said, taking a quick step back from his customer.

Myles Devereux's eyes scanned the doublet sleeves, repressing a smile. Thick black velvet slashed to reveal a dark blue that hinted at royal purple when he twisted his arm and the light on the fabric changed. The effect was created by the deep red silk that lined the slashes, creating an illusion of the banned colour. The double row of gold buttons down the front, that Master Drew had fastened for him, held rubies that matched the silk.

"Next time, ensure the measurements are right to begin with, I'm busy, Drew, and I've little time to spare on the whims of my tailor," Myles said, a scowl fixed on his features for the benefit of his tailor.

Master Drew bowed and spoke as if addressing the floor. "Of course, Master Devereux, my sincere apologies. The error was mine, and I will ensure it doesn't happen again."

Myles waved a ringed hand towards the door. Master Drew flapped his arms at his assistant, and a pile of cloth samples, packs of pins and tape were swept up from Devereux's desk, and the tailor and his assistant quickly exited.

Myles watched the door close before returning his gaze to his sleeves and allowing a pleased smile to brighten his features. It wasn't just the new doublet that was the cause of his good mood, it was Friday, and Myles Devereux liked Fridays.

It was not for any reason related to the end of a week of toil. It was the simple fact that Friday was a day of opportunity. Debts were collected throughout the week by his men with his book-keeper in tow, but on Friday, the petitioners came to him. Some to settle debts, but in the main, to take out new loans. Matthew vetted those who queued to gain admittance to the rooms above the White Hart, where Devereux carried out his illicit commerce. If they had information that might be of interest to Devereux or if Matthew judged their business to be worthwhile, then they were admitted. The rest were turned back out onto the street.

It was an efficient process. There wasn't time to go through every man's case, and Matthew was a good judge.

The opportunities were myriad. Devereux discovered much of what had happened in the city before it became common knowledge, and this was where the profit was to be made. Last year, just before Christmas, his tailor, Master Drew, had arrived in a flurry of creased silk and woe. He had just heard that the *Saint Louise* had been lost at sea on her way from Bruges, taking with her to the bottom of the English Channel the resupply of damask and silk. Drew had wanted money to buy what material was left in London before the news spread, and the prices flew skyward like surprised pigeons from a courtyard. What cloth there was in London was secure in Devereux's stores before the bells struck for prime. It had turned one gold Angel into five. Christmas at Court was a costly affair, and new clothes a requirement. Those wishing for new attire had been forced to pay a premium and be grateful.

Then, Aiden Murray arrived one Friday desperate to borrow money after a fire had left him and his family homeless. Depson's warehouse, behind his home, had burnt to the ground taking with it a large quantity of barrel staves. Needless to say, what staves could be sourced from elsewhere was soon in the possession of a new owner. And when the pond at the back of St Mary's in Cheap Street had overflowed and washed out Jessop Smalt's bakery and several print shops as well, so the streets had run black with dye, Devereux had dispatched men to buy up every available pot of ink they could acquire and set them in the storerooms at the back of the White Hart.

Fridays could be lucrative and kept him in touch with what was happening in his city.

Myles indeed liked Fridays.

It was also an opportunity to check that the rest of his business was running as it should. Matthew spent the week trailing around the city with his complaining book-keeper, Galveston, in tow, collecting and recording Devereux's dues. Then, on Friday, Galveston provided a final accounting of who had and hadn't paid. He was lucky; at the moment, he had very few debts that were not being repaid. Last year would have been exemplary if the shit Partha Crinnion had not decided to throw a rope over a beam and hang himself.

Crinnion owed Devereux two pounds and had been repaying his debt steadily and on time. What really riled Devereux was that he'd hanged himself on the day his next payment was due. Crinnion had left nothing, no family, and there had been nothing Devereux could use to set against his debt. It was actions like this you just couldn't plan for. After the incident with Crinnion, he found himself staring into the eyes of those wanting to take out loans, searching them for a spark of madness hiding somewhere in their depths. A repeat of that incident he didn't need. Striking a line through Crinnion's name in the ledger and watching his money disappear had been an almost physical pain - and one he had no intention of repeating.

On Friday, he was on show. London got to see the Myles Devereux that he wanted them to view. Cold, ruthless, faultlessly dressed and intimidating. Wearing Master Drew's latest creation, he sat behind his desk, waiting for the tap on the door from Matthew that would tell him Galveston had arrived and that the ledger was ready for review.

Myles tugged the sleeve on his right arm down a little further. Drew knew the length he liked but seemed to find that it was against his professional standards to comply, and despite constant complaint, they remained just a little too short. The black band of the sleeve wrapped around his hand, and the line of heavy gold rings that ran across his fingers made a pleasing contrast.

The rings were trophies, all of them had belonged to men of note, and none of them should have ended up gracing the fingers of Myles Devereux. His favourite among them bore a crest easily identified as that of the Duke of Norfolk. Devereux had never had dealings with the Duke, and the ring had found its way to him after being used as a prize in a card game. But no one needed to know that, and it was better if those who saw it just wondered.

The rings on his left hand were plainer. In the middle was one he had liked, crested with a large ruby, until he saw another that made his look clumsy and small in comparison. Myles had a mind to make the owner give it to him, but as yet, he hadn't quite worked out how he might do that. It would look better on his hand than on the current owner's.

The church bells rang for terce.

They were late.

Galveston was always on time.

Myles toyed with a wine glass, thought for a moment about filling it, then pushed it impatiently away. He needed a clear head on Fridays.

Never, ever make a deal with a head full of wine. It was one of his own rules, and he stuck to it. Although he had no qualms at all about striking deals with those who had taken a glass or two too many. If men were fool enough to make of themselves easy pickings, who was he to let the opportunity pass him by?

Myles was pulling down his left sleeve again when he heard a door slam shut. It was the outer door at the top of steps that led down into the open tavern room of the White Hart.

Myles' brow creased, and his eyes fastened on the closed door, trying to hear what was happening outside.

He could hear Matthew's low growling voice, pitched not to carry, but the words he couldn't make out. A chair or table scraped on the floor. The outer door opened and rapidly closed a second time, although not with the vigour of the earlier slam.

Myles rose from the desk, rounded it and stood close the door.

Listening.

He couldn't open the door. That wasn't how the game was played. Myles Devereux did not burst in on altercations. That was Matthew's job. He could hear Matthew's voice still, low and quiet, the words rapidly spoken. The reply was a voice he didn't recognise, higher pitched, young, and shaking with nerves.

Clearly, something was wrong. That Matthew hadn't ejected the youth down the stairs by now said something.

Myles heard boots approaching the door he stood behind and had just enough time to take a quick step backwards before it was pulled open by Matthew.

"Galveston's clerk has just arrived. He said the book-keeper is dead," Matthew announced without preamble. Matthew's muscled frame filled the doorway, wearing, as he always did, a dark leather jerkin held closed with five buckles across his broad chest. Around his hips, a wide belt housed two thick-bladed knives, and a sword belt, currently empty, strapped over this. A chin of neatly clipped greying whiskers made up for a bald head, that was capped with a plush leather bonnet. If the setting was other than the White Hart he could have been taken for a soldier, but everyone knew Matthew as Devereux's man.

Myles stared at him momentarily, then shifted his gaze beyond Matthew to where the youthful speaker stood in the outer room, his face pale, arms wrapped tightly around his body and visibly shaking. The boy looked about sixteen, his lower cheeks bearing a sparse sprout of youthful fuzz, his feet wore clogs and his hose were a tapestry of repairs. The cloak hanging from shaking slender shoulders was a dark respectable fustian, the hem and collar bearing the same evidence of repeated neat needlework.

Myles shifted his gaze back to Matthew. "Dead?"

"Allegedly so, Peter Smythe," Matthew gestured towards the youth, "is his clerk. He says he found him this morning in his office. Dead."

Myles pushed past Matthew. "Dead? How?"

Peter Smythe bent his head and looked at the floor. "I just found him on the floor, he's …. there's …."

"Oh, for the Lord's sake! There's what?" Myles said, exasperated, advancing on the boy.

"It's on his .... I mean sir, there's .... I just ...." Peter's stuttering sentence rambled to a halt.

"Look at me, not the bloody floor, boy," Myles commanded, folding his arms and glowering at Peter.

With evident difficulty, Peter hauled his eyes from the floor, managing to look as far up as Devereux's knees, and there his gaze stopped.

Devereux rolled his eyes.

"Master Devereux said, look at him, you insolent little shit," Matthew's leather-gloved hand grasped hold of Peter's face under the chin and forced his head up so his eyes met those of Myles. The boy's face was filled with fear. Matthew released his hold, and the boy remained where he stood.

"Tell me," Myles said, his dark eyes boring into the blinking tear filled ones of Galveston's clerk.

Peter swallowed hard. "I went this morning when I opened the door and Master Galveston was on the floor, next to his desk?"

"How do you know he was dead?" Myles continued.

Peter shook his head. "I dunno, he wasn't moving."

"He wasn't moving," Myles repeated Peter's unsatisfactory words.

"No, master," Peter stammered.

"Are you sure he's not blind drunk?" Myles said, his eyes narrowing.

Peter shook his head rapidly.

"Why not?" Myles demanded.

"There's blood on his face, here," Peter's hand shot up to his own face, his fingers resting on his right cheek.

"Did you not try and rouse him?" Myles pressed, his fine brows furrowing, an annoyed note in his voice.

Peter shook his head rapidly, his gaze dropping down over again.

"Did it look like someone had broken in?" Myles continued, leaning down in an attempt to look into the boy's face.

Peter shook his head and stammered. "I don't know, master."

"For God's sake! Matthew, take this idiot with you and find out what has happened," Myles commanded, switching his attention from the boy.

Matthew, a hand on the small of Peter's back, propelled him towards the door to the stairs. "Wait outside, and don't bloody move."

The door closed, and Matthew turned to Myles. "I think you'd better come as well. We need to find out what's happened. If he is dead, then the Sheriff will be involved, and it might be wise if we get there before they do. Don't you think?"

Myles' skin was suddenly alabaster against the black velvet. "The ledger!"

"Exactly. The damned ledger," Matthew repeated, already heading towards the door.

CHAPTER THREE

Devereux's men were known locally as Devereux's dozen. It wasn't known whether there were actually a dozen and whether its contingent was static or not. But what was known was that Myles Devereux never left the White Hart without them. Roused to action by Matthew's rough tongue, the group were hastily assembled in the yard of the White Hart, mounted and armed, and ready to follow their master through London.

Galveston occupied two floors above the cobbler's shop, and the local residents saw Devereux's arrival, along with his men. In the narrow confines of Poultney Street, leather-capped heads popped out of windows, linen-coifed women lowered baskets and stared at the oncoming men, apprentices with floppy felt bonnets gawped until a curse sent in their direction caused them to scurry away. Matthew along with a reluctant and pale Peter Smythe entered the building while Myles, still astride his horse, waited impatiently in the street.

Matthew reappeared quickly and beckoned for Devereux to follow; the rest of the men were deployed as a guard on the door.

Myles grumbling, dropped from his saddle, discarding the reins that were collected by one of his men and strode into the doorway, following Matthew from the street.

"Well?" Myles demanded of Matthew's back as he followed him up the creaking, narrow stairs.

"He's dead alright," Matthew announced, turning a corner in the stairs and disappearing from Myles' sight for a moment.

"For God's sake! How?" Myles quickened his pace to catch up with Matthew.

"See for yourself," Matthew held the door open to Galveston's office, and Myles moved past him.

Myles had been in Galveston's office before, but that had been a long time ago, perhaps three years ago, when he started working for him. Myles' brother had found the book-keeper, and as part of the process of appointing him he had visited his offices. It had been no accident that their paths had crossed. Galveston was in debt, having invested unwisely in a ship's cargo. The ship and his capital were languishing at the bottom of the sea. Foolishly he had tried to use what little he had left at the card tables to win back enough to cover his debts, but that had only worsened the situation. He had been ousted from the firm he worked for, which did not want their reputation tarnished by having debtors among their clerks. His debts had been settled in a fashion by Devereux, and the book-keeper worked for him for a pittance in return.

It seemed, however, that the boy had been right. His book-keeper was indeed exhibiting the features of a corpse, the pallid skin a mottled white and grey, the lips now bloodless and one cheek, as the boy had described, crimson with still drying blood.

Myles extended a foot and kicked the corpse. The body was solid, unyielding.

"He's been dead a while," Matthew, folding his arms, come to stand next to him, "the rigor is still upon him."

Myles stepped over the body and peered at the face of his employee. What had killed him was pretty obvious: a cut on his head had leaked blood, streaking his face, but the finality of death had been delivered by the knife impaled in his chest. Myles leaned closer. The blade was wholly embedded into Galveston, only the hilt showing.

Matthew dropped to his knees next to the corpse, his hands on Galveston; he pushed hard at the body. "God's bones, they've nailed him to his own floor!"

Matthew pushed harder. Myles stepped back. There was the sound of splintering wood, and a moment later, the body rolled onto its side. Galveston's guts, disturbed by the movement, sent a wave of gas erupting from his mouth, the sound rattling his vocal cords for one last time, and the corpse emitted a feral groan.

Peter Smythe yelped, jumping backwards he banged into the wall behind him.

"He's dead, lad. It's just a death growl," Matthew's said without looking up from examining the blooded blade that had been impaled in the flooring. "They've used more force than was needed."

Myles leaned over, long fingers on the end of the knife hilt. "That knife has been hammered into him. Even if he'd fallen backwards, the knife wouldn't have impaled itself in the floor. Look, the finials are even pressing his rib cage inwards."

"Poor bastard! Knifed in the chest then pinned to his own floor, and alive by the looks of it," Matthew pointed towards Galveston's hand.

Devereux leaned over and looked at Galveston's right hand. It was still clenched, the fingers arched, and the nails broken and snapped where they had clawed at the floor.

Myles' brow creased. "Wouldn't he have tried to pull the blade from him?"

"He couldn't," Matthew pulled up Galveston's sleeve, and an ugly bruise. "I'd guess someone planted their foot on his wrist, pinning it to the floor while they battered that knife through him."

Myles looked down at Galveston's other hand. It lay empty, palm up, but two of the fingers were at an impossible angle, broken. "And this one as well, by the looks of his hand."

Matthew stood and looked down at the wreckage of Galveston. "It's possible it was one man who did this, but I doubt it. Trapping both of his hands beneath your boots would be a difficult task."

"Why?" Myles said, bending over Galveston to look closer at the smashed fingers.

"Dying men, in my experience, tend to thrash like a fish on a line," Matthew said. He was turning back and moving towards the door. "I would reckon he was hit here and fell backwards. Then, when he was on the floor, they pinned his arms down, and one of them drove the knife so far into him it pierced the floor."

Myles crossed his arms and stared down at the dead man with a look of consternation. "He'd die quickly with that driven through him. I am guessing they pinned him down, broke his hands, threatened him with the knife before they impaled him."

Matthew nodded in agreement.

"Which means this wasn't robbery. Someone wanted him to suffer or wanted to learn something from him," Myles said, his voice suddenly quiet.

"I think you are right," Matthew came to stand next to his master.

Myles turned his head, his eyes locking momentarily with Matthew's, "Do you think this is Bennett's work?"

Garrison Bennett was Myles Devereux's chief rival in the city.

"It could be," Matthew moved towards the desk, his back to Myles.

"Here it is," Matthew had turned and held up the ledger. Myles instantly recognised it as the one Galveston brought to the White Hart each week. It held the details of the men and women of London who owed Myles Devereux money. "If it was Bennett, he wouldn't have left this, would he?"

"At least the shit wasn't robbed of that," Myles shoved a soft leather riding boot into the corpse's side again and added, "Is there anything else we should take?"

Matthew's gaze shifted to Peter, standing with his back to the wall, his eyes fixed on the floor, shaking. "You, are there more records here?"

Peter took a moment to respond. "That box, the one on the floor there, master."

Matthew pointed towards a dark oak joined coffer, the frieze design on the front roughly hand carved. "This one?"

Peter nodded. "Master Galveston keeps all his records in there."

Matthew tried to lift the oak lid. "Where's the key?"

Peter swallowed. "Master Galveston keeps it on a chain .... around his neck."

Matthew grumbling, dropped to his knees next to the corpse, pulling the stained shirt open. It only parted so far, the knife hilt pinning the material to the wearer. Wrapping a fist around the chain, Matthew yanked it hard, separating the links. On the end were two keys.

"The …. largest one…." Peter stammered; his voice held the shrill edge of nerves.

Matthew slid the key into the lock and lifted the oak lid, Myles moving closer to him to view the sparse contents. Two smaller ledgers and a leather bag were all that it contained.

"These are the ones Galveston takes with him when we do the rounds, and that's the collection bag," Matthew said, lifting out the leather bag. The sound of coins shifting inside it was unmistakable.

"There's nothing else?" Myles placed the question to the room in general.

"It should just be that ledger and the ones in here. Those are the only records Galveston keeps," Matthew replied, pocketing the coin bag.

"Boy, is there anything else?" Matthew directed his question towards Peter.

Peter pointed towards the desk. "The Thursday book …."

"What?" Myles said, his eyes following the direction Peter gestured.

Matthew swiped the book from the desk. "Galveston uses these when we collect the dues."

"Nothing else?" Myles snapped at Peter.

Peter shook his head rapidly.

"He has a room above this office. I'll check in there," Matthew said, striding towards the doorway.

Myles' long fingers slid over the few items on the desk. There was nothing of interest. It held the detritus of Galveston's work, broken pens, empty ink pots and stubs of sealing wax. Nothing of value, and nothing that would hint at why a man lay dead on the floor. It was largely undisturbed by what had happened in the room. Galveston's chair was still upright behind it; a pen was laid next to an open inkpot. It looked like he had laid it down when his assailants entered the room. The stopper for the ink was next to the open pot.

Matthew returned quickly.

"Anything there?" Myles asked, looking up and rubbing the dust from his fingers.

Matthew shook his head. "Yesterday's slops, that's about it."

Myles' eyes ran slowly around the room. "We should report this to the Justices."

Matthew's head snapped up. "Are you sure?"

"Yes, we report it as a robbery. Galveston was working late. Some malcontent has broken in and robbed him. I don't want the city believing that my book-keeper has been targeted and may, before he died, have divulged a few secrets, do I?" Myles said. "Report it to the Justice first. Who is the Justice for this area?"

"Daytrew," Matthew replied bleakly.

Myles rolled his eyes. "If you cut him, he'd leak self-importance."

"Daytrew will have to get the Sheriff involved," Matthew said, his hand tugging at his beard.

"Agreed, but there's no rush, is there. Let's gift this little mess to Daytrew first and see what he can make of it," Myles said, slipping his hands back into his riding gloves.

"Fair enough. We'd best make it look like a robbery," Matthew scanned the room.

"Move him over here," Myles pointed to a clear piece of floor before the desk. Matthew, a boot on Galveston's chest, withdrew the knife so it was no longer protruding from his back and, grunting hauled the body across the floor. Myles examined the area where Galveston had laid. Fresh white spikes of wood showed where the boards had been bruised by the knife, surrounded by a sticky patch of blood. "That'll need to go as well."

Myles watched as Matthew ground his boot onto the splinters before using his knife, cutting a strip of fabric from the chair seat, and using it to rub the blood from the floor. It wasn't a large patch, but his efforts made the appearance worse. The blood was nearly dry and refused to be removed from the wood.

"For God's sake! Move," Myles snatched an inkpot from the desk, discarding the stopper on the floor; he poured it over the stain and dropped the pot on the floor. "Search the room, bring anything back you think we need and report this to Daytrew, and make the rest of the room look like it's been ransacked. And don't let him," Myles pointed a long straight ringed finger towards Peter, "Out of your sight."

The boy paled.

Devereux returned to the White Hart and stomped moodily up the stairs and into the outer room. It was Friday, and it should have been full of people. Galveston should have been seated at his small table, ledger before him and with a money box next to it. Behind him, to ensure fair play, would be two of his men, and Matthew would be stood at the back of the room supervising admittance.

And now it was empty.

One of his men stood guard at the top of the stairs, and a number of petitioners waited downstairs in the White Hart tavern. They'd have to let them up as soon as Matthew arrived back with the ledgers. Business had to carry on. Galveston's clerk, with Matthew's guidance, could complete the ledger – he'd not let the bastards think they were getting away without paying their dues this week.

With Peter in tow and three of his men, Matthew arrived in the room. They had the large ledger from Galveston's desk, the two from the oak coffer and the 'Thursday book', along with the leather coin bag.

"You," Myles pointed at the chair Galveston would normally use, "Sit there."

Peter nervously pulled the chair out and lowered himself into it.

"You can take Galveston's place. Matthew will keep you right, and he'll handle the money. All you have to do is write down the amounts in the ledger, no need to work out the balances. We can do that later. Just note down the payments. Matthew will tell you how much. You can do that, can't you?" Myles said to Peter.

"Yes, master," Peter confirmed.

"Give him the ledger and pen and ink," Myles said distractedly.

Matthew banged down the larger books of account they had brought from Galveston's and went to collect pen and ink.

"Master ...." Peter said, the ledger open before him.

Both men ignored him. "Get them organised downstairs. You know who owes the most, get them up here first ...."

"Master ...." Peter tried again.

"Hold your tongue when Master Devereux is speaking," Matthew raised his hand, the threat clear, and Peter cowered over the desk.

"If there are any complaints get the men to deal with it, have another four in the tavern room. We want this to look like a normal day. Have you reported it to Daytrew?"

Matthew nodded. "I've sent a man to his office."

"Good, no doubt the lazy shit will be making his way here later today. When he does, let me know," Myles said. "Now get them up here."

"Master, please ...." Peter's voice was high pitched.

Myles turned on him. "What is it?"

"It's the ledger. Look," Peter's hands lay on either side of the opened book.

Myles stared in dismay at the ripped sheet of paper protruding from the spine.

"Just the last page?" Myles roughly grabbed the book and turned it towards him. His fingers on the bottom of the last remaining page. "The last entry is Wednesday, so it's just the entries for Thursday that are missing. There's no time to debate this now. Start at the top of the next page."

Myles flipped a page over to hide the remains of the ripped one and stabbed the top of the sheet. "Write the date here and record the names Matthew gives you underneath. Do you understand?"

CHAPTER FOUR

Myles didn't want to see anyone.

"Get their bloody money from them and get them out of here," Myles paced across the room, raking his hands through his hair and raising it into untidy spikes.

Matthew caught his arm, pulling Myles to a halt. "Be seen, be normal. Galveston is dead, the matter has been reported to the Justice, and it appears to have been a simple matter of robbery. You are annoyed by the bastard's inconsiderate act of getting himself murdered, and that's it. Let that be what they take away from here today and spread as gossip. Not that Myles Devereux's book-keeper has been murdered and that he's gone into hiding and his business is falling apart," Matthew still had a hand clamped on Devereux's upper arm, and he tightened his hold. "Are you listening to me?"

Myles didn't pull away. There was anger in his voice when he spoke. "I hear, damn you."

"Good. Then let everyone out there know how bloody annoyed you are that the shit, Galveston, has had the effrontery to get himself killed," Matthew said. When Myles nodded, he relinquished his hold.

Myles smoothed down his sleeve where Matthew's hand had crushed the cloth.

"As it happens, I am more than annoyed," Myles said through clenched teeth. "Why is there a page missing? Why has someone murdered Galveston and ripped a page from my ledger? It's Bennett. It has to be."

"It very well might be, and we will find out. But now it's business, and you need to deal with it," Matthew said, heading to the door, "I'll start sending them up."

Myles stared at the closing door and cursed. He'd better things to do than fraternise with London's poor and desperate. He was in no mood for them.

Friday lay in ruins, along with his good humour.

The answer, he was sure, was on the page that had been torn from the ledger. Galveston's clerk may have some idea about its contents, but he couldn't quiz him over that yet. Myles, his hands on the windowsill, stared without seeing across the rooftops of a gloomy London.

His reverie was broken when Matthew knocked and then opened the door, saying loudly for the benefit of not only Myles but those in the room behind him. "Master Devereux, Gaston Clegg would like to speak with you."

Myles cursed loudly.

Gaston Clegg was a pain in the arse! He owned a bakery in River Street, his boys delivered bread, and he paid Devereux to prevent anyone from selling in his area of London. It was a tactic that worked well, it gave his bakery more than its fair share of customers, and Clegg ran a profitable and busy enterprise, so much so that last year he had invested in more ovens and converted the shop next door into an extension of his bakery.

Myles took a long breath, stretched his back out and marched towards the door. The scene, on the other side, was one of organised efficiency. One of his men was herding Mistress Besswick from the room, her debt for the week paid, her business concluded, and only Master Clegg waited for him. No one else had been allowed in, providing Clegg with some privacy for his conversation with Devereux. Clegg was dressed more as a merchant than a baker, yet the dark cloak and fur-trimmed hat did not completely hide the evidence of his profession. Clinging to creases in his leather boots and powdered on his shoulders was the fine dust of his trade.

"Clegg! You do not find me in good humour today," Myles said as he stalked into the room. "Don't worsen it."

"I am sorry. Master Galveston was a good ...." Clegg said, sympathy in his voice.

Myles didn't let him finish. "He was a good-for-nothing shit who didn't have the foresight to lock his door at night. The bloody fool deserves to be robbed. It's a shame only that someone stole his last breath, for believe me, if he'd arrived here with tales of woe due to his own stupidity I would have taken it for him."

Clegg, for a moment, looked slightly taken aback. "Quite, I can see your point. Master Galveston did not live in one of the .... better parts of the city."

Myles leaned towards Clegg. "An open door in London is an invitation you don't want to make. How can I help you today?"

"Err .... Well, I wanted to discuss Munroe and Church Street," Clegg said hesitantly.

Devereux hitched himself up onto the edge of a table and regarded Clegg with cold eyes. "Why? Do you need directions?"

Clegg flushed. "I was wondering if .... It might be possible ...."

"Might be possible to what?" Myles replied, folding his arms across his chest and staring at Clegg.

"I was .... "

"Get to the point, Clegg," Myles snapped. "I can't read your mind."

"I'm having problems in those areas. One of my delivery carts was overturned last week," the words tumbled from Clegg's mouth, his powerful baker's hands crushing the fur of his hat as he twisted it in his grasp.

An evil smiled twisted Myles' lips. "I'd heard."

Clegg's eyes widened. "You did? Can you do something about it?"

"I did do something about it. You pay me to ensure your business runs smoothly, don't you?" Myles said, his tone impatient.

Clegg nodded, his grip on the hat tightening even more. "Of course."

"And so does Hector Feltham, and you were in his area, weren't you? If you had come to me first, then I could have advised you that trying to poach his customers was not a wise idea," Myles said regarding Clegg coldly.

"His customers .... " Clegg stammered uncertainty.

"Yes, his customers. You know Church Street is on the far side of the Parish, and that's the boundary of the area you requested me to protect, isn't it?" Myles replied quietly, a threatening note in his voice.

"Well, yes .... but now I have the new bakery, we have more capacity, and I wanted ...." Clegg tried.

"You wanted to expand your area, and I am afraid Feltham wants to protect his. You should have considered that before paying to have the new ovens built," Myles pointed out.

"But you lent me the money. You knew I couldn't ...."

"I knew nothing of what was in your mind, Clegg. I can't read men's thoughts," Myles said dryly, dropping back to his feet.

"But .... but without those areas, this was a wasted venture. I'll not make my money back," Clegg said, his anger boosting his confidence. "You should have told me you were working for Feltham."

"My business dealings are my own affair. If you've made an incautious decision, then that's not my fault, is it?" Myles said, taking two quick steps towards the baker, and making Clegg stumble backwards, then to Matthew Myles said. "Has he paid?"

Matthew nodded.

"Good, then get him out of here," Myles turned his back on Clegg and smiled as he heard the protesting baker being ejected from the room. Matthew pushed him into the arms of another of his men at the top of the stairs who would, he knew, ensure he left the White Hart in a hurry.

The smile was short-lived. There was a page missing from his ledger, and that fact was burning in Myles' brain. He suffered three more hours of torment before Matthew announced that the day's work was complete and that everyone who had come to the tavern had been dealt with in one way or another. Matthew had forced Myles to meet with two more men during the course of the day, and Myles provided them with similar accounts of his dissatisfaction with Galveston's demise and then finally the torture had ended.

"Get him out, and make sure he doesn't talk to anyone," Myles said, pointing towards Peter.

Finally, he was alone.

The door closed on Matthew, guiding Peter from the room. Letting out a long breath, Myles seated himself where the boy had sat all day and opened the ledger, turning the pages until he came to where the sheet had been torn out.

It was not a neat tear; at the bottom of the ledger, the page was missing from close to the spine, but the rip had run away from the centre, and at the top, a good three inches of the page remained. A ragged reminder of what had been there. The front of the torn sheet bore the remains of some of the entries Galveston had made. The back was completely blank, so evidently, the missing page had been incomplete.

Myles held the tattered remains flat, Galveston's habit was to note the first name and then the family name second.

At the bottom, "Cu" had to be Cuthbert, a common name, and Myles was sure he had at least three by that name who owed him money. Above him 'Ra' had to be Rankin, a stooped-backed man with a printshop and an unhealthy gambling habit. A above him could be Allen, Alwyn or Allison or even ....

Myles sat back in his chair. Bennett. This had to be him. Hearing the name Bennett was enough to sour Myles' mood. Both men had similar businesses in separate areas of the city, and there had been little friction until a year ago. The landlord of the Black Swan, had died owing Myles Devereux money, the inn was on the edge of an area controlled by Bennett, and the bastard had managed to produce legal evidence that the tavern was his. The Black Swan should have fallen under Devereux's control but that hadn't happened.

Bennett had won.

And that had not been the end of the matter.

Along the edges where their territories met, a growing conflict was taking place. In a street where Myles controlled a tavern, Bennett had forced out most of the small businesses, and the tavern and the street were now practically derelict. What had once been a thriving and lucrative business was, for the moment, dead.

Where Bennett used the threat of violence to ensure his wishes were complied with, Myles used cunning. Bennett owned a tannery, and Myles had diverted a stream two streets away to ensure that the next time a forceful rain hit the city, the runoff would head straight through the yard. Which it did with spectacular results. The tannery, on the banks of the Thames, was hit by the water and the entire back wall, along with a stock of cured and curing hides, were sent to a watery grave. The tannery had been out of action for weeks, and Bennett could prove nothing, although Myles suspected he would be attributing the act of God to his rival.

And so, it continued, the tension ever present where their businesses met, those disputed streets in the city where both operated. It was more than annoying. Myles had been happy with his portion of the city, and for years the two had existed in relative harmony until the issue of the Swan.

Was Bennett behind the murder of his book-keeper? If he was, Myles was sure Bennett would want him to know. After all, there wasn't much point in delivering a threat if the origin of it was unknown. But still, Myles' mind couldn't stop circling back to his name. It wasn't his style. Bennett wouldn't have murdered Galveston. He was more likely to have maimed and terrified him into packing up what he could in a hurry and leaving the city. That was more his style. Bennett was quite aware that, on occasion, murders did need to be accounted for, and the fewer there were, the better it was for his continued trade and existence. So, people generally disappeared, of their own volition, in a hurry.

And Galveston had been tortured. Which meant someone had wanted information from him or they had wanted him to suffer for some transgression.

There was a knock at the door.

Myles ignored it and returned his eyes to his ledger and the Al .... Allen, maybe or Allison. He turned the pages back over and found Ainswell listed amongst his clients. Above this was the letter C. That could belong to any number of names, Copeland, Cooper came to mind but there might ....

There was a second, more insistent knock immediately followed by the door opening and the appearance of Matthew's head around it.

"Not now," Myles growled.

"I'm afraid so. That useless fat arse Daytrew is here, you'll need to see him," Matthew advised quickly.

Myles rolled his eyes.

"I'll bring him up," Matthew didn't wait for a reply but disappeared behind the closing door.

Myles sent a curse towards it and slammed the ledger shut. It seemed everything was conspiring to prevent him from discovering what had happened to Galveston.

CHAPTER FIVE

There was a loud knock at the door that Myles recognised as Matthew's warning that Daytrew was about to arrive. A moment later, Matthew entered and behind him, his belly swaying beneath his gown, was Daytrew.

"Good afternoon to you, sir," Daytrew said, entering the room, his pig-like inquisitive eyes roving over Devereux's inner sanctum.

Myles inclined his head in acknowledgement but didn't reply.

It was Matthew who filled the void. "Justice Daytrew to see you, sir."

"I have been instructed by the Sheriff, Thomas Ofley, to investigate the murder of Master Ad-Hyce," Justice Daytrew announced with the gravity of a judge bestowing a death sentence, and ruining the effect by making a poor job of pronouncing the deceased's name.

Myles' supressed a grin, and instead, a confused look on his face he repeated Daytew's garbled words, "Ah-harth?"

"Yes, Master Galveston Ath-hanth," Daytew said, making a worse job of the name a second time.

Myles let Daytrew suffer a moment longer before he said, "Ah, Galveston Ad-Hyce. Of course, he was known simply as Master Galveston, he didn't use his family name, damnably hard to pronounce, from the Welsh perhaps, but who knows? I have heard of his death."

"More than heard. I believe you've been to his offices this morning," Daytrew said, straightening his shoulders and hauling the fabric of his gown upwards over his bulging midriff. Myles wondered idly how long it had been since the Justice had seen his feet.

Before Myles could reply, Matthew stepped forward. "Of course, Master Devereux has been there. Who do you think it was who reported his murder? His clerk arrived here in some confusion, and Master Devereux, concerned for Galveston, went straight to his offices. Naturally, as soon as he saw what had happened, he despatched a man to report the crime."

"Oh, I hadn't realised it was your man," Daytrew replied suddenly, a little crestfallen.

"What have you found out?" Myles said directly, his eyes fixed on the Justice's face.

"It does appear to have been a robbery, thieves have looted his offices, and Galveston seems to have been stabbed during a fight with them. These are sad times when a man is no longer safe in his home. I have yet to speak to his clerk, who you say found the body. No one seems to know where he is unless ...." Daytrew left the sentence unfinished.

"He's here," Matthew said quickly.

"Here?" Daytrew repeated, a frown rippling the fat on his forehead.

"Yes, here. He's a young lad, shocked by what he saw, and worried for his own safety, so we offered him our protection at the White Hart, and he was happy to accept. Matthew, why don't you go and fetch him," Myles said, his eyes locking with Matthew's for a moment, the message clear - if the boy was to be interviewed by Daytrew, then Myles would be present.

"It would be preferable if the boy could be brought to my offices," Daytrew tried. Matthew, his back to them, already had his hand on the door and was leaving the room.

"There's no need, talk to the lad here," Devereux said, uncertainty flitted across Daytrew's face. "Would you care for a glass of wine while we wait? I've just bought some new Gascon wine from the merchant who supplies the Court and I managed to persuade him to send a cask here. You can let me know what you think?"

"I would be delighted," Daytrew said, watching Devereux lift two glasses from a side table.

Myles, his back to the Justice, began pouring out a generous glass and turning, with a smile on his face, held it towards the fat man. "I think you'll appreciate it."

Daytrew sipped at the liquid, his face a study of concentration. "Indeed, delicious."

Myles tried to hide a look of disgust as Daytrew then tipped the glass back, and the contents sluiced down his throat.

"Another?" Myles asked as Daytrew lowered his head back from emptying the glass, his eyes meeting Myles'. Myles refilled the glass that Daytrew held towards him. By the time Matthew returned with Peter, Daytrew had just finished consuming his fourth glass, his upper lip was stained red with wine, and a dark splotch on the front of his gown told where a quantity had slopped from his meaty jowls.

"Ah, here we are," Myles announced as they entered. "Would you tell Justice Daytrew what happened before you came here this morning?"

Peter looked nervously between Daytrew and Matthew.

"Go on, boy, tell Justice Daytrew what you found!" Myles said, his voice filled with false empathy.

"There's not much to say. I went to Master Galveston's office this morning like I always do, the door was unlocked at the bottom of the stairs, and I let myself in and found him on the floor," Peter said. Matthew had clearly advised him precisely what he was to say before ushering him into the room.

"Was the door usually locked?" Daytrew asked, wiping the wine residue from his top lip with the back of his hand.

"Not always, sir. If Master Galveston had been out before I arrived, he usually left it open for me," Peter replied, his eyes fixed on the floor.

"Out where?" Daytrew asked.

"He'd sometimes go to Mistress Penny's at the end of the street to break his fast. If he'd been there, then he'd leave the door open, knowing I'd not be long in arriving," Peter replied. His hands had found the material of his cloak, and he was holding it in a white-knuckled grasp.

"Had he been there this morning?" Daytrew continued. He looked around for somewhere to deposit the empty glass.

"Allow me," Myles stepped forward and refilled Daytrew's glass, a false smile on his face as he watched the waste of wine pouring from the decanter.

Peter shrugged. "I don't know, sir."

"Sounds like that might be worth enquiring about," Myles said, depositing the decanter on a side table with a thud.

"Indeed," Daytrew acknowledged, then to the clerk, "Did you see anyone else?"

Peter shook his head. "There was no one else there."

"What about in the street? Anything unusual?" Daytrew asked before emptying the glass in one smooth movement, his top lip reddened again by the passage of the liquid.

"Nothing, sir. Just the usual people I see every day," Peter said.

"And who were those people?" Daytrew pressed, his small bright eyes buried deep in the flesh of his face were fastened on the boy.

Peter looked towards Matthew, the plea in his eyes clear.

"Just tell the Justice who you saw in the street," Matthew encouraged.

Peter nodded, relief evident on his face. "Handy the water seller was there, and Master Thomas the cobbler was setting his stall up outside his shop. I don't recall anyone else."

"Handy?" Daytrew queried.

"Aye, sir. I don't think it's his real name. We just call him that because he has one missing," Peter said, his eyes examining the floor again.

"One missing? One what?" Daytrew said, evident confusion in his voice.

"I would imagine," Myles drawled, "A hand?"

"That's right, sir, he doesn't have a left hand," Peter said, his fingers still tightly clasping the cloth.

"I see. A thief, then? Is he usually seen in the street? Did your master have any dealings with him?" Daytrew pressed.

"Handy was often around in the mornings. I've seen him a fair few times. My master's house had a well, so there was no need. He'd not buy from a water seller," Peter replied.

"Hmmm, well, I will have to track this man down, it shouldn't be too hard to find a water seller who's been branded as a thief," Daytrew said, sounding pleased with the results of his enquiry.

"Sounds promising," Myles said, trying to sound interested in this new evidence. "As a known thief, he could indeed be the robber."

"Don't worry, sir, we shall find him," Daytrew reassured, then asked Peter, "Do you know of anyone who might want to harm your Master?"

Peter shook his head fiercely. "No sir, he was a kindly man."

"Did you see anything unusual in the room? Did anything appear to be missing?"

"Here, let me fill that for you," Myles slopped more wine into Daytrew's empty glass, then to Matthew. "The justice appreciates fine wine."

"Thank you," Daytrew was forced to say, his attention leaving Peter.

"I don't think the lad stopped to look. He was so shocked by what he saw he ran all the way here. Isn't that right, Peter?" Matthew said on the boy's behalf.

"That's right, sir," Peter agreed quietly.

"What can you remember of the room where poor Master Galveston was?" Daytrew said, trying to regain some control over the conversation.

"Nothing much. I didn't stay, I've always been afraid of dead bodies, and I just ran here to tell Master Matthew what had happened," Peter's voice shook a little as he spoke.

"And you told us, didn't you, Peter, that the room looked like it had been raided in a hurry, and when we arrived, it certainly looked like a thief had been hunting for anything of value. Galveston obviously tried to stop them and, well …. The results are as you have seen yourself," Myles said, then added, "Poor man."

"It appears they might have found something of value, there is a coffer in Galveston's room, and the key was in the lock, and there was nothing inside. I can only assume the thief had taken what they found.

Do you know what Master Galveston kept inside, lad?" Daytrew said before slopping half of the glass of wine into his mouth.

Matthew cut in before Peter could answer. "I can tell you what was in there. As you know, Galveston worked for Master Devereux. He collected rents in for him weekly and then brought the money here on a Friday. So it looks like the thieves have stolen whatever he had collected this week. That's what will have been locked in the coffer."

"That would make sense," Daytrew said. "Would you know how much it might have been?"

"Galveston only collected a few minor rents, trifling amounts," Myles said, "Nothing to me, obviously, but a lot of money to a gutter thief."

"Would many people have known he kept the money in his offith?" Daytrew asked the room in general. There was, now, a decided slur to his speech.

"Well, that rather depends on how well he could keep the matter a secret," Myles said, topping up the Justices' glass, then addressing the boy, "Obviously, you knew. Would you say there would be others who were aware Galveston kept the money he collected in his office?"

"Aye, there would. Those who'd come to his office to make payment would see him lock away the money," Peter said.

"Could you tell me who those were? It would be good to make enquiries of these men firth," Daytrew said, punctuating his sentence with a hiccup that sent wine slopping over the rim of the glass to splat on the wooden boards.

"Of course, I can provide a list. Here, let me refill that for you," Myles glugged more wine into Daytrew's glass and watched as the base was swiped up and the glass swiftly emptied. "I don't have that information to hand, but give me a day or two, and I can have a list of those people sent to your office."

"Perhaps you might remember a few of the names?" Daytrew suggested, wiping the back of his hand across his mouth.

"I'm afraid it would be a guess. Master Galveston was my agent for these matters, and I would have to have records checked. Please, leave this with me, and I will send you a complete list by the end of tomorrow," Myles said firmly, upending the decanter and depositing the last of the Gascon wine into Daytrew's glass.

"That would be mothst helpful," Daytrew conceded, lowering the empty glass.

Myles caught Matthew's eye and glanced towards the door.

"Well, if that's all, Justice Daytrew, let me show you out. I will personally deliver Master Devereux's list to you as soon as we have it," Matthew said. Reaching forward, he plucked the glass from Daytrew's grasp, tucked an arm under his and began to guide him towards the door.

"Go via the stores and get Justice Daytrew a bottle of the Gascon we bought to take with him. It's a genuine privilege to meet a man who appreciates good wine," Myles said through clenched teeth.

"Sir, thath very kind," Daytrew slurred as Matthew continued to steer him towards the door to the stairs.

Myles watched him exit, and the door close on his back, slamming down the empty decanter. "Good bloody riddance."

Myles turned to Peter and eyed him closely. "You just lied to the Justice."

Peter inclined his head to one side. "Not about being scared of dead bodies, I didn't."

Myles grinned. "Really."

"Master Galveston was lying dead on the floor. The room looked like thieves had been through it. That's all I know, sir," Peter repeated the account again that Matthew had told him would be the only one he would ever utter.

"That sounds like an agreeable account. And we both know that Handy the water carrier wasn't branded a thief. God made him like that," Myles said.

Peter shrugged. "I didn't say he was, sir."

"No, you didn't. But you did let that fool Daytrew believe he'd found a possible culprit," Myles said; folding his arms, he regarded the boy with a solid gaze. "Now you help me, and you might get paid, or …. or not."

Myles let the threat hang in the air.

"If I can help with anything, sir. I did a good job recording the names and numbers today, I can be as good as Master Galveston was, and I know who owes what and on what day. I did all the rounds with Master Galveston when he was collecting money in," Peter provided. His hands still had a tight hold on the cloak, but he raised his eyes to meet Devereux's.

Myles picked up one of the day books Peter had called the Thursday book. "The writing in these, it's not Galveston's. Is it yours?"

Peter nodded. "I'd write down the names and amounts in there, then Master Galveston would write them up in the ledger later when he was back in his office."

Myles flicked through the book looking at the lines of tightly packed names and numbers. "When did he start doing this? As far as I knew, he took the ledger with him."

"Shortly after, I started working for him, sir. He said it was too heavy, and it got wet once we went out in the rain. If you look at the front few pages, the ink's run, we got caught in a downpour on St Mark's Street," Peter explained, pointing towards the ledger.

Myles put down one of the smaller books and picked up another, leafing through the pages. "You write very well. How long have you been working for Galveston?"

"A year, sir," Peter said quickly.

"The last page in the ledger is missing. Can you use these," Myles waved one of the day books in the air. "To recreate it?"

"Yes, sir," Peter said, nodding.

Myles opened the ledger, turning over the page Peter had been working on. He took the knife from his belt and drew it down the page, close to the spine, cutting the next sheet cleanly from the book. "Write the names and amounts on here."

Peter hesitated momentarily before relinquishing his hold on the cloth and taking the offered sheet.

"Sit your arse in that chair, and do it now," Myles deposited the three day books on the table. "I'll be in there. Knock when you've done it."

Myles collected the ledger and made to leave.

"Sir, I just need to know the last name on the page before the one that's missing,"

Myles put the ledger down and found the entry. "Peter Crompton."

CHAPTER SIX

Devereux's bed was something he never shared.

It took up a quarter of the bed chamber, with oak-carved posts rising from each corner towards a ceiling that seemed to rest on the wooden frame. The bed looked as if it were a part of the room, fitted as it was between floor and ceiling. The footboard was carved with a hunting scene, and the headboard was draped in a red and green tapestry depicting the Garden of Eden. The hangings along the sides were tied back and loosened only in the colder months. The bed faced the only window in the room, and when Myles awoke, he could see the dawn rise across the city in the knowledge that none could see into his room.

The bed he had taken in settlement for a debt and on a whim had it installed in the room. Matthew had rolled his eyes at the extravagance, but Myles hadn't cared. When he awoke in those early days, watching the fog recede and reveal London before him from the window, he felt like a king.

You had to know discomfort before you could appreciate a bed like this. And Myles did appreciate it. He loved the flatness of it, the smoothness of the mattress, the solid sides, the fact it was raised from the ground, and the way the drapes, when released, swung around it to protect the sleeper from draughts and cold. Myles had spent many years sleeping on the floor, and the value he placed on a warm and dry place to sleep was a high one.

The sanctuary of his room tonight was disturbed. It was Friday. Fridays should be good, the day of promise and opportunity. But this one had been ruined by the dead body of his book-keeper. Why had Galveston been murdered?

Myles dropped the heavy ledger on the bed and lit a candle. Out there somewhere was a man, or men, who knew why Galveston was dead. And Myles needed to find them. If it was Galveston's own actions that had led to his demise, all well and good, but Myles needed an assurance that this was the case. He needed to know if it was his rival Bennett or some other man who wished to strike at him. The missing page could hold the answer. A disgruntled debtor, perhaps? One unwilling to pay who had killed Galveston and ripped the page from the book with his name on it? Maybe, but it didn't make much sense. Those who didn't want to pay usually tried to disappear, not pick a fight with one of Devereux's employees. And it wasn't as if Galveston had been attacked while trying to collect a debt. He'd been tortured first.

It made a lot more sense that Garrison Bennett had murdered Galveston. That would fit. But why would Bennett only have taken a single page from the ledger? Surely, he could have gleaned more if the whole ledger had come into his possession? Unless of course, the men he sent didn't understand his instructions or the worth of the ledger. And Galveston had not had an easy death. He'd been tortured, Myles was pretty sure of that. So what had they wanted to know? What question had they placed while he was pinned to the floor while they stood on his broken hands?

What had they wanted?

The answer could be on the missing page. Bennett could have had business dealings with some of the men who owed Devereux money or paid him for his services.

But who?

Myles swore and paced across the floor, raking his hands through his hair. There were too many questions and not enough answers. Myles returned to the ledger on the top of his bed and began to examine it, page by page. The boy was right. A degree of water damage on one corner affected the first few pages. The names and amounts, although legible, were blurred on the pages, and the white of the page was stained with ink. The ledger was just over half full. He flicked over every page slowly until he got to the missing one. Nothing stood out. He kept turning over the blank pages to see if anything was hiding between them – nothing. The last page was glued to the binding and there was a bulge in the center. Myles turned the hard outer cover over and stared at the back of the ledger.

"My God!" Myles exclaimed, his fingers tracing the deep dent in the binding. The covers were wooden and covered in calfskin, and the dent was deep, fresh and oval in shape. Myles traced a finger around the depression, then suddenly stopped as he realised what the book had been used for. They'd used Galveston's ledger to hammer the knife through him and impale it into the floor. It had been forced into the wood beneath him, which was more than a man could have achieved by hand.

This was something much more than robbery.

Would even Bennett do something like this?

There was a tap on the door.

Myles instantly levered himself off the bed, taking two quick paces across the floor he opened the door. Peter, on the other side, took a step back in surprise.

"Master Devereux, I've written out the page with the missing entries as you requested," Peter said, holding out the sheet.

Myles took it from him and scanned the list. Of course, they were names he recognised, but would any of them have done this to Galveston? Ignoring Peter, Myles stalked across the room and hauled the door open to the stairs that led down to the White Hart Tavern.

"Matthew!" Myles called loudly, his eyes still on the page.

Matthew took the stairs two at a time and quickly entered the room.

"We have the list," Myles announced, holding the sheet.

Matthew's hard gaze landed on Peter. "You, out. Wait at the top of the stairs. Is that clear?"

Peter nodded.

Myles laid the sheet on Peter's desk and read out the names.

"Anne Hesketh, Hal Cooper, Alun White, Rancin Arnwright, Cuthbert Honeywell, Paul Smythe, Benedict Osram, Marlow Sharpe and Prentice Goodson," Myles finished.

Matthew leaned over the sheet, scanning the list of names. "I cannot think that any of those would murder Galveston."

"I know. They all owe a pittance. Anne Hesketh's debt is nearly paid off, as far as I remember, and so is Rancin's," Myles said as he studied the sheet.

"Hal Cooper is a weasel of a man, but I doubt he'd attack Galveston. He's so bent with age I doubt he could have made it up the stairs to his office. Smythe is scared of his own shadow, and White is angling to borrow more from you, so I doubt it is either of them," Matthew said thoughtfully.

"Which leaves Sharpe, Goodson, Honeywell and Osram," Myles tapped the sheet with a long finger.

"Honeywell has a young family, and he's devoted to his wife. I doubt he'd jeopardise his life over this, and Goodson and Sharpe pay to ensure their businesses remain open, and Goodson's son even works for you, so it's not likely to be them either," Matthew said, his brow furrowed with confusion. "I'll check on Osram, but it's not likely. He's a cobbler with three daughters and no wife."

Myles pinned Matthew with a hard stare. "What do you think happened to Galveston?"

Matthew straightened his back and tucked his thumbs into his belt. "It's hard to say. But I don't think it was any of those named on here. None of them have the nerve to try anything like this or a reason to. This must be something Galveston did. That's my thinking. Maybe he brought this on himself."

"Go on," Myles said.

"Well, how did he end up working for you in the first place? He was thrown out by his employer because he'd got gambling debts, remember," Matthew said. "That's perhaps where we should start. If he'd lost heavily, had a debt he couldn't pay, then perhaps that's why he ended up skewered to the floor."

A sudden thought settled in Myles' mind, Galveston occasionally frequented the Angel, a brothel catering to London's elite. Devereux knew that Galveston had incurred heavy losses at the gaming tables there in the past, and it could very well be that incautious gambling had led to him being pinned to the floor.

The more Myles thought about it, the more it made sense. Galveston could have been murdered for a gambling debt he couldn't pay. If that was the case, then it was a straightforward murder and a murder that had nothing to do with Myles Devereux.

It would be a very desirable outcome.

Myles stalked into the Angel, pushed past the bulky door-keeper, and walked straight along the corridor to the main room of the Angel. The woman he wanted to talk to was there, powdered, opulent and smiling. Nonny came towards him.

"Master Devereux, a pleasure as always. It has been too long," Nonny said, sliding an arm through his, her voice soft and the syllables rounded by her French accent.

"A word, madam, if I may," Devereux said, leaning down towards her so only she could hear.

"I 'erd about poor Galveston," Nonny said, lightly touching Devereux's sleeve.

"There's not much you don't know about, is there?" Myles replied, steering her towards a quiet part of the room. "I was wondering if you might know of anyone who could have wished for his demise? He was a poor card player."

"Ahhh, you think he had created an enemy at the gaming tables?" Nonny said, removing her hand from his arm and facing him.

"And did he?" Myles said bluntly.

Nonny shook her head. "I would know if he had. He was here a week ago. He usually meets with Reuban Herd and Martin Fisher."

Myles' eyes narrowed. "And who are they?"

"I believe they used to work together, and meet here about once a month," Nonny replied.

"Reuban Herd and Marton Fisher," Myles repeated the names, "and they only come here once a month?"

Nonny nodded and smiled. "I can read your mind. I shall let you know when they are next here. I do not think I can be of much more help. He was a quiet man, he enjoyed the company of the girls and his friends, and apart from that I don't think there is more I can tell you. There is another man here tonight that you know well, though," Nonny said, gesturing across the room.

Myles' eyes scanned the faces of the occupants, his gaze coming to rest on a small group of card players, one of whom he did recognise.

Richard Fitzwarren. An irreverent and highly dangerous mercenary but also a man amongst his current clientele. With him were two other men. One a merchant, by the look of his garb, with a redhead balanced on one knee and looking decidedly excited by the situation. The other was an impossible blond, his hair white gold betraying some Scandinavian origin, Devereux was sure. Devereux took his leave of Nonny and headed towards them, intending to exercise his temper on Fitzwarren.

"I can see you've been treating yourself, Fitzwarren! Who's the blond?" Myles asked Richard Fitzwarren, his voice dripping insolence.

The blond and the merchant paused their game and stared at him. Fitzwarren, his legs stretched before him, relaxed and, with a glass of wine cradled in his hands, didn't appear in the slightest bit annoyed by his words.

"Devereux! Did anything ever come out of your mouth that was not born from foul thoughts?" Richard Fitzwarren replied, a slight smile lifting one corner of his mouth.

"I try my best," a satisfied smile alighted on Myles' face, and he lowered himself into a vacant seat next to Richard, one leg hooked over the arm and the other booted foot resting on the chair, his knee drawn up to his chest. Devereux was swathed in black saturnine velvet slashed to expose the dark silk of his shirt. His wrists emerged from delicate fringed lace that lay just a little too far down the pale hands. Two of his men stood a few paces behind him, confident and at ease. His appearance at the table had drawn the stares of many in the room, but Myles was oblivious to them.

"Perhaps I shall join your game," Myles suddenly declared, raising a hand in the air; one of his men handed him a red velvet purse, and the other moved the table closer to their master, marooning the cards of the other two players who were now out of reach of the table.

Richard sighed, collected the cards, pulling the deck back together.

"Oh, you disapprove," Myles said, his brows knitted and feigned disappointment clinging to his words.

Richard silently cut the cards and was about to deal a round when Myles reached across and took the deck from him.

"In the name of fair play, I cannot allow you to deal," Myles said smiling, then he held the cards towards another man. "You deal, blondie."

The blonde's eyes darted between Richard and Myles, confusion evident on his face as he was forced to rise and pull his chair closer to the table. Taking the offered pack, he shuffled the suits and then dealt a neat hand.

Richard won the first game and Myles the second. The conversation had stopped, and the only noise was the clatter of coins on the wood. Myles won the next round. He left his winnings in the middle of the table. After collecting the cards, the blond slid the coins towards Myles.

Myles' eyes, dark as coal, flicked towards the coins, and a moment later, quicker than a ferret, his hand trapped the blond's wrist in a tight hold. Twisting it for a moment, angling the fingers towards him so he could better view the heavy ring before the man could wrench his hand from the unwanted touch.

"Well, my treasure, where did you get that trinket from, I wonder?" Myles cooed, leaning back in his chair, an evil smile twisting his mouth.

The blond ignored him and sent another set of cards across the table to each player.

Richard won the next two games.

Myles cast his cards on the table in disgust and quickly unfolded himself from the chair, and stood looking down at Richard. "Come on then, if you want to know what your money has bought."

Myles used a private room on the first floor and closed the door when he entered it. The man, Fitzwarren, stood in the centre of the room, his arms folded. He said, "So, Devereux, what's put you in a foul temper this evening?"

Myles stalked across the room. "You won't have heard. But my book-keeper has been murdered."

"That was careless. Didn't you have a guard on him?" Fitzwarren replied.

"Hindsight, Fitzwarren. He was a book-keeper, that's all," Myles stated.

"I'll lay a wager, though, that he knew more about your business than you would like to share with the world. Ergo, carelessness on your part," Fitzwarren said, his voice light with amusement.

Myles ran his hands through his hair. "Alright. You win. I need to find out who murdered the useless shit and why?"

"Undoubtedly, a good idea," Fitzwarren replied in agreement.

Myles coming to the end of one of his traverses across the room, turned abruptly towards Richard. "You could help me? You know people I don't, and can go places I can't."

Fitzwarren had crossed the room and taken one of the chairs near the fire, his legs crossed at the ankle, and he regarded Myles with a quizzical gaze. "Tell me what happened?"

Myles dropped down into the chair opposite without his usual aplomb. "His name is Galveston Ad-Hyce. He has an office in Poultney Street and lives above it. He accompanies Matthew three days a week to collect dues, records these in a ledger, and then presents this every Friday at the White Hart. This week he failed to arrive, and his clerk delivered the news that the shit was laid dead in his office."

"Was it simple robbery?"

Myles shook his head.

"Go on," Fitzwarren said, his voice resigned.

"The bastard's who killed him drove a poniard through his chest, pinning him to his own floor and holding him down while he died. I can only guess they wanted information from him," Myles said morosely.

"The poniard was still there?" Fitzwarren asked.

"Was what still there?" Myles said, exasperated, his voice raised.

"The poniard?" Fitzwarren repeated patiently.

"Yes, it had been hammered into the floor. They even used my bloody ledger to do it," Myles said angrily.

"Interesting, don't you think?" Fitzwarren mused, his fingers tapping the chair arm.

"No .... I don't."

"The poniard, did you recognise it? Could it have belonged to Galveston?" Fitzwarren questioned.

Myles shrugged. "I don't know. I can't say I've seen him with one. There's no need. He's always got Matthew or his men with him."

"The fact it had been hammered into the floor tells us his murderer didn't want it back, and if it was robbery, then why leave such a valuable item that could so easily be sold? Anything else?" Fitzwarren summarised.

"They ripped out the last page from the ledger," Myles added.

"That's got to be your starting point. Any ideas what the entries were?" Fitzwarren said, sounding more interested now.

"I do. His clerk kept day books and could recreate the entries, but they are nobodies," Myles explained.

"In what way?"

"They owe pittances," Myles replied quickly.

"It's all relative, Devereux. What is a pittance to you is a King's ransom to a hungry man," Fitzwarren said carefully.

"This wasn't the work of a hungry man, Fitzwarren," Myles shot back. "As you pointed out, if it was they'd not have left a sellable poniard impaled in Galveston's guts."

"I agree. Nor was it a chance robbery. However, you still need to review those debtors on your missing page. It must have been torn out for a reason. How many of them are there?"

"Six," Myles replied.

"That's not so many. Any business rivals of yours that could have done this?" Fitzwarren said, his grey eyes fixed on Myles' face.

"You're thinking this has something to do with Garrison Bennett?" Myles eyed Richard coldly.

"Have you been stepping on his toes again?" Fitzwarren said, laughing.

"Very much the other way around," growled Myles in reply. "This isn't Bennett's style. He doesn't send messages; he just kills or persuades people to be elsewhere. Can you see what you can find out?"

"How?" Fitzwarren replied, exasperation creeping into his reasoned tone.

"You know many men in London," Myles continued.

"Not so many amongst the thieves of the city, Devereux. That is much more your province," Fitzwarren replied, laughing softly.

"I know men connected with Bennett, but they'd not give me honest words," Myles said.

Fitzwarren laughed. "Christ! Myles. Honesty is not a commodity you trade in, is it?"

Myles scowled at the other man. "You've got contacts. If you hear anything, let me know? Remember it is you who needs me as well."

Cold grey eyes regarded him for a moment before he spoke. "I will."

"Thank you, Fitzwarren," Myles said, leaning heavily in his chair.

"Well, then. May I return to the card table?" Fitzwarren asked, one eyebrow raised and a slight smile twitching one corner of his mouth.

"If you must," Myles replied, watching the other man leave.

How long had he known Fitzwarren? Most of his life, he supposed. He was older than Myles, but he would guess not by more than three or four years. And if the man had ever suffered hard times, and Myles knew he had, it annoyingly didn't show. He knew Fitzwarren had enjoyed a career as a mercenary, and the last he had heard, he was in France. An able leader of men, it had come as a pleasant surprise when he had turned up in London asking for help, wanting to hire some of Myles' men to ensure a merchant's security

He refused to say where his own men had gone, but he looked far from destitute and had coin to pay Myles. He had refused to tell Myles why he needed them, and Myles knew from experience that persistence would not change that, so there was little point in asking the question again.

CHAPTER SEVEN

The visit to the Angel had not helped. When he placed his boots on the steps leading to the Angel's door, Myles had been sure that he was about to find out why Galveston was dead. But that wasn't the case. He'd been there, that was a fact, but he'd not lost heavily and didn't seem to have left owing any money. It was a dead end.

Myles dropped heavily into his chair and pulled the ledger towards him, opening it at the place where the page was missing. They'd not found the page that had been torn out. That fact made it important; he was sure of that. But why not take the whole book? Or even more pages? Why rip out the incomplete page?

None of it made any sense.

Myles looked back at the previous page. It had been neatly completed in Galveston's own hand, the names of all those who had paid, the date of the payment, the amount and their outstanding balance. The bottom of the sheet bore a total, and this had been agreed to the amount of money collected. It was a process carried out every Friday.

Myles stared at the figure.

Five crowns and sixteen pence.

Next to this were his initials. MD. Every week he checked to ensure the ledger totals agreed with the amount of money that had been collected. It was always right. Galveston counted the money; Matthew checked it, and Myles agreed it to the ledger.

Every week.

There was never a discrepancy.

It always balanced.

Peter had compiled the missing sheet from the day books. They sat at the end of the desk, and Myles pulled one towards him. Inside were tightly written lists of names, each headed with a date and to the right of the names the payment amount. The last page was the one Peter had used to complete the missing list, and his eyes found the name of Hesketh. Anne Hesketh, and next to it the amount of 4 3/4d, a groat and three farthings. Peter had transcribed it onto the sheet Myles had given him.

Myles flipped the page back to reveal a previous week's entry. Anne Hesketh's name was there again, and a payment of 2 3/4d, half a groat and three farthings. Frowning, Myles turned the page forwards. Anne had paid more in the most recent week. That was unusual. It was generally a fixed agreed amount, any reduced payment being discouraged by Matthew and his men, and no one ever paid more. Why would they?

Yet Anne Hesketh had paid 2d more. Myles' blackened fingers leafed through the ledger. Every previous week the amount was 2d 3/4d; only in the final week was the amount higher. Myles pulled the daybook towards him, and found the entry for Anne Hesketh for the previous week in Peter's tight neat characters. It was higher than the ledger amount, 4d 3/4d

Myles' heart missed a beat.

He found the name of Rancin Arnwright, the figure in the daybook agreed to the ledger. Then Sharpe. Sharpe's payment didn't agree; the amount in the daybook was higher, 6d, and the figure in the ledger 4d, and just like Anne Hesketh, the previous pages were all a lower amount, but the day books showed the higher figure next to his name.

Slowly Myles added the figures up on the page in the daybook. Then he totalled them for a second time, then a third and then a fourth. The week's ledger pages total was 30d lower than it should have been.

Whipping the page over, he began to add the previous page up.

Same again. 30d short.

By the time he got to the bottom of the eighth page, the hand that held the pen was shaking so much that the nib split when he tried to write down 240d. In eight weeks, he was 240 pennies short, a full pound!

Sitting back hard in his chair, he discarded the pen across the desk and glowered at the ledger. His long ink-stained fingers raked through his hair. The bastard, Galveston, had been robbing him. Every week, systematically, by the same amount. The debtors' payments in the day books were higher by 30d weekly than those Galveston wrote in the ledger. The amounts were wrong for Hesketh, Sharpe and Goodson.

Myles pressed the heels of his palms into his eyes. Cursed and then stood so suddenly that the chair toppled behind him.

"Matthew," Myles bellowed before he had the door open. "Matthew, where the hell are you?"

Myles Devereux's rage was complete. A long index finger stabbed Anne Hesketh's name in the daybook. "She paid 4d 3/4d, the clerk wrote it down, and then the shit, Galveston, wrote a lower amount in the ledger, look, 2d 3/4d."

Matthew frowned, his response too slow for Myles, who continued. "You went with Galveston, or if not, one of your men. How the hell did this happen?"

"I don't understand ...."

"You blind fool! How could you not understand! That fat shit, palmed money, my money, into his bloody pocket right under your damned nose," Myles stormed.

"But .... how. I don't...."

Myles picked up one of the day books and brandished it towards Matthew. "The shit got his clerk to write down the correct amounts in here, then in his office, when he was alone, he wrote a lower figure in the ledger. The woman, Hesketh, has been paying me 4d 3/4d all year, and he wrote it down as 2d 3/4d. So where did the difference go?"

Myles finished by flinging the book towards Matthew. The older man, refusing to match Myles' temper, scooped the book from where it landed on the floor and put it back on the desk. "Show me."

Myles spun back towards the desk, his voice furious. "I've just explained it!"

"Well, explain it one more time, slowly and then, perhaps, I'll be able to follow you," Matthew said patiently, pushing the day book towards Myles.

"For God's sake!" Myles fumed.

"Tell me again once more," Matthew said firmly, opening the day book.

Myles took in a deep breath and tried to settle his temper, pulling the book towards him. "According to the day book, she paid 2d more, then if you look in the ledger, Galveston has written down a lower amount. And it's not just her; there's another six I've found so far, and God only knows how many more there are."

Matthew didn't look up, his eyes switching between the documents, comparing the numbers. "The crafty old ...."

"Crafty! If the shit wasn't dead, trust me, he'd take a long time to die at my hands. Christ, Matthew, how has this happened?" Myles said flinging his arms in the air.

"And there's another six more debtors he's wrongly recorded, you say," Matthew said, raising his eyes from the books.

"Six that I've found so far," Myles' eyes were bright with temper. Matthew though, was still studying the accounts. "The first eight pages I've checked are all 30d short; that's half a crown every week. One coin, that's all he had to take."

"We don't collect in half-crowns during the week when we do the rounds. It's only ever farthings and pennies and the odd groat. If he was taking half a crown, we'd have noticed," Matthew said, his right hand tugging at his short beard.

"I don't think he took it from the money when he was out collecting the dues, he'll have helped himself to half a crown from here on a Friday, and because he's written the amounts down lower than those he collected, it means it would all balance," Myles turned and stalked across the room.

Matthew had one hand on the daybook and another on the ledger. "How far does this go back?"

"I don't know! Since that ledger started, which was February last year, since that date, these six, at least, have been wrongly accounted for, and that bastard has kept the money," Myles growled. "His clerk told me when he started this ledger, he began using these books," Myles' finger stabbed the day books. "Before then, he wrote the amounts in the book while you watched."

Matthew frowned. "That's true. Then he brought these; they were easier to carry. It made sense."

"I thought *YOU* took the payments, and then he'd write the ledger amounts?" Myles said, his tone accusing.

Matthew held his hand up. "Alright, perhaps I've not paid as much attention as I should have, and it wasn't always me with him on some of these collections. The amounts are low value. He'd take the coins and write the books up, then I or one of the lads would bring the purse here at the end of the day."

"Who carried the purse? Did Galveston have access to it?" Myles continued.

"Some of them handed the money to him, that's true, most gave it to me or the lads .... so you mean he was taking something from each of these six before it went into the purse, every week? I can't believe that," Matthew said, shaking his head.

"He didn't have to. He's marked these six down in the ledger by an amount that adds up to 30d, so all he had to do was take one half-crown every week, just one when he was here on Friday, and then the amounts in the purse would balance to the ledger, and if you checked while you were with him, the amounts the clerk wrote down were correct. These books and the ledger were never together, so the discrepancies would never have been picked up, and the purse always balances to the ledger," Myles explained through gritted teeth.

Matthew met Devereux's gaze. "He could have done that, I admit. And don't forget, a couple of them came to his offices to pay, only small amounts, but it was all added into the weekly total. He could have taken it from there."

"No. Those who paid at his office during the week wouldn't give him enough to do that. The filthy bastard would take his half-crown from here, every bloody week," Myles announced with finality

"Indeed," Matthew agreed.

Myles turned on him. "I can't believe he fooled you. You! God's bones, Matthew, over a year at the very least, this shit was stealing from you."

Matthew had paled. "From us. Do you know how much?"

Myles shook his head. "Not yet. It'll take me hours to match the entries from these books to the ledger."

Matthew was already heading towards the door.

"Where are you going?" Myles demanded of Matthew's retreating back.

"You find out how much he stole, and I'm going to find out what his clerk knew about it," Matthew said; his eyes were dark, and for a moment, a very fleeting one, Myles almost felt sorry for Peter.

It wasn't a problem Myles was about to share. There was a certain amount of shame in having been robbed, and even worse when you didn't know how much the amount involved was. The fire was banked high, every available candle holder was on his desk, and the shutters were drawn back to let in what light they could from a dreary London day.

Myles was vain.

He'd seen too many hunched-backed scribes over the years, their noses dipping ever closer to the pages, unable to see, and he had no intention of becoming one of them. Rumour courted Myles as lazy and idle. It also listed his notable qualities as violent and vindictive, which suited him well. There was little point in being a moneylender and having a reputation for philanthropy. However Myles was far from lazy, and very rarely idle.

He had cleared the desk of anything he didn't need. Before him was the ledger, day books, the sheet the clerk had prepared, pen, ink and several spare sheets of vellum.

He'd started with Hesketh. Making a list from the day books of each payment and comparing them to the values in the ledger, they were all wrong by the same amount. On a sheet, he had a list of names and next to it, the notation after he had checked them. Either correct or incorrect, and the value of the anomaly. From the final page, he had found six debtors that had been under-recorded in the ledger, and by the time he had compared two of the day books, he had discovered he had a total of twenty instances where Galveston had been applying the same process. The third book, however, did not produce any anomalies. Every entry in it agreed to the ledger.

Matthew had interrupted him before the first hour's work was completed and told him he thought it highly unlikely that the clerk was complicit in what had happened. Myles didn't ask him why he was confident that was the case. Matthew had his methods. But he did ask him why the book that related to Monday's debt collections would be correct compared to the others and found the answer simple and believable. Matthew accompanied Galveston on Mondays. It was one of the biggest collection days, especially from businesses after they had the weekend takings, and so Matthew was always present and brought whatever was collected in dues back to the White Hart.

It was starting to fit together rather too well.

Galveston was not stupid enough to try and dupe Matthew. Instead, he had kept his deceitful dealings to the days when his escorts were simpler men to deal with, easier ones to deceive. Galveston would be accompanied by three of Devereux's men when he was out collecting; those involved varied. It depended on who was available, and according to Matthew, there wasn't a set routine.

Myles sat back in his chair and surveyed the neatly written names and numbers he had produced. If you looked at it in terms of amounts per debtor, per week, it was small. But those small amounts were adding up to a sum that Myles was having difficulty believing. Why? Galveston's office was nondescript, his room above it was frugal – so where had he been spending Devereux's money? He'd not gambled it at the Angel; that much seemed to be clear. So where had it gone?

Myles ran his fingers through his hair, and when he raised his head, he realised he was looking straight at his bed. The drapes drawn back and the covers invitingly smooth the mattress comfy. The window behind him was still unshuttered, and the sound of the bell tolling for vespers sounded through it. The hour was late. Myles was tired, yet he wasn't at a point he wanted to stop. There were still too many unanswered questions.

Rising from the chair, Myles rounded the desk and took a Venetian wine glass from the side table he had relegated both wine and glasses to earlier. Filling it, he emptied it quickly. Taking the bottle by the neck, he flopped down on the bed. Knees drawn up, he stared through the open shutters into the darkness of London. A waning moon cast white light on the city. It was enough to highlight the White Tower and the steeple of St Bride's.

Myles emptied the glass and let his head fall back on the pillow, eyes closed. Why was this riling him so much? He'd dealt more than his fair share of thieves over the years? But not within his employ. Those who worked for him, the systems he'd put in place, he had been sure were secure. And they bloody well weren't. A damned book-keeper had not only the ability to deceive him but the nerve to do it. How many more were there? If there was one, you could be sure there would be others.

Myles pushed himself up, filled the glass from the bottle and balanced the base of it on one knee. Things were going to have to change, and at the same time, the change was not one that he wanted anyone to notice.

CHAPTER EIGHT

Myles had worked until common sense told him to stop. The hour was late, the bells had rung for compline, and his mind could no longer keep track of the numbers. His addition was wrong, and he knew he was making mistakes. Myles closed the day book using his pen as a marker. Three of the candles he had set on his desk had burnt down hours ago, and the remaining two he neatly extinguished with his fingers, filling the room with a sudden caustic aroma.

Taking a glass of wine, Myles flopped down on the bed, his back against a pile of pillows, his gaze on a night-time London.

Outside, the wind was playing around the tavern, its passage noisy against the walls of the White Hart, extracting low notes from the roof tiles as it rushed by. The pitch rose a degree as the wind pressed harder against brick and wood, and a sudden exploratory gust drove down the chimney making the embers glow and sending a plume of ash into the room. Revived, the fire glowed orange, and Myles watched as the grey dust driven by the wind rolled from the fireplace. The white flash from beyond his window drew his attention back. White hot, the first finger of lightning split the dark sky arcing from clouds to somewhere beyond the city, the noise a distant rumble akin to the stampede of hooves. The sound rolled towards him, the herald of the assault to come.

Myles sipped the wine, his eyes on the dark window and the unseen vista of the city. The hour was such that no windows were marked by light escaping around shutter edges. Closer this time, not far from the city walls, a forked spike of light pierced the night, the hoofbeats of its vanguard closer.

Rain fell like archers' arrows on the roof. The onslaught was sudden and violent. Drips falling from the tiles above his window quickly became a steady stream, pouring down to begin an assault on the yard below. The lightning was closer now. A single spike from clouds to ground struck somewhere amongst the packed streets, the cannonade of sound quick on its heels. For a moment, London was illuminated. Roofs, houses, and spires were all suddenly revealed in the night. Lit up as if the storm were seeking some particular place.

You can't hide from lightning, Myles thought, taking another sip of wine. The next bright blast was just behind the spire of St Bride's, lighting up the Church in harsh relief. The path the storm was making was heading directly towards the Church. Myles wondered if the next bolt might split the spire. If it did, he would have the perfect view. Then, remembering that he was using the Church for his own purposes, he sent a silent prayer for it to miss the landmark.

The storm was matching his mood. Thoughts in his head were landing like lightning in different places. Why had Galveston done this? How much had he stolen? Were there others doing the same thing?

Who else knew? Was this why he had been killed? Did he owe money to someone?

Myles growled and pinched the bridge of his nose. He needed to pursue these lines to their conclusion, one at a time. First, he needed sleep; he couldn't focus on the problem adequately. Resting his head, he listened to the rain on the roof and the slurry of ejected water as it drained to the yard below. The lightning pierced his closed lids two more times before the storm moved to the south of London. Myles didn't hear the retreating drum beats of the thunder. He fell asleep, propped up, head pillowed in goose feathers and the glass in his hand.

He awoke cold. The fire was out, the embers dead, and the room chilled. His right hand was coldest. Realising why, he cursed. He'd let the glass slip from his grasp, and the covers around his hand were soaked in wine. Rising, he deposited the glass on the table, slewed the shirt over his head, discarded his hose and slithered beneath the covers, carefully avoiding the soaked ones. There were a few hours left before dawn lay a brittle winter light on the cold city.

Matthew brought the unwelcome news to him early. It wasn't an issue he wanted to deal with. But deal with it, he must. A messenger had arrived at the tavern early with a demand from Ivan Candish, the Parish clerk, that Myles Devereux attend him at his offices. Myles would have to make an uncharacteristic visit to see this particular client. The White Hart was not a venue the clerk would frequent, and unfortunately, the business transaction was lucrative, and as such, Myles couldn't avoid the meeting.

Arriving at the clerk's office, he was rapidly appraised of the problem.

"We pay you, Master Devereux, to remove the bodies of the unfortunate and safely inter them," Candish, the clerk, said.

"You do, I agree," Myles was in no mood for the clerk's indignant tone. "And that is what I have been doing."

"But you haven't. That's the issue, and complaints have been made. Complaints that have made their way to me, and I need to take action," the clerk complained.

Myles sneered. "Complaints? Who from? I doubt it was from those you handed into my care."

"Master Devereux, this is a serious matter. The Parish pays you well to dispose of the victims of the sweating sickness, and you've not done this; bodies are being stored in the crypt at St Bride's. It's not what you are paid for. They need to be properly interred," Candish finished.

Myles seated himself on the corner of the clerk's desk, leaning over him. "And can you remember what I pay you for?"

Candish paled.

"Exactly. I pay you to ensure this transaction runs smoothly. So, if there is a temporary problem, it's yours to deal with," Myles said bluntly.

"But .... but what can I tell the Parish councillors," the clerk stammered.

"Tell him what you like. I don't care. You know there is a lack of space," Myles said, dropping his gaze to the desk and leafing through the papers.

The clerk went red. "Master Devereux, they are private matters relating to Parish business."

"Then it's a good job that I am here on Parish business," Myles said, turning one of the sheets towards him so he could read it better.

"What shall I report back to the Parish," the clerk said, a distinct edge of nerves in his voice.

"Anything you like that you think they'd wish to hear," Myles had taken another sheet and was reading it.

The man made to snatch the paper from Myles' hand. Myles, quicker than the clerk, dropped from the desk, the paper still in his grasp. "This, Candish, is telling me you have not been entirely honest."

"I don't know what you mean?" Candish's voice shook.

"Don't take me for a fool. You've made a payment to Carson in Newgate Lane, and we both know what that payment will be for, don't we?" Myles, flung the paper down on the desk, his cold eyes fastened on Candish's face.

"It was six bodies, that was all. You said yourself there wasn't any space, and he said he could ...."

Myles took a quick step towards the clerk. "You idiot. If there's no space to dump these bodies, then that's the same for Carson as it is for me. Until new pits are dug, we need to store them. Where did you think he was taking them? He'll have weighted them and dropped them in the river, you bloody fool."

"He said he had access ...." The clerk's voice trailed off.

Myles slung the paper in Candish's face, the man flinched. Then, a long finger pointing towards the clerk, he said, "I'll overlook this, but if it happens again, and trust me, I'll know if it does, the rest of the Parish will be getting to know about our arrangement."

The clerk swallowed hard and paled even further.

Myles folded his arms. "Now, was there anything else you wished to discuss?"

Candish shook his head wildly.

"Good!" Myles turned on his heel and left.

"Matthew!" Myles bellowed as soon as he left the clerk's office.

His horse was brought forward from where it was being held by one of his men. Mounted and without a backward glance towards the Parish offices or his men, Myles pressed his horse into a brisk trot heading back the way he had come. Rather than turning left to the White Hart, he crossed several more streets until he was beneath the steeple of St Bride's.

Slipping his feet from the stirrups in one smooth move, he was on the ground, one of his men rushing to take charge of the abandoned reins. A gravel path went around the graveyard and then gave way to churned mud. Myles used two overturned gravestones to keep his boots clean, arriving on top of a flat-topped tomb sided with cherubim. From there, he could survey the excavations that had gone so wrong, according to the clerk, Candish.

Myles cursed.

The man he wanted to speak to was Clegg, who had already noted Devereux's arrival and was making his way around the edge of the monstrous pit towards him, his pattens sliding on the mud. What had once been a smart red cloak earlier in the day was now splotched with ochre and the fur trim drooped with the rain.

Devereux watched his progress with ill-concealed impatience, tapping a riding crop against the leather of his boot.

Clegg, noting his master's impatience, tried to hasten his arrival, with disastrous results. The pattens, already weighted and clogged with mud, stuck fast momentarily, unbalancing their owner and leaving him scrambling, hands and elbows in the quagmire.

"Lord bloody preserve us!" Myles cursed, looking skyward. "Clegg, please, bless me with good news."

Clegg, the feather from his hat now firmly attached to a muddied cheek, arrived in a flurry of wet and mired drapery.

"Master Devereux, a pleasure to see you," Clegg said, rising from a clumsy bow, his pattens threatening to pitch him face down in the mud again.

Myles, towering above him from the top of the templar's tomb, pointed with his whip towards the flooded pit. "What is that?"

Clegg swivelled back towards the excavations. "It's all under control. The rain has created some problems, and unfortunately, it means extra work for Hill and his men. I have negotiated a good rate with them, and they assure me that an extra trench will be dug to drain it by tomorrow."

"By tomorrow," Myles repeated the words, disbelief in his voice.

"Yes .... Hill assures me ...." Clegg was suddenly uncertain.

"Can I speak with Hill?" Myles said, his tone making it quite clear this was not a request.

It took a few minutes to locate the man, and he didn't want to speak with Devereux, as evidenced by a heated argument with Clegg. However, after a few glances towards Myles Devereux, who was still on top of the tomb backed by several of his men, he seemed to change his mind. Stabbing his spade into the mud bank, he made his way with more grace than Clegg had managed towards Myles.

Myles waited until he had arrived and stopped before the marble edifice, cap held tightly in both hands and eyes firmly on the ground.

"Hill," Myles announced loudly, glaring down at the man.

"Yes, Master," Hill mumbled in return.

"It seems that some confusion has arisen. What did I pay you to produce?" Myles asked, his voice clear and loud enough to carry across the graveyard.

"Well it's …." Hill tried.

Myles cut in, his voice hard. "What did I pay you to produce. In two words, tell me?"

There was a brief pause. "A pit."

"A pit," Myles repeated. Then pointing with his whip towards the excavations, he said, "Look over there, Hill, and tell me what you have produced?"

Hill reluctantly turned his gaze towards the pond where, on one bank, he was being observed by Clegg and his men.

"In two words, Hill," Myles growled.

"A pond, Master," Hill mumbled in reply.

"A pond," Myles said in agreement, then dropping down onto his haunches, he glowered at Hill. "A bloody pond. And you had the damned effrontery to argue with Clegg for more money. I think you should perform the job you agreed to do. Otherwise, I'll not be paying you at all. Do you understand?"

"Yes, Master," Hill said, returning his gaze to the ground before his feet.

Myles rose. "If I'd wanted somewhere to put ducks, I'd have asked. Now get that damned pit drained as Master Clegg requested."

Hill mumbled an inaudible reply.

"Don't bloody stand there. Go and find a shovel and use it. Now!" Myles' final word rose to a shout.

Hill jumped and, turning, ran back to his men.

Myles, shaking his head, surveyed the sorry state of the churchyard for a few moments. Then he made his way back using the gravestones to preserve the dryness of his boots.

Clegg's full name was Thomas Cleggston. He was related, albeit by marriage, to Henry Courtenay. His wife was Courtenay's cousin, the Marquess of Exeter, before an appointment with the axe. His wife, Jane, had brought Clegg a modest estate in Leicester. Clegg, however, had lost not only his wife but also his land, when he had made the ill-advised decision to back Northumberland and the Grey's claim to the throne in an effort to improve his standing. Mary had removed his land, his wife had left him and moved to France and was living with her sister and Clegg had been interred in the Tower. That he had not been dispatched was due more to his uselessness than his use. Mary had decided on a degree of clemency to help ensure that those nobles who had aligned themselves with Northumberland would now switch their allegiance, and Clegg had been among a number of worthless political prisoners who had been released. Shortly after, bereft of money, he had found his way to the White Hart, where Devereux had recognised his usefulness.

Clegg might be disgraced nobility, but he was still nobility. And he added a certain legitimacy to some of Devereux's dealings. The man was a fool but a useful one. The Parish officers he dealt with were happy to allow themselves to believe they were dealing with Thomas Cleggston and not Devereux. So the man might be a fool and an idiot, but he was profitable. Clegg lived at the White Hart in humble accommodation, and Myles paid him a pittance. Still, he provided him with food and, to ensure his continued usefulness, the services of his tailor, Master Drew, so that Clegg could continue to emulate a member of the noble classes. And Clegg might be a fool, but he was also vain to the core and would do anything to retain even a shell of his noble veneer.

Sam Burnell

CHAPTER NINE

It hadn't been an ideal morning. Myles had wanted to continue finalising his work on the ledger and not spend two hours supervising the digging of the burial pit and rectifying Clegg's poor work. There would be more words with Master Clegg. He had been lucky today that Myles wanted to do nothing more than return to his room and find the answer to a question burning in his mind. How much, exactly, had Galveston stolen from him? Now he had found the fraud he very much wanted to quantify the extent of it. Clegg had no idea how lucky he had been.

When he returned to the White Hart, he found the fire had been lit in his room, and the wine-stained covers on his bed had been changed in his absence. It was well known that he hated servants in his room while he was present, and Matthew, arms folded, his attention never leaving the servants, would have overseen their ministrations. There would be no opportunity for straying eyes or fingers to examine the contents of Devereux's desk. Myles preferred to believe that no one, apart from himself and those he invited in, ever entered the room. It helped to preserve his feeling of sanctuary, and Matthew aided Myles' self-deception.

The papers he had been working on and the ledgers and day books were still on his desk, exactly where he had left them. Crumbs from when he had eaten whilst working were still scattered around them, and a soiled wine glass still sat next to the ink pot. Matthew knew better than to disturb the desk at the moment.

Myles discarded his doublet on the bed and, sitting at the desk, began to finish the task he had set himself. Three hours later he had finalised his summary on one piece of paper. It comprised a list of names of people who owed or paid Myles for services who's payments had been incorrectly recorded, an amount of how much this was since the start of the ledger and then, at the bottom, underlined in thick black ink was the total. Galveston had diverted exactly half a crown every week for forty-six weeks from the money collected. He had been systematic, methodical, and the deception was elaborate. Twenty-three crowns in total.

If any of the errors had been detected, it would not have raised the alarm as the amounts were small, and it would have been viewed as an accounting error. Galveston would have had his errors pointed out to him in short order, Matthew would no doubt have added an unnecessary threat, and Galveston would have made up the missing amount. But that would have been it.

Galveston knew that Myles examined the ledger weekly, knew that he reviewed them and signed the pages off. So if an error were ever found, it would be limited to the current week and unlikely to be tracked back over. Myles never saw the day books. Indeed he hadn't even been aware of their existence until yesterday. Galveston never brought them to the White

Hart on Fridays. If he had disposed of them, there would have been an excellent chance that Myles would never have discovered the deception. What would have happened? Debtors would have tried to argue they had paid more? They could claim they owed less if they dared, and who would have believed them? Not Matthew; certainly he wouldn't have believed their tales. Most couldn't write let alone understand Galveston's notations in the ledgers.

Myles shook his head – what had happened was hard to believe.

"Matthew!"

Matthew arrived immediately from the outer room.

Myles held up the sheet. "I have the total; that bastard has taken twenty-three crowns since the start of this ledger."

Matthew's eyes widened. "Are you sure?"

"Of course, I'm bloody sure. Look for yourself," Myles said, handing him the paper. "All those names had the wrong amounts written down in the ledger. He wasn't greedy, Matthew. He was just persistent, half a crown every week."

Matthew shook his head. "I can't believe this."

"Believe it, it's a fact," Myles said, stretching his back and dropping back in the chair.

"But why? He knew if this ever came to light, you'd have him torn apart," Matthew's face was lined with confusion.

"I was hoping you might have some idea," Myles said grimly, accepting the page back from Matthew. "Over time, it's a significant amount, but weekly, day by day, was this worth risking your life for? He set up an elaborate deception, Matthew, and there was a reason for that – and I want to know what it was."

"We've tried the Angel and had no luck there. If this was gambling, then it might be somewhere else. I'll get the lads on to it," Matthew said, tucking his thumbs into his belt, happy to be taking on a task he knew how to carry out.

"It's not gambling," Myles said, shaking his head.

"How do you know?" Matthew said, unhooking a thumb, he stabbed the sheet on the desk where the total was written. "The shit had nothing to show for that amount of money. He's got to have gambled it away."

"If he'd lost heavily, then with this scheme he'd not be able to steal away enough in a week to cover any large debts, and gamblers, Matthew, do not stockpile money to offset their future losses. Trust me, I have some experience in this area," Myles said sarcastically.

"True," Matthew conceded, inclining his head, then he changed the subject, "Did you sort out Candish and Clegg?"

Devereux rolled his eyes. "Don't remind me! How bloody hard is it to dig a hole? That man Clegg has a monopoly on idiocy."

Matthew laughed. "Luckily for us, he is not alone. Don't forget that's where most of your clients come from."

"The pit should be ready today, tomorrow at the latest. Keep an eye on it, and let me know. That snake at the parish has started to use Carson to dispose of bodies," Myles grumbled.

"Carson! But if you can't find a space in a burial pit, where exactly is he going to put them?" Matthew exclaimed, flinging his arms wide.

"Exactly. I don't want him using St Bride's either, I paid for that. Knowing Carson, he'll be weighting them and heaving them into the river. It would serve the Parish right if a few washed up around the bridge piers," Myles mused, tapping his fingers on the desk. "Indeed, I might just make sure that happens."

"Be careful," Matthew advised, "Also it had nothing to do with Osram."

"How can you be so sure?" Myles replied.

"Osram fell from his roof a week ago trying to fix a hole in the thatch and broke his leg, so I doubt very much that he could have made it up the stairs to attack Galveston," Myles said, heading towards the door.

Myles turned the sheet he had shown Matthew back towards him, his eyes fastened on the total. Twenty-three crowns, just over three pounds. Galveston was paid eight pounds a year, and the shit had helped himself to near enough half again from the dues he collected. Myles felt his temper rising again, the pressure throbbing at his temples. It was lost money. There was nothing he could do about it now. Galveston was dead.

A tap on the door, followed by the appearance of Matthew's face around it forced him to still his temper for a moment. "What now?"

"It's Fitzwarren," was all Matthew said.

Myles groaned, sat back heavily in the chair and waved his hand towards Matthew. "Send him in."

When his visitor arrived at the other side of the desk, Myles pushed the sheet towards him. "That shit, Galveston, has been robbing me all year, and Lord knows what he's stuffed into his pockets before that."

Richard Fitzwarren's eyebrows raised a degree. "That was uncharacteristically careless of you."

"Every week, he wrote down the amounts incorrectly in the ledger and kept the difference," Myles flipped open the ledger where a knife had been inserted between the pages. "Here, for example, next to the name Miller he has written 3d when the amount should have been 5d."

Fitzwarren leaned forward to look at the entry, frowning.

"Why are you smiling?" Myles said, annoyed.

"Come on, Myles, there's a certain amount of humour in this, I thought you were the Prince of trickery and deceit," Fitzwarren said, then added. "How much?"

"Twenty-three crowns this year alone," Myles replied, his voice taught with temper.

Fitzwarren whistled softly. "That must have hurt."

Fitzwarren was still examining the ledger, running an index finger down the list of names.

"What?" Myles exclaimed, rounding the desk and coming to stand next to him. "I can read your face, Fitzwarren. What are you looking at?"

Richard flicked the ledger back several pages and then forwards again. "He's not using Pacioli." The words were spoken more to himself than to Myles.

Myles rounded the desk and tried to meet the other man's eyes, but Fitzwarren was still intent on examining the book of account. "Who the Hell is Pacioli?"

Fitzwarren ignored him, tapping Devereux's signature on the page. "I assume from this that you check each week and then sign it off."

Myles' gaze was drawn back to the book, the lines across the pages, and his signature. "Yes, the totals from there were agreed to the money weekly. But the errors would never have been apparent as he kept a second set of records that he didn't bloody show me."

"Where did you get your book-keeper from?" Fitzwarren asked.

"Does that matter?"

Fitzwarren raised his gaze from the ledger and met Myles' eyes. "Well, given that he's robbed you and then been murdered, I think it might have some bearing on the events."

Myles huffed and turned his back on his guest. "He owed money."

"For God's sake, Myles! You employed a man in debt to keep your books? I thought you were a little cleverer than that," Fitzwarren scoffed.

Myles turned and slammed his fist on the desk. "It's not quite that simple. And neither am I. Galveston was a friend of my brother's, he'd invested in the *Saint Louise,* and the ship sank, leaving the investors responsible for the losses."

Fitzwarren finally met Myles' gaze. "Andrew was a good judge of character. I doubt he would have foisted a charlatan on you."

"My thoughts exactly. Galveston worked for Oldcastle & Peel, in Shore Lane, near Lincoln's Inn. When it became known that he owed money, he lost his position. Andrew asked me to help," Myles said, then added, "It wasn't as if he got into debt by his own agency, the *Saint Louise* was lost due to poor navigation by all accounts. The fool tried to make up the losses by playing cards, worsening his situation. I paid his debts off, and he's worked for me for the last three years."

"You are, of course, known for your charity," Fitzwarren said acidly.

"Don't, Fitzwarren, I'll not be goaded by you. Andrew asked. I needed a book-keeper. The arrangement was a good one," Myles said bluntly.

"The missing ship, *Saint Louise*. Did you check it?" Fitzwarren asked.

"Do you think I was born last week! Of course, I did. The ship sailed from Bruges in bad weather and was lost. Galveston wasn't alone amongst those where he worked that had invested. It just so happened he was the only one who couldn't cover the debt," Myles said, then added. "And who the Hell is Polario?"

"Not Polario, it's Pacioli. His protocol is used in books of accounts to ensure there isn't an error or a fraud, and your Galveston, if he worked for Oldfield & Peel, would have been very familiar with Pacioli," Fitzwarren said thoughtfully, an index finger still tapping the ledger.

"Pacioli, and how do you know about Pacioli," Myles said, irritation in his voice.

"Does that matter?" Fitzwarren said.

"It might," Myles replied sulkily.

"I spent some time working for a lawyer in Madrid, and these are not good records, Myles," Fitzwarren said directly, raising his eyes from the ledger.

"I know that now," Myles accepted.

"Who do you have to keep your books of account now?" Fitzwarren asked.

"Galveston's clerk, I've got him here under lock and key. He's amenable to the arrangement and he'd not dare cross me. Matthew would cut his hands off if he did, and he's well aware of that fact," Myles said.

"I am sure Matthew would," Fitzwarren said in agreement, still sounding distracted.

"It won't happen again. Matthew will collect all the money in now, and the boy writes down what he is told to," Myles said.

"You know what they say about money,"

"No, what do they say,"

"Never let anyone else play with yours," Fitzwarren said, closing the ledger with a bang of finality.

"Lesson learned, Fitzwarren. I won't," Myles said, bitterly

Fitzwarren reached inside his doublet, retrieved a page, unfolded it and held it towards Myles. When Myles didn't take it, he cast it on the desk between them, "Read it."

Myles picked it up. A single sheet, it had been nailed up by the look of it, and both of the top corners were torn away.

In printers large capitals, the title declared –

The Falsehood of the Catholic Church

"Just skip to the bottom ...." Fitzwarren advised, folding his arms and watching Myles read.

Myles' eyes took in the final lines.

"I attest to this falsehood and place my name against it Ad-Hyce."

Myles looked up from the document.

"Ad-Hyce – there can't be many of them in London, can there? And this one is trying very hard to have his heels warmed with this Heresy," Fitzwarren said. "It's a particular failing of the radical that they feel they need to pin their names to their actions."

"I can get Matthew to check this. It shouldn't be too difficult," Myles said. Turning the sheet over, he asked, "Where did you find this?"

"Nailed to the door of a carpenter's shop. They are all over London. Someone was busy last night," Fitzwarren said. "I wasn't that interested until I overheard the name Ad-Hyce"

"There could be a connection," Myles conceded, tossing the page to his desk.

"How was he connected to your brother? Was it religion? Your brother would never have involved himself in something like this, but that doesn't mean he didn't know people who would," Fitzwarren stated bluntly.

Myles was shaking his head slowly. "He heard of Galveston's plight through a friend who used Oldcastle and Peel's services, Andrew only met him twice. I will get Matthew to ask some questions and see if he can find anything that links Galveston with this Heresy."

CHAPTER TEN

Matthew's initial enquiries drew a blank. Peter didn't know if Galveston had any family, and none of the residents in the street near his office knew either. Galveston's life had been a solitary one. He didn't do much besides leaving his offices on Devereux's business. He bought his food locally, took meals in the Inn at the end of the street where he would sit alone, and occasionally met at the Angel with men he'd worked with at Oldfield & Peel.

The tavern at the end of the street, the Havelock Inn, was where Galveston habitually took his evening meal, apart from on a Sunday when he'd take some food prepared by the Inn on Saturday to eat in his rooms.

Master Black was the landlord and knew Galveston well, and he was horrified by what had happened to one of his regular patrons.

"Did you know of anyone who might have had an argument with Galveston?" Matthew asked of the innkeeper.

Black shook his head. "He was a quiet man, took his meals in peace, paid his bills and never had a crossed word with anyone. I told Justice Daytrew the same."

"Daytrew's been here, has he?" Matthew said, then asked. "An' what questions was he putting before you?"

"He just wanted to know if I knew of anyone who might do him harm, or if he owed money or if anyone had come asking for him. He'd even thought it had something to do with the poor water seller, until he found out the man was a fool and born with one arm. I can only tell you what I told the Justice that I can't help. Myself and Goodwife Black are appalled by what has happened, robbery it was, so they say, and in a respectable street like this," Black did indeed sound appalled by recent events.

Goodwife Black was a neat but dumpy woman, with a head now too small for her body, who wore a white starched coif around her head that was of a style that had long since been abandoned. Scenting gossip, she arrived at her husband's side. "He were a lovely man, really appreciated my cooking, and always had a kind word."

"Did he always take his meals alone? You never saw him with anyone else?" Matthew asked.

The woman shook her head, the wings of the white headwear drafting the air. "Sometimes, the lad who worked for him would come in, I can only assume he'd sent him on some errand or other, but he never stopped. Master Galveston always supped alone, same meal, every day."

"The same meal?" Matthew repeated, surprised.

"Yes indeed, sir. My game pie is the best in London. If you'd like to try it, we've some ready," Black's wife said, a proud smile on her pudgy face.

Matthew was about to brush her aside, but something made him change his mind. "I've a hunger on me, as it 'appens."

"You'll not be disappointed. Husband, find him a good table near the fire," tucking a straying strand of grey hair back inside the neat coif, the sizeable mistress Black turned and waddled on thickened ankles towards the kitchen.

"Where did Galveston sit?" Matthew asked quickly.

"Just here, near the fire, the best table in the inn. It seems a little wrong to have another in his place; perhaps you'd like to sit on the other side of the fire," Black suggested pointing to a different table.

"I'll take this one," Matthew settled into Galveston's accustomed seat.

"Of course, sir. As you wish," Black replied, clearly unhappy with this new man in his favoured customer's chair. The landlord brought a cup, a jug of cool ale, and shortly afterwards, a platter was carried to him with a pie, steam pluming from the slit crust, oozing a scent that was a true delight to the nose. Matthew smiled. "Join me, Master Black. I'm not a man who likes to take his meals alone."

Shrugging, Black accepted the invitation and pulled a chair to the opposite side of the table, pointing towards the pie he said. "You'll enjoy that. There's no finer cook than my Molly."

"Galveston always ate here, alone," Matthew said, cutting into the pie, filling the air with an even thicker aroma of game.

"I told you that already," Black sounded a little put-out.

"I just need to be sure. His employer, Master Devereux, is very keen to find those responsible," Matthew said, taking his first mouthful of the famed pie.

At the mention of the name Devereux, the smile fell from Black's face, and he sat in silence, his eyes fastened on the table.

"You're right, fine fayre," Matthew said between mouthfuls, and he wasn't lying. "So, Galveston had this very meal every day?"

Black nodded. "Apart from Sunday. My wife wrapped one for him to take with him on Saturday for his evening meal on Sunday."

"He didn't come in on Sundays?" Matthew asked between mouthfuls.

Black shook his head. "He was a man of habit, came in every day at the same time. My wife always had his meal ready, and we kept this table for him, and on Saturday, he'd pay for all his meals for the week."

Matthew's brow furrowed. "You trusted him to pay?"

"Of course! Master Galveston always paid on a Saturday, in full, never missed, never short and no excuses, not like some of my customers," Black grumbled, his eyes straying around the sparsely occupied room as if looking for the bad customers he was obviously thinking about.

Aye, Matthew thought, and he paid you with Devereux's coin, but he didn't share the thought. Instead, he said. "So, do you think it was robbery?"

Black seemed a little taken aback. "What else could it be? Master Galveston was a respectable man, sir."

"You said his clerk came in here sometimes, but he didn't stay. Any ideas why he came?" Matthew asked, tucking the last of the pie into his mouth and licking his fingers.

Black shrugged. "It wasn't often he'd call in, when he did he'd just exchange a quick word with Master Galveston and leave again."

"No idea why?"

Black shook his head. "If I recall rightly, he called in one day last week, just before the poor man was found dead."

Black's wife breezed over, admiring the empty platter. "I told you that you'd not regret it. Famous hereabouts are my pies."

Matthew smiled. "It was good. I can understand why Master Galveston would take one home with him on Saturday."

Black's wife waved a finger. "Not one, sir, but two. He loved my cooking, that poor man."

A tear sprang to her eye.

Matthew left shortly after, resolved to have another word with Galveston's clerk.

***

"He what?" Myles spluttered when Matthew told him what he had found out.

"He had a client from a print shop. Every three of four weeks, he would bring his accounts book over, and Galveston would make out the bills. He gave the lad the job to do. Then after he was finished, the lad dropped the key into the Havelock Inn where Galveston always had his evening meal," Matthew said, then added, "I've spoken to him. He told me he dropped the key at the Havelock Inn two nights before Galveston was murdered."

"Get that boy in here, now!" Myles growled.

Matthew returned with Peter fairly quickly. "Tell Master Devereux what you told me, lad, how you used to go into the Havelock Inn seeking your master."

Peter shrugged. "Master always took his meals there. If I'd work to finish, then I'd get it done and bring the key to him. That's all."

"What work did you do on your own?" Myles rounded his desk and stood over the boy.

"Master Galveston did some work for the printer on Chase Street. He had a book he kept, and Master Galveston would prepare the bills from it," Peter sensing the immediate danger in front of him, took a quick step backwards, away from Devereux.

"Galveston was working for a printer. Which one?" Myles said, taken aback.

"Master Preston, sir," Peter supplied.

"Are you sure?"

"Yes, master. That was the name I always penned a the top of the bills," Peter said quickly.

"Did he have any other clients?" Myles said. "Was this knave working for everyone and anyone!"

"I don't think this was a client, sir. I think he did the work as a favour," Peter said quietly.

"What makes you think that? What exactly did you overhear, lad?" Myles took a step towards the boy.

"Nothing, sir, I've not been listening at doors. Master Galveston used to grumble to me about doing the bills. That's why he got me to do them for him. He hated writing them out," Peter's voice was shrill and his explanation rapid.

"How often did he do them?" Myles retreated, leaning against the edge of his desk.

"Every three or four weeks. One of the print shop apprentices would bring them over and then collect them when they were done," Peter's hands had found the edge of his cloak again and fastened themselves in it.

"Were there any on the week he died?" Matthew asked.

Peter nodded. "I'd finished them and called into the Havelock to give Master Galveston the key back."

"So that was Thursday?" Myles said.

Peter shook his head. "Wednesday."

"Tell me what they looked like?" Myles said.

"Just bills. The name of the Printer, Master Preston, was at the top, then I'd copy out the services he had provided from his book. Master Galveston would have already noted the amounts down and done the reckonings, so I just needed to make a neat copy of them," Peter said, his voice worried now.

"Where did you leave them?" Myles asked.

"On his desk, I always just left them there. I think this week there were eight bills in total," Peter said, trying to be helpful.

"Well, they weren't bloody well there when we arrived. There was nothing like that on the desk, just the ledger and one of those day books," Myles said.

"The print shop could have collected them on Thursday, the day before Galveston was murdered," Matthew suggested.

"Possibly," Myles was heading across the room. "Let's call at Master Preston's print shop, shall we, and find out."

"Goodwife Black, at the Havelock, told me that on Saturday Galveston took home two pies with him. Did he meet with someone on Sunday?" Matthew asked, watching the boy closely.

Peter shook his head. "I don't know, sir. I didn't work on Sunday's and Master Galveston never said anything about it to me."

CHAPTER ELEVEN

When Peter was out of the room, Devereux produced the Protestant Declaration from beneath the ledger and pushed it towards Matthew. "Fitzwarren brought me that. Apparently, they've been nailed up all over London."

Matthew looked at it, puzzled.

"At the bottom, look, the writer shares the same surname as Galveston AND I'm wondering if they came from the same print shop he's been doing the bills for? Surely this can't be a coincidence?" Myles said. "If Galveston was tied up with this Heresy, that might well have been the cause of his death."

"You could be right," Matthew conceded. "This would get you thrown in the Tower. If Galveston was involved with this, then there is no telling who he has fallen foul of."

"Perhaps, the name is not common, and we have a link with a printer now. So perhaps Preston was producing these for Ad-Hyce in exchange for him producing the bills he wanted?" Myles said thoughtfully.

"There's only one way to find out," Matthew replied, turning towards the door, "I'll get the men ready."

If Devereux thought he would get an answer to his questions soon, he was mistaken. Arriving at the White Hart accompanied by two armed men was Justice Daytrew. Matthew expedited his passage through the Inn, up the stairs and into Myles' presence and his men were neatly disposed of to the yard at the back of the Inn with a promise of ale. The Justice's armed men on display in the tap room of the White Hart was just bad for business.

"Justice Daytrew, a pleasure," Myles said, managing a broad and almost convincing smile as the Justice waddled through the door.

"Thank you, Master Devereux, and I wish I could be here on more pleasant business," Daytrew said, his voice filled with sadness and the puckered fat of his brow furrowed with concern. The Justice's eyes, Myles noted, had already come to rest on the wine glasses on the side table.

"Do you have news regarding Galveston's murder?" Myles asked, his dark gaze fastened on the fat man.

Daytrew shook his head, jowls swaying. "A mysterious affair and I am afraid to say there has been another murder."

"What! In London, you do surprise me," Myles failed to keep the sarcasm from his voice.

Daytrew took the words at face value. "We live in uncertain times, Master Devereux, London is not the haven it once was. Even our Parish is suffering. Streets that were once safe are no longer so."

"True, true," Myles said, wondering when Daytrew was going to get to the point.

"And today, another murder, another life taken," Daytrew said, his voice saddening further.

Myles tried not to groan. Daytrew was going to have his moment, that fleeting instant when the bearer of news has the listener at a disadvantage. What men like Daytrew failed to realise is that the moment is soon gone. A moment of power, but a moment only. Myles selected one of the glasses and poured wine into it; raising it to his lips, he asked, "Pray tell, Justice Daytrew, what has happened?"

"Sad news, Ann Hesketh, has been found murdered in her home this morning," Justice Daytrew delivered the news slowly, enjoying each word as he uttered it. His greedy eyes had again flicked back to the wine and the glasses.

Myles' face remained blank; taking a sip from the glass, he asked, "I am sure the passing of Mistress Hesketh is a sadness to her family, but I am not sure why you are bringing me this news?"

A look of disappointment slackened Daytrew's features. "We've been told that you must know Anne Hesketh. She has borrowed money and was in the habit of receiving a weekly visit from your book-keeper, Master Galveston."

"I am sorry, I am not acquainted with the names of all those who owe me money. Matthew, and before his sad demise, Master Galveston, would have dealt with them. So the name would be known to them. Let me call Matthew," Myles said, his tone helpful.

"Of course," Daytrew said, still sounding disappointed.

Myles opened the door to the outer office and made the pretence of calling Matthew's name. There was, of course, no need, as Matthew had been diligently listening to the conversation on the other side of the door.

"Matthew, Justice Daytrew has just come to tell us of the untimely demise of Anne ...." Myles paused and looked at Daytrew.

"Hesketh," Daytrew provided. "Anne Hesketh."

"Anne Hesketh," Myles repeated, smiling, then to Matthew, "Is that name familiar to you?"

"It certainly is," confirmed Matthew. "Anne Hesketh's son was in the debtor's gaol at Marshalsea, and she borrowed money for his board and lodge. He was released about a few weeks ago, I believe."

"And she owes you money?" Daytrew questioned.

"Apparently so," Myles said simply, his empty hands, palms up over, held out before him.

"Was she up to date with her payments?" Daytrew ventured a little nervously.

Myles eyed him closely. "It would take me a little time to check, having had my book-keeper removed from my employ rather suddenly."

"Of course, I understand. If you would make it a priority, Master Devereux, it would be appreciated," Daytrew replied, his eyes resting on the glass in Devereux's hand.

When a disappointed Daytrew had left, Myles turned on Matthew. "Hesketh is on the list of people Galveston used to rob me. What does this mean?"

Matthew held his hands up. "It doesn't mean anything. Anne Hesketh lived near the butcher's shop on Folgate Lane, a poor area. Her son owed money for gambling debts, and Lord knows what else. And you didn't deal with Daytrew very well, either. It's better to keep him well disposed towards you, and you set to annoy him."

"Did I?" Myles said, draining the wine glass and setting it down with a clink.

"You damned well know you did," Matthew said heatedly.

"Nothing more than the fat shit deserves," Myles shot back.

"That very well might be the case, but that doesn't mean to say it was wise, does it?" Matthew rebuked. "Your book-keeper is dead, and now one of your debtors is, and the only common link I can see between the two is you, and I'm not the only one who is going to be thinking that either."

Myles pressed his palms into his eyes. "Why is this happening, Matthew?"

"I don't know. I'll find out what happened to Hesketh. If you'd given Daytrew the opportunity, he would have been more than happy to give you all the details," Matthew said, annoyed.

CHAPTER TWELVE

Ann Hesketh's house was a poor affair, crammed between a carpenter's warehouse and a butchers shop in Folgate Lane. What had been a yard or open space had been roofed to provide a small one-roomed house. The front showed only a door, and there were no windows in the wooden walls. It had an appearance of dereliction, despite the current occupant having been absent for less than a day.

Matthew headed first towards the carpenter's shop, where a man already regarded him with suspicion. The carpenter, sandy-haired and freckled, with bare strong arms and wearing an apron that bristled with the tools of his trade, watched his approach.

"You knew Anne Hesketh?" Matthew asked, walking towards the carpenter.

"Aye, she was a good, hardworking soul. An' who are you to come askin' after 'er?" the carpenter said, sliding an awl into the tool pocket on his apron.

"My Master is interested in finding out what happened to her, that's all," Matthew answered, squaring his shoulders, his thumbs finding his belt.

"An' who'd that be then?" the carpenter drawled.

"Master Devereux," Matthew said, and watched with some satisfaction as some of the colour left the carpenter's face, then asked, "Her son went into Marshalsea, is he still in there?"

"That good for nuthin', no, unfortunately. The Good Lord should have made sure he stayed in there and rotted for what he did to poor Annie," the carpenter said, then spat on the ground to underline his depth of feeling on the matter.

"What did he do?" Matthew asked.

"Worked herself to death, at least she would have if …. " the carpenter stopped abruptly.

"And that was her son's fault?" Matthew pressed.

"Of course it was! The poor woman was always trying to find money for him. Every penny he ever had, he'd gambled with, and then she'd be left trying to pay off his debts time and time again," the carpenter's tone was bitter.

"Do you think that had something to do with what happened to her?" Matthew asked, his head inclining in the direction of her tiny house.

The carpenter looked at him nervously. "I can't say, but she didn't do that to herself."

"What about her son? Have you seen him?" Matthew asked.

The carpenter shook his head. "Not for a few days, he got out of gaol, came here to see what he could scrounge from his poor mother, and I've not seen him since."

"He doesn't know his mother is dead?" Matthew asked.

"No, I don't think he will, not until he comes back to see if he can get some money from her," the carpenter said, folding his arms across his chest.

"I heard she'd been found hanged. Maybe the trials of life had become too much," Matthew suggested.

"I am sure they had become too much for her a long time ago, but she didn't commit the sin of killing herself," the carpenter crossed himself. "Annie was a good Christian and a God-fearing soul. She'd not have added an eternity in purgatory to her life's sufferings. Anyway, she couldn't have done it."

"How can you be so sure?" Matthew asked.

"Well, if you are going to throw a rope over a beam and hang yourself, then you'll need something to step up on," the carpenter said bluntly.

"What do you mean?" Matthew asked, frowning.

The carpenter leaned forwards, his face hard. "There's not a stick of furniture in there save a pallet on the floor. Anne burnt what there was last winter. So tell me, how did a woman who barely came up to my shoulder hang herself four feet from the ground?"

Matthew frowned. "Are you sure?"

"Of course, I'm sure. The poor woman had one stool, and she sold that to me a month back, not that it was worth much, but I felt sorry for her and couldn't see her starve. She'll have needed the money to pay that robbing bastard …. " the carpenter stopped himself just in time before mentioning Matthew's employer. "She'll have needed the money to feed herself, what with her son being in Marshalsea."

"Did anyone come looking for her son? People he owed money to?" Matthew continued with his enquiries.

"Oh yes," the carpenter shook his head. "He's a witless fool. Part of me thinks poor Annie is better off now rather than worrying about who would come knocking on her door next."

"Do you think she was killed because of his debts?" Matthew asked.

The carpenter's face twisted. "I wouldn't have thought so. He usually owed money to the lads in the Havelock tavern. Why would they do that? Without Anne, they've no chance of being paid. And they're violent, but killing an old woman is a stretch even for them."

"So you know who her son owed money to? What was his name?" Matthew asked.

"If you are lookin' for the lads from the Havelock he owed, then you ask for Jeddie Tansin, and don't be going saying you got that name from me neither," the carpenter said firmly.

Matthew turned his head towards the small house crammed between the two shops. "Is it locked?"

The carpenter shook his head. "Nah, there's a wood latch holding the door shut, and that's it. There's nowt in there to steal."

Matthew stepped towards the ill-fitting door and lifted the wooden latch. The door, badly hinged, swung open on its own.

The carpenter was still behind him. "It was me who found her. Annie was always up and about early. When I didn't see her or get an answer at her door, I let myself in."

Matthew stepped over the threshold into the small interior. At the back, a hole in the roof had let the smoke out from a fire set in nothing more than a small pit dug in the earth floor surrounded by cobblestones. The room smelt damp. A rustle in the corner told of rats, they had moved into the mouldering low pallet bed covered in dank rags that was now vacant.

"She was tied up there. You can still see the rope. They cut her down, but the knot is still there round the beam," the carpenter said, pointing.

The only solid-looking part of the structure was the thick beam that ran between the carpenter's workshop and the butcher's shop. It had been used as the support for the roof, and around the middle was still wound the remains of the hemp rope.

Matthew reached up. His hands were a good two feet short of the beam, and as the carpenter had said, there wasn't a stick of furniture in the room. The rope had not been looped over the beam. It was knotted around it, which meant someone had been close enough to do that. So she'd either had help and, more than likely, that help had been unwanted.

"She'd not broken her neck neither," the carpenter continued, "She'd choked, tongue hanging out all purple and swollen, looking like a cows. Her eyes were red and looked ready to pop and her fingers trapped in the rope round her neck. It was a sight I'd rather I'd not seen."

Matthew frowned. "Trapped?"

"Yes, like she'd been trying to pull it off, and it had tightened before she could get her hand out of the way," the carpenter said, "I don't care what anyone says, it wasn't Annie that did this to herself, even that idiot Justice could see it was a case of murder."

"Justice Daytrew?" Matthew asked, "What did he want to know?"

"Same as you, and I gave him the same answers I told you. She'd not killed herself. She couldn't have," The carpenter said, shaking his head sadly.

"I agree. It doesn't sound like it at all," Matthew said.

As he left, securing the latch, Matthew was aware of a man across the street watching him closely. Broad chested, a leather jerkin neatly buttoned and a dark feather-topped cap pulled over his head, shadowing his face. Matthew met his gaze momentarily, running his eyes over the man from head to foot before stepping towards the butcher's shop.

Outside, attesting to the freshness of the meat on offer, were two heads on spikes still leaking blood into the gutter. Stepping around them Matthew entered the shop.

"Now then, sir, what can I be getting for you?" A large man asked, his hand's blood-stained, a knife in one, was in the process of butchering the pig whose head now graced his shop front.

"Did you know Anne Hesketh that lived next to you?" Matthew asked, gesturing in the direction of her house.

The butcher's face soured, and the knife that had been cutting through the meat stopped. "Aye, I did."

"Know anything about what happened to her?" Matthew continued, keeping his tone conversational.

"Why don't you ask that nosey shit?" the butcher retrieved the knife and pointed towards his neighbour's shop with it, sending blood splats towards Matthew, "The damned carpenter, he found her, called the watch. If you want to know anything you go and ask him," the butcher said bluntly turning the knife back to the fresh kill. "Who are you to be askin' about Annie? Anyway, you don't look like the Sheriff's man."

"I'm Master Devereux's man, and that's why I'm asking," Matthew said bluntly.

The butcher stopped in the act of pulling the sharp blade through the meat. "Aye, well, I knew Annie, but I don't know what happened. I don't live here. My house is two streets away. All I know is that when I came to open the shop, the street was full of people, her door was open, and they were carrying her body out."

"The carpenter said her son owed money. Do you know anything about that?" Matthew asked, watching the butcher's face closely.

"That good for nothin' owed money to anyone who was fool enough to lend it to him or play cards with him. The boy's an idiot," the butcher said, forcing a knife through and separating the hock from the rear quarter of the pig he was butchering.

"The carpenter doesn't think she killed herself. What do you think?" Matthew asked.

"I don't rightly know. I wasn't here, and the poor woman didn't have much to live for. Her son, a wastrel, owing money to the likes of your master with little means to pay and working every hour God sent, not much of a life, and it wouldn't have been a long one the way she was going anyway," the butcher said, trying to turn his attention back to his work, and making it obvious he didn't want to talk to Matthew.

"What do you mean?" Matthew asked.

"She was ill, had a swelling on her back, couldn't walk right anymore, it wasn't going to be long before she couldn't work, and then what was she going to do?" the butcher said.

"Sounds like you knew her fairly well?" Matthew said.

"I did. She was a close friend of my mother. She ran a respectable laundry shop next to the Havelock until her husband died, and then her son stole away what little she had and she was left to live out the last of her days in that dank hovel. That damned carpenter should be ashamed of himself for charging her to live there," the butcher growled.

"She was his tenant?" Matthew asked, looking in the direction of the carpenter's workshop.

"Yes, she was. God rest her soul," the butcher said with feeling.

"He said some of her son's debtors would come looking for him. Do you think this could have had anything to do with them?" Matthew asked.

The butcher straightened and impaled the bloody blade in the side of the wooden block. "Very possibly, he had no sense. He'd borrow from anyone with not a thought about how he would settle the debt. Plenty over the years came here looking for him, and many of them had a threat on their lips."

Matthew nodded towards the carpenter's shop. "He seemed to think it was just the lads at the Havelock Tavern, her son was involved with, and he didn't think they'd harm the old woman."

The butcher spat on the floor. "They wouldn't, but he was involved with things that don't end right, if you know what I mean."

"No, I don't," Matthew said.

The butcher leaned towards him and whispered, "Sedition."

Matthew's brow furrowed in confusion. "How so?"

"He'd do anything for money, that one, and worked for a preacher nailing his words up around the city after dark. And no doubt that's why he's not been seen for a few days. I told the Justice the same?" The butcher said.

"You said sedition? What do you mean?" Matthew asked.

The butcher cast his arms wide. "I don't know, and it's not my business. The idiot said he'd taken money from some foolish preacher to spread his Lutheranism ramblings. Said he'd charged the man twice what he'd asked for, but the preacher didn't object as long as he got the job done."

"Do you know which preacher?" Matthew asked.

The butcher shook his head.

"How do you know this, then? Did Annie tell you?" Matthew asked.

"No. That boy, Danny Hesketh, was a fool, and he was in here treating himself to cooked mutton, and I very much doubt he took any back for his mother. He was bragging about his work and the money he made from it. He said he made half a penny for every nail he banged in. Bloody fool," the butcher said.

"Annie might have died because he was involved in this. Do you think that is possible?" Matthew asked.

The butcher shrugged. "Maybe. You never know who he spoke to, and there's a lot take more than a passing dislike to these Protestant words being nailed up on church doors on the Sabbath."

Matthew asked a few more questions. When he was satisfied that the butcher had little more to tell him, he left the shop, sidestepping the dripping pig's head. Across the street, the man with the feathered cap still stood, back resting against the wall, arms folded across his chest, one leg raised, the booted foot on the wall. The man was looking directly at him. As Matthew watched, he removed his feathered cap and performed a slight bow in his direction, smiling.

Matthew looked up and down the street. The man appeared to be alone. What other activity there was seemed in keeping with the area, and there were no more loitering strangers, at least not within his line of sight.

Matthew strode across the road and stood before the man who was fitting his cap back to his head.

"You wished to speak with me," Matthew said, his thumbs finding their habitual home in his belt.

Feather Cap smiled again. "Not me, sir, no, but my master said that if you've a mind to meet with him, the welcome will be a warm one."

"Does he now. And do I know your master?" Matthew asked.

The man's smile turned into an ugly leer. "I'm sure you do."

A cold feeling ran up Matthew's spine, and his expression hardened. "Tell me?"

"Master Bennett," Feather Cap said, then performing another mock bow, he turned and walked up the street, leaving Matthew staring at his back.

Matthew returned to the White Hart via the Havelock Inn. Goodwife Black, who had now been informed by her husband of the name of Matthew's employer, was not pleased to see him again. However she did know the name Jeddie Tansin, unfortunately she also knew he'd been interred in Bridewell Prison for knifing a man in the back and stealing his purse. The attack, about a month ago, had been witnessed, and Jeddie had been caught not long after.

Another dead end.

An hour later Matthew was back at the White Hart.

"It's not good," he announced after he'd closed the door to Myles' room behind him.

Myles flopped down in one of the chairs near the fire. "Go on."

"She was murdered. There's no way she could have hung herself, Daytrew might be an idiot but even he can see it was murder," Matthew said, "But I did learn something else. Her son, Danny Hesketh, the one who was in and out of Marshalsea. Apparently, he got out of Marshalsea a week or so ago, and he's been working for a preacher nailing his teachings up on church doors and the like. Got well paid for it, apparently."

Myles rose from the chair. "Did you find out what the preacher was called?"

Matthew shook his head. "All I know is that Danny gossiped with the butcher, telling him he was being well paid to nail up this preacher's word. More than that, he didn't know."

Myles crossed to the desk and picked up the folded sheet Fitzwarren had brought him. "It has to be these?"

"There's a link. But what it is, I don't know. Galveston shares the same name as the writer of that Heresy, and one of your debtor's sons, who is now dead, distributed them ...."

Myles held his hand up, stilling Matthew's words. "There is something we have not considered. I think we have missed the obvious .... Could Galveston have been the author of these? Was that why he was tortured and murdered? Then Anne Hesketh is murdered because her son was involved in distributing them?"

"I would never have taken Galveston as a religious man at all, but you never know ...." Matthew replied thoughtfully, one hand tugging at his beard. "And it does explain the manner of his death and Anne Hesketh's murder as well. Her son hasn't been seen for days, it could be he is well aware of the danger he is in, and that's why he's not to be found."

"And the boy told us Galveston did the work for the printer as a favour, so was this what he was getting in exchange for preparing the bill?" Myles groaned and waved the creased sheet in the air.

"I think that sounds very likely. We should tell Daytrew, I doubt very much he has made the connection. All he has to link these two murders is you," Matthew advised.

"Perhaps, first, I think a visit to Galveston's printer is in order. We can deliver him to Daytrew as proof of the scheme?" Myles' relief was visible. He dropped into the chair, one leg looped over the arm. The tension of a short few moments ago draining from him. It wasn't Bennett. It wasn't a threat to himself or his business.

"The printers will be shut by now, and it will easily take us an hour to get there. If we go now, and he's not there, we could alert him to the danger, and he could evade us tomorrow. Better to arrive in the morning when his business is open. I'll get the lads to check in the meantime, though, to make sure Preston is still there," Matthew suggested.

It seemed a sensible course of action, Myles nodded slowly. "Alright, we'll go in the morning, and if you find out he's already gone then we can take that as evidence to Daytrew."

"Agreed," Matthew said, a smile on his face. He, too seemed to be sharing in Devereux's relief that the situation was one that had little to do with his master.

The bed was a testament to the fleeting visit sleep had paid Myles during a long night. It had stalked in with a false promise of peace, then prodded and poked him, turning him this way and that until the bed looked like a battleground.

Pillows had fallen to the floor, and a fur that ordinarily covered his feet had slithered down to join it. The linen had been fresh but was now creased, the covers laying on the top like an angry sea filled with spiked waves. His agitation during the night had dislodged several feathers from the mattress, and the sharpened quills had found soft flesh to scrape and jab at. And worse, he was cold.

The sensible course of action would have been to retrieve the fur from the floor, but that would mean leaving the bed, and Myles had no intention of giving up what warmth there was. Myles pulled the blankets closer. It was his own fault. The servants would not venture into his room while he was there, if he'd been absent the night before, even for a short time, the fire would have been banked up, fresh wood added to the hearth, and his bed would have been warmed. But he hadn't left his room, he'd been too busy to notice that the fire had burnt down, too distracted to realise that the room was cold and too annoyed to recognise how chilled he had become before he slithered into his icy bed which had served only to remove the last of the warmth from his body.

If Myles had once looked through the window across the rooftops of London and felt like a king, that was no longer the case, now he felt more like Lazarus. Pushing himself up on his elbows, he leaned forward and tried to rearrange the pillows into something more comfortable before he sat back. The maneuver failed, the pillow ejected itself to the floor, and his shoulders pressed against the cold and uncomfortable carved headboard, the pointed relief biting into his back.

Devereux cursed. Even his bed didn't want him. Flinging back the covers, he swung his legs over the side, a snapped quill from the feather mattress delivering another painful scrape to his legs before his already cold feet slapped on the floor. Snatching a bed robe from where it hung over a chairback, he applied himself to the task of setting and lighting the fire. There was plenty of wood. A large basket filled with axed chunks of white dry pine, aged bark peeling from the outer edges, the other next to it held kindling, crisp, dry slivers of wood eager to take a flame.

Rising, he examined his work. Thin twists of grey smoke rose from the centre of the small pyre, where a fierce orange flame began taking hold of the shavings and thin slices of wood he had added. He watched it for a few more minutes, confident it was set, he balanced two larger pieces of wood on the top and pulled the robe tighter around himself. The fire, as yet, had little impact on the room.

Yesterday he had wanted to go to the printers, but after Daytrew's visit, Matthew had advised against it. Myles was regretting his decision to postpone the encounter.

CHAPTER THIRTEEN

Devereux stopped on the threshold of the printer's workshop and waited while Matthew disappeared inside. The noise of the press, the smell of the ink along with an undercurrent of damp and rot seeped through the doorway to where he waited.

Matthew appeared, saying quietly, "The shop's owner, Preston, is in his office waiting for you."

Devereux began pulling the riding gloves from his long fingers and stalked through the print shop towards the office at the back. Inside, standing near the opened doorway, wearing an ink-stained apron that stopped below the knees and a close-fitting felt cap, was the print shop owner.

Myles said nothing. Entering the office, he closed the door behind him, reviewed the available furniture, and then pushing a pile of neatly stacked papers from a chair he seated himself.

"No ...." Preston took a step forward, the pain on his face evident as he watched his endeavors slither to the floor.

Myles crossed one leg over the other, fastened his linked hands around his knee and regarded Preston with a cold stare. "Many would argue that heretical papers deserve to be in the gutter, don't you agree?"

"They .... those were ten volumes of legal treatise for Chadwell's at Lincoln's Inn," Preston stammered, looking in horror at the scattered sheets.

"Really?" Myles leaned down and fished one of the pages from the floor. "I see you are right, it will be the Devil's work to put those back in order."

"Indeed," Preston lamented, his eyes still on the mound of disorganised pages, "How can I help you, Master Devereux?"

Slowly, Myles slid a hand inside his doublet and retrieved the folded page Fitzwarren had left with him. "I wondered," Myles said, smoothing out the page, "If you might recognise this. I think this is your work."

Myles held the unfolded sheet out towards Preston.

The printer's hand reached out, the response automatic, accepting the offered sheet.

"Well? Do you recognise it?" Myles demanded, watching the printer closely.

Preston put the page down on the desk, fished in his apron pocket for glasses which he found, and pressed them onto the bridge of his nose. Lifting the page from the desk, he examined it, without raising his eyes from the sheet, he said. "This is not something I have produced, nor would I if I were asked to."

"Why's that?" Myles said, studying the printer carefully.

Preston raised his gaze from the sheet, his eyes meeting those of Myles from behind the smeared lenses of his glasses. "This is Heresy, Master Devereux. I would be a fool to print this."

"I think you were that fool," Myles settled himself back in the chair and watched with some satisfaction as Preston paled. "Galveston? You knew him?"

Preston's eyes opened in alarm. "I had heard of his unfortunate murder, robbery so they are saying."

"So they are. That didn't answer my question, though, did it?" Myles said, his voice threatening.

"Umm …. he often prepared bills for me for my clients," Preston said quietly, avoiding Devereux's cold eyes.

"Indeed," Myles paused, "Did you pay him?"

"Of course, sir. I'd not take work from a man without recompensing him for it," Preston replied defensively.

"His clerk tells me that one of your men brought over bills to be made out just before he died. Is that right?" Myles continued, narrow eyes fixed on the printer.

"It is. Master Galveston would produce bills for my clients. Some of the work we do is for the Parish, and they won't part with so much as a groat unless they have a bill for the works," Preston explained, his empty palms open.

"Just the Parish?" Myles asked.

Preston shook his head. "Just for my larger clients, the Parish, some of the Legal Chambers at Lincoln's Inn and the Bishop of Winchester."

"Did you collect the bills yourself?" Myles asked.

Preston shook his head. "The first I knew of the unfortunate events was when I sent one of my lads over to collect them, and they came back and told me what had happened."

"So he hadn't prepared the bills?" Myles said.

"I don't know if he had or he hadn't, there's no one to ask, and it seems a rather trivial matter when the poor man has been murdered," Preston said.

Myles leaned back in the chair. "I understand. But surely you would need your notes back so you could get the bills drawn up elsewhere?"

"Luckily, I keep a copy here," Preston retrieved a wax tablet from the desk and held it up, I used this to make a list for Master Galveston and luckily didn't destroy this, so I still have the list of clients and their requirements. Otherwise, it would have been a problematic issue for me."

"I think he prepared the bills for you in exchange for printing these," Myles stabbed the sheet with a finger.

"I can assure you, sir, this is not my work," Preston stammered.

Myles didn't reply, but just fixed the printer with a cold stare. Preston continued, his words a rapid ramble refuting any involvement. "I didn't produce these, sir, I can assure you .... It would be too foolish to involve myself .... My business is a respectable one. Many of my clients are clerics. I do a lot of work for the Bishop of Winchester. I'd never jeopardise my reputation by being involved with this."

Myles glared at Preston. It wasn't the reply he'd wanted. "Someone was a fool. If it wasn't you, then who was it?"

Preston reversed the sheet, examining the paper and shrugged.

"Come on, man. You trade in the printed word. You must be able to tell me something about it. Prove it was not your doing," Myles said, his voice raised, and he leaned over the desk towards the printer. "And you'll need to. I imagine you'll get a visit from the Justice very shortly asking the same questions."

Preston looked between the page and his visitor, realising he would not be easily satisfied; he relented, the hands that held the sheet shook violently, the paper rattling in his hold. "The paper is Dutch ..... Certainly Dutch .... most of the paper in England comes from there."

Preston stopped.

"That hardly proves you did not produce it, does it?" Myles said, folding his arms.

Preston swallowed hard, and returned his gaze to the trembling sheet. "It is of the cheapest and poorest quality. Look here at the top; there is staining. The paper arrives in bales, it's well wrapped in linen and tied closed, but sometimes the outer pages are either marked or deformed, and these are generally sold separately," Preston said, "I would suspect that it was part of a quire that's been sold together."

"A quire?" Myles' brows furrowed.

"Yes, a block of twenty-five sheets. Do you have any more of these?" Preston asked, looking up nervously from the page.

"No, just the one. Why?" Myles demanded.

"I would suspect the other sheets will be similarly marked, have poor edging or other damage to the pages," Preston explained, pointing to an imperfect edge that bore a brown stain.

"Where would this have come from? Do you sell paper?" Myles asked.

Preston shook his head. "The Stationers Guild control all the suppliers of paper. Everything that comes in from overseas is recorded, and they set tariffs on it. I buy my paper from Harker's in Fleet Street, a large printing workshop that also deals in importing paper. It might be that you could match this to supplies they have. The watermark is not one I've seen before. It's a circle with a cross through it."

Myles took the page from Preston and held it up. "Where? I can't see anything."

"Here, towards the top, in the middle, if you hold the sheet near the lamp, you'll see it more easily," Preston said, helpfully pushing an oil lamp on the desk towards Devereux.

Myles found the watermark, smaller than he had thought it would be, a circle containing a cross, the edges of the cross reaching the outer rim of the ring. Myles fished one of the legal treatise from the floor and held it near the lamp, his eyes searching for a watermark. When he found it, he was disappointed to find it looked like a ship and nothing at all like the one on the page he had brought with him.

"Or you could try and track down the compositor," Preston continued while Myles examined the documents.

"The compositor?" Myles said, lowering the page and fixing Preston with a hard stare over the top of it.

"The compositor sets the type, and there are some unusual spellings in this document," Preston said, an inked forefinger pointing to the page, "If this type was set in London, these words would be set differently."

Myles leaned forward in his chair. "Which ones?"

"Get, had, set and also ...." Preston's finger hovered over the page, "yes, here it is, fit."

Myles waved his hand towards a pen on Preston's desk. "Show me how you would set those words for type."

Preston reversed the sheet, found a pen on his desk, dipped it and wrote.

"Gette .... Hadde .... Sette .... fitte."

Myles rose from the chair. "So, in London, those words would be set like that?"

Preston nodded. "That is the convention." Preston picked up a sheet from his desk and held it toward Myles. "You can see here how those words have been printed. This is a sheet from one of ten volumes I am printing for the Bishop of Winchester, at the top is the word Hadde."

Myles cast his eyes over the page and smiled grimly. "We all know you charge by the letter!"

"Sir, it's the current style," Preston protested defensively.

"So you are saying this compositor didn't know the current style. So either these were not printed in London, or they were printed by someone who doesn't work in a print workshop," Myles said, "Do you agree?"

"That would be a fair assessment. If you can't match the paper, then perhaps they were imported," Preston said, "But I can't say for certain. I wish I could be more help."

"Undoubtedly," Myles said sarcastically, then added, "Do you know Galveston's surname?"

"I do now, sir, Ad-Hyce. Before his unfortunate murder, I'd only known him as Master Galveston," Preston said, taking the glasses from his nose and wiping them on his apron.

"And where did you meet him?" Myles asked quickly.

"He used to work with a firm of book-keepers, Oldcastle & Peel if I remember rightly, they are in Shore Lane just to the left of the Hammer and Anvil Tavern, I used them for preparing bills, then when Master Galveston left their employ, I approached him directly, it was a good arrangement for both of us," Preston said, breathing on his glasses, he tried again to polish the smears from them.

"Did you see the name at the bottom of that sheet," Myles pointed towards it.

Preston frowned and picked it up again. "My word, the same name, I'd not noticed."

Myles scowled, he doubted very much that Preston had missed it. He'd found the watermark, and a myriad of misspelt words, it was unlikely he would have overlooked the name at the bottom.

"Perhaps a relative? Did Master Galveston ever mention any?" Myles asked.

Preston shook his head. "Our discussions were just confined to our business."

"I am sure they were," Myles said, his words heavy with sarcasm. "I will try and trace the paper as you suggest, but if anything else occurs to you, it would be wise to let me know before I find out - and believe me, I will find out."

Myles, the sheet refolded and stowed inside his doublet, left the print shop. There was no direct proof of Preston's involvement, and presenting him to Daytrew wouldn't resolve the issue. There wasn't enough to link him to the sheets nailed to the church doors. He needed more proof.

Riding back to the White Hart, Myles leaned his head close to Matthew. "I can't believe he hadn't noticed the name at the bottom of the sheet."

"Agreed. Preston knows more than he's admitting to. I'll have a couple of the men keep an eye on him and see what he gets up to," Matthew said, glancing over his shoulder towards the print shop.

CHAPTER FOURTEEN

The covers were smooth on his bed. Myles flipped them back and ran a hand over the mattress. His complaints had been heeded, it seemed. The feather bolster that graced the top of the bed had been re-sleeved in fresh linen, and the broken quills that had launched a sharp assault on his legs were gone. A fire burnt gently in the grate, the wood baskets were refilled, and from somewhere, the sweet scent of rosemary was infusing the air in the room.

Myles pulled the sheet from his doublet and, dropping down into a chair near the fire, examined it. On the back now was the list of words with the standard printers spelling added by Preston. Myles reversed it. His eyes wandered over the name at the bottom and then were drawn to the opening line.

"A truth defiled by the Pope will lead all men down the path to Hell, there will be no salvation for the misguided. There can be no excuse when men can hear the true word of God and choose to ignore it. I beseech you to free yourself from this diabolical Heresy woven by the Church in the name of God. Release yourselves and find salvation in the truth ...."

Myles read the rest of the religious rant, and when he finished, he wondered exactly what the writer was trying to convey? Surely they could have stated their message in simple terms in about three line? The Pope is lying to you. Don't believe him. If you do, you'll go to Hell. It would have been a quicker summary.

So what was linking this together?

So far, he had a dead book-keeper and now a deceased debtor. He was reasonably sure Preston had seen the name at the bottom of the page of print and had chosen to ignore it. So the printer knew something. Plus, his bills were missing; the clerk had completed them, and left them on Galveston's desk, and the printer said he had not collected them before Galveston was murdered. So where was the truth? Had Preston collected the bills? Was he a part of this religious conspiracy?

It was possible. Galveston knew Anne Hesketh; he'd no doubt known her son and been aware that he had been released from Marshalsea. He was known to be a man who would do anything for money and also a fool, so he could have recruited him to nail up the sheets he obtained from Preston. It could be that the money he had stolen from Devereux had been used to fund this religious endeavor and that the coins had paid for the paper and printing costs and Danny Hesketh's fees. It did fit together rather well.

Why had Galveston been murdered, though, and by who? And then there was the missing page in the ledger.

Myles looked towards the book of accounts, now sitting closed on his desk. If it had been on Galveston's desk on the night of his murder, it would have been natural to be open at the most recent page. If someone had tried to pull it from him and Galveston had resisted, that could explain why the page was missing, torn out in the struggle. He was reasonably sure the ledger had been used to hammer the knife into the wooden floor.

But that left two loose ends.

Two annoying items, and both of them were missing. The torn-out page and the bills that had been prepared for Preston.

Devereux tapped his fingers on the desk. It had to be Preston or someone closely linked to him. If the bills were on Galveston's desk, then they had a value to him, and if he had been there, he wouldn't have left them, and they also gave the printer a legitimate reason to visit Galveston in the first place. It couldn't be proved if he had taken them, but why would anyone else take a pile of bills when they had left the ledger?

An image, of Garrison Bennett wandered, unwanted, into Devereux's mind.

The evidence, thank the Lord, was beginning to move away from him as the perpetrator of Galveston's murder. He may have taken the bills but Bennett wouldn't have left the ledger. That would have been a treasure trove for him, details of all of Devereux's dealings, the names, the amounts. He would not have taken half a page; he'd have taken the whole ledger.

Then there was the locked coffer. Galveston would have had the lid ripped off to find out what lay inside if he had not found the key around Galveston's neck. If it was a robbery, a tortured Galveston would have told them where the key was. But that hadn't been their motive. They'd wanted to learn something, but it had nothing to do with money.

Heresy.

His mind kept on coming back to that one word.

Heresy.

Galveston and Preston must have been involved in promoting the Protestant cause, and in Mary's Catholic England that was dangerous. The Queen had eyes and ears everywhere, men were paid to inform on their neighbours, and the Queen's thirst for purging Protestant souls with fire seemed never ending.

Devereux pressed the palms of his hands into his eyes to stop his train of thought. Stop his mind conjuring for him the blazing faggots, jeering crowd, stoney-faced mounted officials, the running of blood released from flesh .....

Stop .... Stop .... Stop.

He didn't, couldn't, watch his brother burn again.

Myles blindly crossed the room. One shaking hand found a glass, the other the wine. The heavy Venetian decanter chattered on the rim of the glass, and a glug of wine slopped into the bowl a second before the glass cracked. Myles, blood-red wine running through his fingers, was left holding only the broken stem.

With a guttural cry, he flung the remains of the glass across the room and raised the decanter to his lips with two unsteady hands. He took three deep mouthfuls of wine before lowering it and letting out a shaking breath. He slowly filled another glass, and raising it in a trembling hand, took a seat by the hearth.

After a few moments, his breathing had steadied, and his train of thought was stopped by the sound of a tap on the door. For once, it was an interruption that he was thankful for.

Another thing Myles never did, was to eat in public. His meals were brought to the outer room and left on the table. Thus preserving the deception that the servants never entered his room. Rising, Myles pushed the door open, and the aroma of warm food met his nostrils. Sitting on a table on a tray was his food. Whoever had delivered it had tapped on his door and then immediately left.

Gathering the tray, Myles returned to the room and set it on his desk next to the ledgers and the damnable Protestant lament Fitzwarren had brought. Devereux lowered himself into the chair behind the desk, took another long, steadying draught of wine, and set the glass down with a firmer hand next to the tray. Pulling the ledger and his notes towards him, he began to leaf through the pages while he ate. Behind him, the bells of St Bride's struck for compline, and Myles' hand reached towards the plate.

It was empty.

Myles scowled at it. His attention had been on the list Preston had made on the reverse of the sheet, and he'd been contemplating those rather than giving any attention to his meal, which was now gone, and he had little recollection of having enjoyed it.

An hour later, backed by his men, Myles stalked into the Angel, where he found the man he wanted to talk to.

"You do like to ruin my game?" Fitzwarren complained as he followed Myles into his private room.

"To hell with your game, Fitzwarren," Myles grumbled, kicking the door closed with a slam.

"What's happened?" Fitzwarren asked.

"It's created more questions than answers?" Myles produced the sheet Richard Fitzwarren had given him a few days ago.

Richard's eyes flicked down to the sheet, but he didn't take it. "How so?"

Myles hitched himself onto the edge of the table. "The printer accepts that he used Galveston to produce bills for his clients and says he had a batch to collect, but Galveston was murdered before he did. Those bills weren't in his office. We'd have seen them."

"Burnt?" Fitzwarren asked.

"Possibly," Myles conceded.

"A man had been murdered, and you didn't check to see if anything had been disposed of in the fire?" Fitzwarren said, an incredulous note in his voice.

"No, I didn't," Myles said heatedly.

"What did you find out from the printer?" Fitzwarren asked.

"That the Printer is a liar. He clearly saw the name at the bottom of that sheet but professes that he didn't know Galveston's surname until after he was murdered. He identified a watermark which might allow me to trace the paper, and the spelling of the words are not commonly used amongst London printers," Myles summarised.

Fitzwarren raised the sheet from the desk holding it over the candle, evidently searching for the watermark.

"It's towards the top, in the middle," Myles advised, pointing. "It's a circle with a cross inside it."

"That has to make it easier to trace," Fitzwarren said, his eyes on the page.

"Hmmm, perhaps. Preston advised me to take it to the Stationers Guild. They control all the paper imports, so they might be able to trace this to a shipment from the watermark," Myles said, looking up from the sheet and meeting Fitzwarren's gaze.

"And ...." Myles hesitated.

Fitzwarren looked at him closely. "And what?"

"One of my debtors, one that Galveston was falsely accounting for, has been found dead," Myles said bluntly.

"Killed or died, there is a significant difference," Fitzwarren questioned, a slight smile on his face.

"Murdered. Hanged from a beam in her house. The fat shit, Justice Daytrew, brought me the news?"

"A short-sighted man would be looking towards you as the culprit," Fitzwarren said thoughtfully, laying the sheet on a table.

"I know," Myles said gloomily. "When he came to the White Hart, he had armed men with him. And there's more. Her son, who has now disappeared, seems to have been the man who nailed that religious Heresy up around the city. Galveston worked for the printer, and I think he was stealing from me to have these printed. He'd know the murdered woman's son was short of coin and would be easy to persuade to put them up for him."

"It fits together, I agree. It doesn't answer one question, though," Fitzwarren said.

"What question?" Myles asked.

"Why was your book-keeper murdered," Fitzwarren said.

"I don't bloody care," Myles shot back.

"You should. Everything is pointing in your direction now, and your reputation is not a polished one, is it? I would say your Justice Daytrew is waiting to see what you do next?" Fitzwarren stated.

"What do you mean, what I do?" Myles said indignantly, "This has nothing to do with me."

"Be careful," Fitzwarren warned, "Because that isn't how it appears."

"I don't need warnings from you, Fitzwarren," Myles said, dropping from the table's edge.

"You don't need to heed them. That's very much your choice. Can I ask you about the extra men I wanted?" Fitzwarren said, suddenly changing the subject.

Myles folded his arms. "I am guessing you believe you've helped me, so I'll send them to you for no cost? Don't think I am indebted to you, Fitzwarren."

Fitzwarren fished in his doublet, pulled out a purse, loosened the strings, and poured the coins onto the table. Ten gold angels rumbled onto the wood.

"Looks like you are good for your word. I never doubted you," Myles said, a thin smile on his lips.

"Will you send the extra men over to Carter's house that I have requested now?" Fitzwarren asked.

Myles picked up one of the coins from the table, examined it, and collected the others. "I shall have them sent over tomorrow. Will that be soon enough?"

"Today would be preferable," Fitzwarren said bluntly.

"Alright, today. Are you going to tell me why the security of Christian Carter, one of London's lesser merchants, is your concern?" Myles asked, then added, "What happened to your own men? Last time I heard, you had quite a mercenary troop at your back."

"I misplaced them," Fitzwarren said bluntly, his tone telling Myles this was not a topic he wished to be pursued on.

"Not all of them, though. That blond you have with you looks very able to look after himself if pressed," Myles said, unable to resist the jibe.

A half smile crossed Fitzwarren's lips. "Indeed he can, so take some advice, and don't press him."

"Keeping him to yourself, are you?" Myles said a sly smile on his face.

Fitzwarren shook his head. "I'll make enquiries at the Stationers Guild on your behalf."

"I can do that myself!" Myles said indignantly.

Fitzwarren laughed. "They'll be too worried you are there with other ideas. These men, these merchants, are, on the whole, honest men, Myles."

"What is that supposed to mean," Devereux's fine eyebrows had raised a degree.

"We both know how you conduct your business and what your business is, and so do they. None of them will want to be associated with you, Myles. It won't be good for trade. It's unlikely that you will find them overly helpful," Fitzwarren said.

"I can be very persuasive," Myles said.

"Under the circumstances, I don't think that is wise. I told you there is an excellent chance that the Justice is waiting to see what you do next. If you start threatening the Stationers Guild, that's not going to help. If I find out anything, I will let you know." Fitzwarren took the sheet, folded it and stowed it inside his doublet before leaving.

CHAPTER FIFTEEN

The message from Clegg was a verbal one delivered by one of his men. Clegg was requesting Devereux's presence regarding a "delicate matter."

Myles fumed.

What could be so delicate about digging a bloody pit to throw the dead in? How hard could it be?

Myles' first impulse was to send Matthew to deal with it, but the warning words that he needed to be seen in control echoed in his mind.

Damn, Matthew – and damn Clegg even more.

This "delicate" matter better be important; otherwise, Clegg would be swimming in the pond he had overseen the construction of.

The graveyard was still much the same. The piles of mud, mired with rain, banked the sides, and the pit was still a pond. The water level had not fallen; if anything, Devereux estimated it had risen another half-foot since he had last been here. The sight did little to improve his mood. Neither did the figure of Clegg clambering across the muddy banks towards him, pattens still clogged with clay.

"Clegg," Myles spat the word when the man was within earshot.

"Master Devereux, I am so pleased you have come. This is not an easy matter, and I really do need some help," Clegg said, closing the remaining gap between them.

When Myles spoke, it was through gritted teeth. "Why has the pit not been drained?"

"Ah, you see, this is where we've hit a snag ...." Clegg said, attempting a smile.

"A snag!" Devereux bellowed back. "God help you if you ever encounter a real problem. Go on then, tell me about this snag?"

Myles' sarcasm missed its mark, and Clegg continued, still with a slight smile on his face. "Well, it's Saint Agatha; she's rather in our way. Hill and his men dug the trench as you directed, but then we were forced to stop when we came upon her."

Myles stared at Clegg, incomprehension on his face. "Saint Agatha?"

Clegg smiled even more.

"You might find this humorous, Clegg, but I don't. Tell me quickly why a bloody Saint is stopping you from draining that pit," Myles growled.

"Well, sir, St Bride's church is constructed on the site of an earlier one, doubtless of wooden construction and long ...."

"Get on with it; I am not here for a history of the city!" Myles interrupted.

"Yes, quite. Saint Agatha was buried in the original church before the altar," Clegg swivelled extending an arm, "and that rowan tree in the churchyard marks the spot of the original altar where Agatha was laid to rest. Our channel would cut through it, and for obvious reasons, we've had to stop," Clegg explained, lowering his arm and turning back towards Myles.

"Saint Agatha!" Myles was breathing heavily. He stood on top of the Templar's memorial as he had last time, and he turned his back to Clegg for a moment, struggling to contain his temper.

"To drain the, err, pit, we would need to go through where the burial site is, and Father Hugh is obviously not very happy with this. So I did need to speak with you, Master Devereux," Clegg explained.

Myles turned back, his arms flung wide. "Why? Why do you need to speak to me?"

Clegg looked utterly confused. "Sir, you told us to dig a trench through where we now find the saint is buried, and as we can't really do that, it is a significant variation, and I thought ...."

"You thought!" Growled Myles. "I doubt very much, Clegg, that a coherent one has ever strayed into your mind! For God's sake, vary the trench path to avoid the Saint's rotting bones, is that not the obvious solution?"

"Yes," Clegg nodded vigorously. "But with it being such a significant change from the plan you gave us, I thought we needed to check with you what the new direction should be."

"Direction?" The colour in Myles' cheeks had risen, and his raised voice shook with temper.

Clegg suddenly became aware of his master's displeasure with the situation, and he squeaked, "North or south."

Myles dropped from the tomb, his right hand catching hold of Clegg's cloak and hauled him close. "Did you summon me here simply to tell you whether to dig to the left or the right of that bloody rowan tree? Did you?"

Suddenly, realising the enormity of the error he had made, Clegg tried to avoid Myles' gaze and kept his mouth shut.

Myles brought his face within inches of Clegg's, his words softly spoken. "If you do not want to be in that trench alongside Saint bloody Agatha, drain that pit, and bring me word that it is done by tonight. Do you understand?"

Clegg nodded vigorously, the long feather on his cap prescribing erratic arcs in the air above his head. Myles released Clegg, who staggered back and slithered on his pattens. His arms windmilled in an attempt to keep his balance, but his left foot slid from beneath him, and he sat down heavily in the mud.

"I'm warning you tonight," Myles said before turning and remounting the Templar's tomb and exiting the graveyard.

Fitzwarren, after a brief wait, had been admitted to Devereux's room.

"Hold it up at the window," Fitzwarren said, offering Myles a blank sheet of paper.

Myles hesitated a moment before he took it from the other man's hand. "Why? What am I looking for?"

Myles turned his back to Fitzwarren and held the sheet up towards the light at the window.

"The watermark at the top," the other man said.

"I know, I've seen it before. Indeed I told you about it," Myles said, his eyes finding the watermark at the top of the sheet.

"You did. You told me the printer said it was a circle with a cross inside it," Fitzwarren said.

"It is," Myles turned on Fitzwarren, "Get to the point."

"It's a spoked wheel. It happens to be the mark of the Cretia company, the largest importer of paper into England, and your printer would have recognised their mark," Fitzwarren said.

Myles turned back to the window, the sheet held before him. Now he knew what he was looking for, he could see the other fainter spokes in the watermark. It was a wheel.

"So your printer was using a certain economy with the information he gave you," Fitzwarren said.

"Thank you, Fitzwarren; I will be placing a few questions regarding this shortly. Is there any way to trace the buyer of the paper?" Myles asked.

Fitzwarren shook his head. "That is part of a large consignment that came into London last year; it is sold to nearly every printer in London. It's a lower quality sheet and highly sought after as it allows for a greater profit. Your printer, more than likely, will have more of those sheets."

"But it wouldn't prove anything, not if they are as common as you say," Myles replied.

"Sorry, I can't be more helpful," Fitzwarren replied, spreading his arms wide.

"I think I need to go back to the printer's and find out what that shit knows that he has not told me," Myles growled, pacing across the room.

Myles crossed London, Matthew and his men behind him. The pace was a little quicker than he would usually travel. Myles Devereux rarely wanted to be seen to be in a rush to see anyone, but today he urged his horse a little quicker through the streets, rounding obstructing wagons and market stalls with impatience. Behind him, his men, to keep up, were causing chaos in the busy streets.

Handy, the water seller, in a cacophony of clanging and chiming cups, was forced to flee in a noisy and chaotic clatter of pewter to avoid Devereux's horse as it rounded a flat-bed wagon laden with fresh cut timber. Another wagon, the fat driver, seated precariously on a hogs head barrel behind a ponderous dray, turned to curse at the man who had ordered him to pull aside. When his eyes met those of Myles Devereux he flung himself backwards, drew in the slack leather of the reins and hauled the startled elderly mare to the side of the road.

Myles dropped from his horse outside the print shop, abandoned the reins, and stalked towards the door. The earthy smell of ink and damp paper drifted through the open doorway, as did the press's noise and the boys' chatter as they hung the freshly-inked sheets up on the pegs to dry.

Myles stepped over the threshold.

Two boys turned towards him, as did the man operating the press. Myles recognised none of them.

"Where's your Master?" Devereux demanded.

The occupants exchanged quick reluctant glances, and then the man standing near the press wiped his hands on his apron and stepped forward.

"Master Preston hasn't been in today, sir," The man stammered, "He left word he had gone to meet with a client."

Myles glared at the man. "And does he do this often?"

The man looked confused. "It's not for me to question, sir."

Myles slapped his gloves off the edge of a table. "Is your Master in the habit of leaving you in charge of his print shop while he leaves to visit clients?"

"Not usually, sir, they normally come to him, but he left word …."

"And who, exactly, did he leave word with?" Devereux demanded, eyes raking the room.

"Sir, he told me he would be back in a few days," the man with his hands wound in the apron said. He was years younger than Preston, clothes neat and tidy beneath the ink-marked apron, and some accident in his youth had scarred his forehead leaving a thin white line severing one eyebrow.

"A few days," Devereux repeated. "And he trusts you with his business in his absence, does he?"

"Aye, sir. We've work to complete, and I know what needs doing," the man said nervously.

"Where's he live?" Devereux demanded.

The man raised his eyes towards the ceiling. "Master Preston lives above the shop, sir, he moved here after his wife Martha was taken by the sweating sickness."

"Matthew," Myles called, knowing the other man would be standing close behind him. "Go and see if Preston is out."

Myles cast his eyes around the interior of the dank shop before stepping towards the doorway. Above him, they could hear the creak of timbers as Matthew made his way up the stairs to the rooms above.

Matthew came down moments later, addressing the man near the press. "How long did he say he'd be gone for?"

The man shrugged, his eyes fixed on the ground, twisting the apron in his hands. "He didn't, sir. He just said a few days."

"And you've no idea where he went?" Myles questioned.

"I don't know, sir, he didn't say," the man replied.

"Was he visiting a client in London?" Myles continued.

"I don't know ...."

"Come on, man, you must have some idea? If you worked for Preston, you'd know his clients and his habits? Does he have clients outside the city or just in London?" Myles continued.

The man's knuckles were white where they had wound themselves into the stained fabric of his apron, his face distorted into a mask of obvious distress. "I wish I could help, sir; I really do."

There was a wooden block on the desk, weighing down a pile of paper. Myles' right hand found it and flung it across the print shop; it clanked off the top of the press, and, redirected, it headed towards the two boys who dived backwards out of the way, wet sheets in hand, disappearing between the hanging pages, smearing the wet ink.

Myles was about to turn on his heel and leave when the swaying sheets caught his attention. Striding across the print shop, he snatched one from where it was pegged to dry and carried it to the doorway. Holding it up the light from the street was enough for him to see the faint outline of a watermark towards the top of the page. It wasn't the same paper.

The sheet he held was a legal treatise that Preston had shown him on his last visit. Nothing heretical or seditious in that. Myles balled the page and discarded it on the floor, the wet ink staining his hands. "What else has Master Preston left you to print?"

Myles didn't wait for a reply. Instead, he advanced towards the drying pages, still swinging after the boys had escaped through them. Pulling another one from a peg, Devereux scanned the lines, the same sheet as the one he'd already crumpled.

"They're all the same, sir; it's an order for Lincoln's Inn," the man near the press said haltingly.

"And what other work has he left you?" Myles demanded.

"None, sir, it's a large order," the man said.

Myles looked around; every sheet hanging from the strings in the shop's roof was the same, and the dried pages had been collated in a box on one desk. Myles leafed through them. All the same. With nothing more to be learned, Myles strode from the print shop and remounted his horse.

"We found nothing there. Preston has disappeared and has left his print shop in the hands of idiots," Myles said, riding next to Matthew.

Returning to the White Hart, Devereux's mood was further soured when he found a messenger from the Parish waiting for him. An update was required on the likely internment of the deceased of the Parish. The message had come from the Parish clerk, Candish, who had at least been wise enough not to summon Devereux to his offices this time. The messenger was sent away without a reply for his master.

Shortly after another arrived from Clegg, one of Hill's men, still caked with the churchyard's ochre clay, left a message that the pit was free of water. Clegg, it seemed, had literally and metaphorically dug himself out of a hole; the messenger was returned with a summons for Clegg. Devereux had no intention of making a third personal appearance at the graveyard.

"Clegg. Well done," Myles' words were heavy with sarcasm.

Clegg rose from a deep bow, the plume on his hat dancing above his head and a pleased expression on his face. "Master, the pit drained successfully in a trice, just as you predicted."

"There's a surprise!" Myles continued in the same sarcastic tone, regarding Clegg with a cold stare. "Let us put it to use, Clegg. I don't want any space wasting; pack them in tightly, do you understand?"

"Yes, sir," Clegg replied rapidly.

"Clegg, explain to me how you will do this," Myles demanded.

"Err …. Well, we will collect the bodies from the crypt and put them in the pit. And I'll ensure Father Hugh says the words over them before …."

"I don't give a shit about Father Hugh. How will you put the bodies in the ground?" Myles pressed.

Clegg looked utterly confused. "Well, I can use Hill and his men to lower them in …."

Myles held up his hand, stilling Clegg's words. "No, you fool. Lay one head first and the next feet first to take up as little room as possible. Do you understand?"

Clegg's face creased with dismay. "But master, I'm not sure Father Hugh will allow that; it would be more fitting for them to all face east, surely …."

"I don't give a shit about the second coming. At least half of them will be ready to meet Christ! Pack them in as I direct, and then, and only then, fetch Father Hugh," Myles said heatedly.

"But what if he ...." Clegg tried.

Devereux threw his arms in the air, strode towards the outer door and bellowed down the stairs. "Someone fetch Matthew. Now."

Matthew was not long in arriving, casting his eyes over the nervous Clegg, his hands fidgeting and not knowing quite which way to look.

"Matthew, I need you to go and oversee Clegg's work at St Bride's. I want the bodies lying head to toe; no point in wasting space. Get the job done before there is a chance for complaint," then to Clegg, an evil smile on his face, "It's always easier to ask for forgiveness than permission."

"Yes, master. I'll head over now with Clegg," Matthew said.

"And that trench you dug, before you fill it in, make full use of it," Myles told to Clegg.

Clegg continued to look confused.

Myles rolled his eyes. "Give Saint Agatha some company and pack it with bodies, you bloody fool."

It was later when Matthew returned. His boots a testament to his afternoon in the graveyard at St Bride's.

"That fool, Clegg, you need to get rid of him," Matthew said, closing the door.

"He's useful, Matthew; just put up with him," Myles replied.

"He's also a bloody idiot; just think how much money you could have lost on that venture?" Matthew replied.

"While I have dealings with the Parish, I'll keep him. I know the man is a fool, but it seems London is full of them. That printer, Preston being among them. Never, Matthew, leave control of your business to anyone. It's a hard learnt lesson, and one Master Preston is about to suffer for," Myles said, shaking his head.

"What do you mean?" Matthew asked.

"When I was at his print shop, they were printing a page of a legal treatise, hundreds of them, all the same. Dried sheets in boxes, freshly printed ones hanging from the drying lines, all identical," Myles explained.

"I don't understand," Matthew said.

"It was the same page. Why on earth would you print hundreds of the same one. Preston told me he was printing ten volumes, so those idiots, in his absence, have produced hundreds of the same page. That mistake is going to cost him dearly; I've no doubt they are still at it."

Matthew was staring at Myles. "That could be bad direction or …."

Myle's eyes opened wide, a look of horror on his face. "Dear God! Or without a master, they continue like sheep. Keep the print shop running; make it look like Preston is away for a few days. Nothing seems amiss."

"You could be right," Matthew said.

"I am sure I am right. Why would he disappear and leave his shop in the hands of witless idiots? How much money do you think they have wasted duplicating that sheet? Surely Preston would have left his business in the hands of someone who knew what they were doing?" Myles was on his feet and lifting his cloak from a chairback.

"You would think so," Matthew said in agreement, "Let me go back, and see what I can find out."

"I'll not be lied to, Matthew," Myles said, "Get the men together; I'm coming as well."

CHAPTER SIXTEEN

The interior was in darkness, the press silent.

"Find a lamp, Matthew," Myles said impatiently while waiting on the threshold.

Instead, Matthew flung open the front shutters to the workshop, and the grey light of London filled the abandoned interior.

Myles stepped inside. Sheets hung from the ceiling in neat rows pegged to the lines that crisscrossed the roof. Large, unmanned, and silent the press stood open at the back of the room. The wooden frame raised, the printing plate blackened with ink, still in place. Myles snatched one of the sheets from the ceiling; it was the page from the Legal Treatise book, he discarded it and took another and another. All the same. The box on the desk he had leafed through was now full, pages rising to the top, all identical.

"There must be hundreds of them." Matthew, too, was examining the sheets. "Why?"

Myles stalked around the room. There were two tables; one wall was filled with angled racks containing lead letters and shelves with paper waiting to be placed in the press. Myles picked up a blank sheet, and he easily found the faint impression of the spoked wheel. The same paper as Fitzwarren had brought him.

"Someone," Myles said slowly, "Wanted it to look as if Preston's print shop was in use, that nothing was amiss. That's why they have continued printing these. And they knew Preston had mentioned this watermark to me, so this paper was hidden."

Myles walked slowly around the empty, quiet print shop. His eyes missing nothing. Pots of ink had been left open without their stoppers. Brushes, black with ink, lay next to them, unwashed, abandoned when the user had finished with them. At the end of the table, scattered across a pile of the identical sheets were crumbs and the edge of a dried pie crust. Grease from the pastry had marked the paper below, spreading through the fibres and darkening the sheet.

"Whoever it was didn't care about the sheets they'd printed. They ate a meal here, using this pile as a platter. And look, the brushes from the ink pots have also splattered the sheets there," Myles pointed, adding "And they didn't put the stoppers in the bottles or wash the brushes, so they had no intention of coming back here."

Myles placed himself at the end of the bench. The press was to his right, the ink pot to his left with the dry brushes. "Someone stood here, eating a meal. Then reached over dipped the brush in the ink pot, trailed ink across these pages and I suppose inked the plate in the press."

Matthew came to stand next to him.

Myles was staring at the plate. The letters were reversed, the whole facia blackened with ink, and yet he could see the pattern of the lines and the letters seeping through it. Whipping one of the sheets from the desk, he held it next to the set letters in the press.

"This isn't the same, look, these sheets all have two half-empty lines mid-way through, and that one doesn't," Myles said.

Then discarding the sheet, he crossed the room and took a handful of blank sheets from the stack on the shelf. Putting one on top of the letters in the press, he rubbed it hard with the heel of his palm before lifting it and examining the reverse. The ink had dried, and although the letters had cut into the paper, it was impossible to discern the words. He dipped the brush in the ink pot and pasted ink across the lead letters.

"The sheet would go on to the top, but how does this come down?" Myles said, stepping back and examining the plate above, which should close down and press the paper firmly against the letters.

Matthew, on the other side of the press, said. "The lever is above your head. Reach up and pull it down."

Myles found the smooth worn wooden handle just above his head and pulled it down, the top of the machine closed on the top of the letters. The top of the press was weighted with lead blocks, and it closed with a loud bang. Raising the leaver again, Myles could peel the sheet from the letters. He'd used too much ink, and the sheet was running with black; the impact of the top plate on the letters swathed in thick ink had sent it splattering across the page. He could see the odd impression of half a word but not enough to decipher the document.

Myles took another sheet, fitted it to the press and lowered the plate; the result was much the same. After five more repetitions, the letters were still clogged with ink, and the words were unreadable.

"Pass me that jar," Myles pointed to one on the shelf stuffed with sheep's wool. Matthew passed it to him, and with a handful, he began to dab the letters and soak up excess ink. Lifting it away to review the plate, the wool fibres snagged two lead letters and pulled them free from the set. Cursing, Myles examined them, uncertain which way round they went, he pressed them back into the black holes.

"I think you need to use these," Matthew held up two leather spheres by their wooden protruding handles.

Myles just looked at him blankly.

"Next to those sheets, there's a dish cut into the workbench, the ink goes in there and then onto these and then they ink the letters in the tray," Matthew said.

Myles glared at him. "When did you become an expert on printing presses?"

Matthew, ignoring him, cleared space on the bench away from the dished recess that had been cut in the wood. "I've been here before; I saw them using these."

Matthew used the brush to slop ink into the dish. Satisfied there was enough, he picked up one of the leather pounders and slapped it on top of the ink.

Ink escaped from beneath it, spattering Myles in the face and delivering a line of black wet dots across Matthew's chest.

"You bloody fool! You've no idea what you are doing," Myles said accusingly. Pulling a white linen square from his pocket, he attempted to wipe his face.

Matthew looked towards the floor, hiding a grin.

"Get out there, you fool, and find someone who knows how this works!"

Matthew was gone for only five minutes; he returned with a confused-looking man, obviously a printer by trade; his apron was darkened with ink, and his fingers stained black to the knuckles. A tight-fitting felt cap glued his hair to his head and beneath the rim, two thick bushy eyebrows protruded.

"Show Master Devereux the workings," Matthew said as they entered Preston's print shop.

"Well, I'd rather not, sir. These are Master Preston's, and it'd be wrong for me to lay my hands on another man's press," the man said.

"Do you know who you are talking to?" Matthew growled in the man's ear; with a heavy hand on his shoulder, he applied an uncomfortable pressure and said, "Now, tell Master Devereux how this works."

"Yes, quite," the man wriggled quickly from Matthew's hold.

"The plate is still in place; how do we obtain a print from it?" Myles asked.

"Dear me. What's gone on here? You'll not get a print from that; the letters have been drowned out," the man said, peering at the plate.

"What's that mean?"

"Too much ink. I'll need to clean it back. Otherwise, the ink will mark the paper, and you'll not get a clean copy," the man said.

"I don't care how good it is, just so long as I can read it," Myles said, stepping aside so the man could get closer to the press. As he watched, he extracted a cloth from his apron and cleaned the ink from the letters.

"The risk is, sir, that there's so much ink on here that it's run down behind the letters, and when the pressure from the press is applied, it will spill forward and spoil the print," the Printer said.

"Do what you need to do," Myles grumbled.

"I need to reset the plate, really," the Printer said.

"How long is that going to take?" Myles said.

"Well, about an hour to take it apart, clean it and reset it will take another two, maybe a little longer," the Printer said.

"Can't you just clean it where it is? Do you really need to take it apart?" Myles said, then added, "What if you drop it or mix the letters up? Then it will be lost. Is there no way to take a print from it now?"

"I assure you, sir, I'd not make a mistake. I've been setting letters since I was a lad. They say round here that there's none quicker or more accurate than Dale," Dale declared proudly, thumping his chest. "If I use it as it is, the ink will spoil the print."

"I accept that, but will it produce a readable copy. That's all I care about," Myles said.

"Well, it might be readable, but the quality would be very poor," Dale said.

"I don't care about the quality; just take a print," Myles said, standing back and waving an arm towards the press. When the man didn't move, Myles quickly stepped towards him. "Go on, then."

Jolted into action, Dale jumped back and then turned towards the press and the business of producing the page. He was old, methodical, and liked to talk. All characteristics that were like a hot poker to Myles' impatience.

The Printer stooped over the over-inked plate. "The letters are filled with ink, so they'll not produce a clean impression when the press brings the paper down onto them."

As Myles watched, he fished in his pocket, produced a thin spill of wood nicked at one end, he plucked some wool from the ball on the desk and rolled it between his fingers, forming it into a tight ball. Then, squinting, he pressed it into the end of the spill and began to use it to dab the ink from the filled letters.

Myles paced up and down the room. Dale replaced his wool wad four more times before he was satisfied that the letters were clear of an excess of ink.

"That should be fine, now sir, although I'm fairly sure there'll be a lot of ink in the tray behind that's going to spoil the print, but if you are sure …. "

"I'm sure," Myles said, standing next to the Printer.

Dale took another sheet from the pile and fitted it to a wooden board to the press's right.

"Doesn't the paper go onto the letters?" Myles' brow furrowed.

"It does, but first it goes onto this board, there are two pins to hold it in place, then when we reverse the sheet to print on the other side, we can be sure the print will be even on both sides," the Printer retrieved a thin frame from the floor, dropped it over the sheet and secured it in place with four wooden lugs.

"Now we have the tray ready for print; it slides in here like this," Dale slowly slotted the tray above the lettered board, face down; above the Printer's head was the polished wooden lever; grasping it, he pressed it forward slowly. "I'm just doing it gently, like, otherwise all that ink will shoot forwards and spoil the print. There that should be fine."

He released the lever and lifted the wooden board from the lead letters. It was released with a sound like a kiss as the sticky ink let go of the paper. Reversing it, he shook his head. "As I said, sir, the ink has spoilt the print."

"Give it to me," Myles demanded, trying to view the sheet still attached to the board.

The Printer removed the frame and lifted the sheet from the two pins. Myles snatched it from his hands.

"Careful, sir, it's wet," Dale said, alarmed.

Myles, his hands on either side of the wet sheet, walked slowly across the cluttered print shop as he read. It was another religious diatribe entitled "The Heresy of Religion." Myles read the first few lines only before his eyes dropped to the bottom of the sheet, and he found the name "Ad-Hyce," attesting that these were his words alone.

Myles handed the sheet to Matthew. "Make sure that makes it back intact."

The Printer had a coin pressed into his hand by Matthew and was ushered from the print shop.

"Find out where they've gone, Matthew," Myles said, his eyes on the plate still holding the ink-blackened letters in their tray. He was about to turn and leave when an impulse made him lift the heavy tray from the press and tip it up; once beyond the vertical, the letters spilt from it like water over the falls. Myles shook it to free the last, then let the tray fall to the floor.

It was Preston who was producing these religious prints, and the name Ad-Hyce tied them to Galveston. The two of them had to have been working together. The question now was where had Preston gone? Had he fled, knowing that the truth was about to emerge? Had he returned to his print shop at the end of the day and produced one last batch of these Protestant Proclamations before he disappeared?

CHAPTER SEVENTEEN

"It's more of those bloody Protestant ramblings Fitzwarren brought me," Myles said, riding next to Matthew as they returned to the White Hart. "Preston wasn't here during the day, he knew we were close to discovering the truth, and he was hiding somewhere, making it look as if it was business as usual; then, after the shop closed, he's come back and produced another batch of those Heretical prints."

"It does look like that," Matthew agreed. "I'll find out where he's gone. The printer might have disappeared, but you can be certain those two lads working the print shop will still be around, and they'll have seen plenty of what was happening. I'll find them."

"And the man Preston left in charge, find him and find out what he really knows," Myles said.

Myles fell silent, considering what he had learnt. Ad-Hyce, who he presumed was Galveston, was writing Protestant Declarations. The book-keeper had stolen plenty of money from him, enough to fund his scheme and pay for the printing and distribution. The printer, Preston, had disappeared, or at the very least didn't want to be found, and Galveston was dead.

He was sure Preston held the answer as to why Galveston was dead. He hadn't been robbed; Myles was sure of that, he had been murdered, along with Anne Hesketh. She also must have known who her son had been working for. She must have been able to connect Preston and Galveston, so she'd ended up swinging from her roof beam. Her son, Danny, was missing, but there was no reason not to suspect that he, too, was now dead if he knew of the link between Galveston and Preston.

If his brother had been alive, he might have been able to help; Andrew had been a Protestant and had spent time in exile. He had been a quiet man, he kept his principles and his friends close and had never felt the need to rant to others about his religious convictions. But that opportunity was no longer available, Andrew was gone, and Myles had little idea who his friends had been or who he had been connected with in London.

The problem remained that the only connection Daytrew was likely to find was Myles Devereux. There was no doubt that Ann Hesketh had been one of his debtors that Galveston had been falsely accounting for. He'd told Daytrew that he had little knowledge of who Ann Hesketh was, but that had been untrue. He remembered her well. A small spare woman, hunch-backed, overworked and driven to an aged look by a wastrel son. She'd needed money for his board in Marshalsea, and Myles had loaned her the small amount. Her son had been released, but again after only a few months of freedom, he had gambled his way back into Marshalsea and his poor mother was queuing at the White Hart to request another loan.

Myles doubted Ann Hesketh harboured any fervent religious principles, the woman didn't have time for them. She worked as a washer woman and would have toiled as many hours as possible to support herself and repay her debt. Now she was dead. It seemed her son had been released from Marshalsea a few weeks ago and ended up working for Galveston.

Myles leaned close to Matthew. "Ann Hesketh's son, see if you can find out where he is."

Matthew nodded and looked as if he were about to say something. His expression suddenly changed, his hands tightened on the reins, and he sat upright. "That's Daytrew."

Myles switched his gaze forward. They were nearly back at the White Hart, and sure enough, in the street at the back of the Tavern near the open gate was Daytrew. Mounted uncomfortably on a sizeable horse and surrounding him half a dozen armed men.

Matthew instinctively reached out and pulled Myle's horse to a stop. "Go right here, down Crisson Street; I'll find out what he wants."

Daytrew already had his eyes on the approaching riders, and he'd found Myles amongst them.

"It's alright, Matthew; I'm not going to dart off like a criminal. Let's go and greet Justice Daytrew and find out what the shit wants," Myles said, his eyes narrowing.

Justice Daytrew looked less than happy on the top of his heftily built mare, and not all of it was owing to the saddle he was in.

"Justice Daytrew, a good day to you," Myles announced when they were within earshot.

"And a good day to you, Master Devereux," Daytrew replied hesitantly.

"How can I help?" Myles said, his eyes scanning the the men around Daytrew.

"I've come .... I mean the Sheriff has sent me .... It seems that ...."

Myles closed the gap between them, saying for the benefit of Daytrew's men and his own, "You seem a little confused, Justice Daytrew."

There was the unmistakable sound of laughter, and Daytrew reddened.

"Come now, Justice Daytrew. What brings you to my door? The Sheriff's business? Your own? Or have you forgotten?" Myles continued loudly.

"There are questions to answer," Daytrew said, the words tumbling from his mouth.

"There are always questions, but remember, as Plato advised, or maybe it was Aristotle, I forget, it is not the answers that enlighten, but it is the questions. So place them, Justice Daytew, and we can be enlightened together," Myles announced, drawing his horse next to Daytrew's.

"The Sheriff .... err .... the Sheriff has the questions," Daytrew stammered.

"Enlightenment will have to wait then," Myles dropped from his horse, discarded the reins and couldn't resist placing his riding crop across the rear of Daytrew's mare. The animal wheeled around, and the Justice, wide-eyed, was clinging to his saddle pommel.

"Be still, stop!" Daytew's shrill voice served only to further panic his unhappy mount, and the men with him tried to hide their smiles.

Daytrew had lost a stirrup, and his weighty bulk began pouring from the saddle.

"I think one of you should dismount and help your master," Matthew declared loudly, sidestepping the uncontrolled horse.

One of Daytew's men slithered from his own saddle, catching the bridle of the spooked mare, and he pulled it to a halt.

Myles chuckling, strode across the yard of the White Hart, calling over his shoulder to Daytrew. "I'll come when I am ready."

"You are not going with him, are you?" Matthew said, following Myles into his room.

"I don't have much choice. Daytrew is not arresting, is he?" Myles said, unbuttoning his doublet rapidly.

"No, but I don't think it's wise to go and step inside the Sheriff's office, do you?" Matthew said, taking the doublet from Devereux and depositing it over a chair back.

"Daytrew has a dozen men with him. If I don't go, the implication is I have something to hide, and he'll be back with more. I'll go on my own terms, Matthew. Now round up the men. I intend to arrive at the Sheriff's office with more than Daytrew has," Myles selected another doublet and began pulling it on.

"Alright," Matthew said, not sounding convinced.

"I'll be about an hour. I am sure Daytrew will enjoy the wait. Make sure the fat shit stays in his saddle, and don't invite him in," Myles said, beginning the task of fitting silver buttons through embroidery-edged holes.

Just over two hours later, Myles left the White Hart. He was immaculately dressed and rode at the head of his men flanked by Matthew. A flustered Daytrew and his men rode behind.

Daytrew had attempted to arrive in the Sheriff's presence before Devereux. However, he was quickly robbed of that small victory. While he was still trying to shake a boot loose from a stirrup, Devereux had dropped to the ground, and was heading towards the steps leading to the Sheriff's office. Devereux's horse, held now by one of his men, was in Daytew's way, and he was forced to bend over the bulk of his stomach and duck beneath the horse's neck in an attempt to take the shorter path to the Sheriff's door. Emerging from the other side of the animal, his watery eyes, filled with disappointment, found that Devereux had already bounded up the steps and made his way through the doorway without waiting for his escort to catch up with him.

Devereux, black leather riding gloves in one hand and whip in the other, stalked across the outer room towards a man seated at a desk.

He slapped his gloves on the oak table, the draft disturbing a pile of papers resting on the desk, and the sudden noise making the elderly man behind the desk jump in fright.

"The Sheriff wished to see me? Well, here I am," Myles announced loudly.

The small man looked up, opened his mouth, thought better of whatever he had been about to say and closed it quickly.

"Come on, man. I've not got all day. Go tell your master I've answered his summons," Myles continued, gesturing towards a door with the whip.

The small man rose quickly, the chair legs grating on the wooden floor. "I'll go and tell him, sir."

Myles had not supplied his name, but he had little doubt that the man seated at the desk would not recognise him, and anyway, he had been expected. Justice Daytew, accompanied by a force of men, had been sent to retrieve him, and they had obviously expected him to resist.

"You do that," Myles said, pushing the papers and an ink pot to one side, he seated himself on the end of the table.

Behind him, Justice Daytrew, breathing heavily, after forcing his fattened body across the yard and up the steps to the Sheriff's office with as much speed as his fattened legs could provide.

Myles ignored him.

Daytrew, unsure of himself, stood, in the middle of the room, his hat in his right hand.

A few moments later, the small man emerged, and behind him, neatly attired and with a chain that declared his status, was the Sheriff. His eyes took in the scene for a moment. Devereux, sitting on his clerk's desk, one leg swinging below him, tapping his gloves against his hose, and Daytrew, red and puffing, still standing in the middle of the room, his hat screwed up in one plump hand.

"Master Devereux, thank you for coming. Please," The Sheriff held the door to his office open, and after a moment, Myles dropped from the desk and sauntered across the room.

Daytrew made to follow, but the Sheriff held up his hand. "I wish to speak with Master Devereux privately, Justice Daytrew."

The Sheriff followed Devereux into the office, closing the door behind them.

"It is good of you to come. Did Justice Daytrew explain why I wished to see you?" The Sheriff asked as he rounded his desk and seated himself.

There was a chair next to Myles, and without waiting for an invitation, he dropped into it, one leg hooked over an arm, leaning back, a hand on the raised knee, he regarded the Sheriff over it, smiling broadly Myles said, "No, he didn't."

The Sheriff regarded him with a severe gaze; he didn't return Myles' smile. "There have been murders in this Parish, and it is my duty to investigate them."

Myles frowned. "I thought Daytrew was investigating the murder of my book-keeper? Has he got anywhere? It was not a convenient event."

The Sheriff's eyes narrowed. "I am sure Master Ad-Hyce was more than inconvenienced by his recent demise."

Myles raised one hand and waved his gloves airily. "Indeed, poor Ad-Hyce."

"Daytrew tells me you have not seen him for some days. Is this right?" The Sheriff asked.

"That's right, he failed to keep an appointment with me on Friday, and his clerk arrived after discovering his body," Myles said, idly tapping the gloves against his thigh.

"You went to his offices, though. Apart from his clerk, you were the first person present when his body was found?" the Sheriff asked.

"I was," Myles confirmed.

"Don't you think you should have reported his murder first?" the Sheriff pressed.

Myles rolled his eyes. "We didn't even know if he was dead. The boy babbled like an idiot and told us he thought his master had hit his head; he hadn't even checked to see if he was dead. So, at that point, there was nothing to report. And if you check, my men reported the incident shortly after we arrived and found the poor man deceased on the floor."

"Did you take anything from his office?" The Sheriff asked.

"Nothing that did not belong to me," Myles said; his voice no longer held any trace of humour.

"What exactly did you take?" The Sheriff said.

Myles stopped tapping the gloves against his thigh and fixed the Sheriff with a steady gaze. "He had my books of account. I am hardly going to leave those unattended, am I?"

"The boy hadn't seen or heard anything?" the Sheriff asked.

"He's already been quizzed by your man, Daytrew. He arrived and found his master on the floor, then he came straight to the White Hart to report what he had seen," Myles said, then added, "I went, with my men, as I explained. We found him dead when we arrived and reported his demise."

"You said you took your books of account with you, were they intact?" Sheriff asked.

Myles frowned. "Intact?"

"Exactly that. Were they?"

Myles waved a hand in the air. "As far as I am aware, I don't spend a great deal of time examining them; I have, or at least, had a book-keeper for that. Why do you ask?"

The Sheriff leaned back and pulled open a desk draw; his eyes dropped from Myles as he reached inside and drew out a creased piece of paper, he lay it on the desk, holding it flat between his hands. The ink had run in places, and the page was torn and stained, but Myles still recognised it. The missing page from the ledger.

"We found this, and I was wondering if it might be from one of your books of account," The Sheriff asked, his eyes fixed on Myles.

Myles unhooked his knee from the chair arm and leaned across the desk. As he did, the Sheriff drew the paper towards him, out of Myles reach.

"If I can't see it, how I am I supposed to know if it belongs to the books or not?" Myles said, dropping back heavily in the chair and making the back rock, lifting the front feet from the floor to clatter back down a second later, refusing to return his eyes to the page.

"Perhaps you recognise the names. Although it is somewhat damaged, it is quite legible," the Sheriff asked, turning the sheet towards himself.

Myles shrugged. "Perhaps I might."

"Let me see, some of them are incomplete, but among them are Paul Smythe, Benedict Osram, Marlow Sharpe, Prentice Goodson …. and Anne Hesketh."

Myles interrupted, "Smythe, perhaps, but then it is a very common name."

"If you have the account book to hand, we could check together," The Sheriff suggested.

"We could, indeed. I shall have it brought here for you from the White Hart," Myles said, his voice steady.

The Sheriff smiled. "No need to trouble yourself, I've sent men to bring them here already."

The false smile on Myles' face froze. "I think, sir, without my word, it would be unlikely that my servants would willingly give your men access."

The Sheriff shrugged. "I have sent word that they are required as part of my investigation. On the orders of Her Majesty, I find it unlikely that they would resist."

"If you have made all the arrangements, then why bother telling me?" Myles said, failing to keep an edge of irritation from his voice. He'd been duped. Most of his men were with him, if the Sheriff had sent men in force to the White Hart there would be few to resist a search of his rooms. The Sheriff had wanted the ledger and he'd wanted to get hold of it before Myles had a chance to dispose of it.

"Are you not interested in where we found this?" the Sheriff raised the sheet from the desk and waved it in the air for a moment.

"Not particularly; however, it seems to be of some importance to yourself," Myles said calmly.

The Sheriff smiled; his eyes, though, were cold and fixed Myles with an intense gaze. "You have heard Mistress Hesketh was found dead recently, and it seems that it was another case of murder. Two in a week, first your book-keeper and a lady who owed you money."

"Did she? I am not familiar with all the names ...."

"We both know she did, and her name appears on here," the Sheriff held the crumpled page up between them. "I would lay a hefty wager that this page is from your ledger that Galveston Ad-Hyce kept for you. And do you know where it was found?"

"Do tell?" Myles managed to keep his voice level.

"Folded up, and in the poor woman's mouth," the Sheriff said, slamming it down on the desk.

"How that happened is very much a mystery that I doubt I can help with," Myles replied; his right hand had tightened into a fist, the knuckles white, and he lowered it slowly beneath the edge of the table, and out of the other man's sight.

The Sheriff smiled, and this time there was a degree of satisfaction on his face. Placing his hands on the desk, he rose. "If you would remain here, I will find out if my man has returned. And we can check your ledger together."

Myles watched the Sheriff make his way across the room, as the door opened, he could see the two armed men on the other side, and he was left in no doubt that he had little choice but to remain in the room.

Myles rose as soon as the door closed. The last glimpse the two guards had of him before their view was obscured was one of him lolling in the chair. The moment he was out of sight, Myles erupted from the chair, ripped a cloak from a pen on the wall, rounded the desk, and flung open the closed shutters with both hands.

As soon as the door opened, the Sheriff addressed the man he expected to find inside the room. "As I said, sir, your men were most happy to provide …."

The Sheriff's words trailed off as his eyes scanned the empty room, took in the shutters flung side and the casement window swinging open, the long iron latch dangling free.

CHAPTER EIGHTEEN

Two of the Sheriff's men stood guard on the midden at the end of Brinton Lane. A group of three inquisitive children who had found the body had been quizzed for what they knew, which was very little, and shooed from the site. Their backs to the muck heap, the armed men stood shoulder to shoulder, their presence enough to deter most of the local population from idle curiosity.

Daytrew had been informed a body had been found, but little more, having been in the middle of a supper at the Guild Hall it was nearly two hours before he finally arrived where the men patiently waited. Daytrew came by litter. An expense he would not have usually indulged in, but the lateness of the hour and an attack of gout in his right foot made travel by horse uncomfortable and on foot untenable. He had spent far too much of the day on his feet.

The sudden disappearance of Myles Devereux from the Sheriff's office had been blamed on him, which he felt was hugely unfair. The man had been in the Sheriff's office; he had left him alone near an open window, not Daytrew. But Daytrew had taken the blame for not securing the building; had he posted guards around it, they would have prevented the man's escape, as the Sheriff had stated. Daytrew had attempted to argue his case, but the Sheriff had not been for listening and made it very clear where the fault lay. Daytrew had spent the rest of the day organising searches for the missing fugitive. His disappearance, however, did very much resolve the issue of the murders. They had to be attributed to Devereux, otherwise, why would the man have fled through an open window?

The litter was set down near the two armed men, the wooden frame jolted slightly as the men sought to lower it evenly.

"Be careful, you dolts," Daytrew's words emerged from inside, and the wooden frame tipped him to the right, a solid thump from the interior attesting to the fact the occupant had been slung against the side by the litter's careless handlers.

The two men on guard exchanged mirthful grins, which were quickly hidden when Daytrew flung the litter curtain aside and swung his feet towards the road.

"There had better be a good reason for summoning me at this time of the night. I was supping with Master Gardner at the Guild Hall," Daytrew grumbled, turning sideways and squeezing his stomach through the gap of the litter entrance. "So, who's death couldn't wait until tomorrow?"

"Sir, it's the printer you questioned earlier this week," one of the men said.

"Preston? What about him?" Daytrew said, his voice irritable as he stepped down from the litter into the road, pudgy hands smoothing out his creased clothing.

"He's here, sir," the man on the right jerked his thumb over his shoulder.

Daytrew frowned at him, confusion on his face.

"He's in the midden," the man said, then when Daytrew still remained silent, he added. "Dead, sir."

Daytrew's eyes widened. "Preston is dead?"

"Yes, sir. That's why we thought you'd want to know immediately," the man on the left said.

"Where is he?" Daytrew peered across the midden.

"Over there, we left him where the boys found him," one of them said.

Daytrew approached the edge of the rotting mound of rubbish and stopped before his boots were mired from the ouse leaking from the stinking pile. Daytrew peered in the direction pointed. "Where? I can't see him."

"Just to the right of that mound, he's partly buried," one of the men said helpfully, pointing in the direction.

Daytrew looked down at the ground again, considered stepping towards the body, wavered, and changed his mind. "Well, don't just stand there! Pull him out."

The two men exchanged glances, hesitating for a moment before turning and stepping as carefully as they could over the unstable pile of muck and debris to where the unfortunate printer was laying. Daytrew stretched his neck, trying to see the body they were heading towards, but he could see little in the midden that was recognisable as human.

The men stopped; one turned back to Daytrew and called. "He's here, sir."

Daytrew flung his arms wide. "Well then, pull him out. We can't just leave him there!"

As Daytrew watched, he could see two white pallid arms being raised by the two men who began to try and tug the body free from the pile. Daytrew recognised the printer when the men finally hauled the body free from the midden and lay him in the road. What had killed the man was plain to see, his forehead, just above his right eye, was stove in, the wound angular; he had been hit with something solid. Daytrew swivelled his body around his stomach in an attempt to view the body closer. It wasn't a blow from a weapon, whatever it was had left a square impression where it had cracked his skull.

Daytrew straightened up. It looked as if Devereux had another murder to answer for. The Sheriff was not going to be pleased when he broke this news to him in the morning.

Nonny opened the door to one of the private rooms at the Angel and closed it quickly behind her. "You can't stop here, my lovely."

Myles Devereux, seated by the fire, and swathed in a nondescript cloak eyed her closely. "Why's that, then?"

Nonny lowered herself into a chair opposite him, arranging her skirts about her, before lifting her gaze and meeting his. "I might not report that you are 'ere, and Nathaniel will probably keep his counsel as well, but there are too many eyes and ears at the Angel. Molly, recognised you, no doubt she's already mentioned your appearance to at least one of the girls, and when it becomes widely known that the Sheriff is looking for you, they'll trade that news for silver."

"My appearance?" Myles questioned.

Nonny laughed. "Myles Devereux without his finery is something to raise a comment, Myles Devereux without six men behind him will make tongues wag, and Myles Devereux seen sneaking through a back window of the Angel is going to be wildly reported. And I 'ave already heard that you escaped from the Sheriff's office today and made a fool of that idiot Daytrew."

"I had little choice," Myles said, then, his voice serious, asked, "Is Fitzwarren here tonight?"

Nonny shook her head. "When I see him, I will tell him you are looking for him. Can I tell him where you will be?"

"I don't know myself yet. Where is Fitzwarren lodging?" Myles asked, taking the glass of wine Nonny had brought with her and emptying it in a single gulp.

"I don't know. He is not at his father's house, that much I do know," Nonny replied.

Myles rose from his chair and strode across the room towards the closed shutters, turning to regard her with dark eyes, he asked. "You know everyone in the city. Did you hear about the printer's sheets nailed up around the city last week?"

"That is not an irregular occurrence, but I did hear that the Queen's men are looking for the perpetrator to burn him. Why?" Nonny asked. "These were not your doing, were they?"

Myles suddenly paled. Weak knees took him two steps forward, and his hand reached blindly for the chairback.

Nonny was out of her chair in a flurry of silk and perfume, catching his other arm. "My poor man, what have I said?"

Myles allowed himself to be helped into the chair and waved away the glass of wine she held towards him. He felt too sick to even think of drinking, and his throat closed tight, probably would refuse to let the liquid pass.

Nonny was kneeling in front of him, a gentle hand on the side of his face; her voice was full of genuine concern. "What has happened? Should I fetch a physician?"

Myles shook his head.

"Do you want to tell me?" Nonny asked quietly.

Myles was about to shake his head again, then changing his mind, he said simply. "I think someone is trying to kill me."

Matthew had learnt nothing when he had tracked down the boys who had worked in Preston's print shop. He had yet to respond to Bennett's summons, and the more he thought about it, the more he realised he had no choice.
Myles had disappeared, and if there was information in Bennett's possession about the murders, any of them, then he needed to find out. Matthew arrived at Bennett's leather shop accompanied by a dozen of Devereux's men.

Bennett was the son of a London baker; he had grown up in the city delivering bread from a basket before dawn every day; now, the bakery was a pawn shop, and the room at the back where the ovens had once been was where Bennett could be found. The front of the shop was both a pawnbroker's, a money lender's and a leather goods shop. Among Bennett's more legitimate business's was a tanning yard, and some of the goods produced by the leather workers were hung up for sale in the shop, filling it with the aroma of fresh hide.

Bags, belts, bridles and boots hung from wooden pegs in neat rows along one wall. From nails hammered into the roof beams, harnesses, head collars, reins, and girths dangled, causing the taller of Bennett's patrons to duck to avoid them. The rest of the room was given over to shelving and the chattels that had come Bennett's way through the pawn shop. Cups, earthenware and pewter, variously dented and chipped, crowded together next to a pile of wooden trenchers topped with a cracked pot holding a stack of dulled lead spindle whorls. Beneath these ran a shelf filled with dusty wooden-soled shoes, and below that, another holding small woven baskets filled with pewter, bronze and copper oddments – strap ends, buckles, clog clasps and thimbles. Along the floor under these were a series of empty cages, the fowl and rabbits they had housed long since gone, but not the filthy straw.

Matthew's eyes took in the poverty as he stepped over the threshold onto the worn wooden floor, feeling the planks give beneath him. Bennett's shop was not just packed with goods, it was also crowded with people. His arrival was noted by a man standing before a closed door at the back of the shop, arms folded across a broad chest, one of Bennett's men. Matthew caught the man's eye, and he immediately pressed through the throng towards him. A woman, a basket over one arm, was shoved roughly aside as he walked across the crowded room towards Matthew.

Behind the door was Bennett's office. Once, it might have been lime-washed and white; now the daub was grey, falling away from the walls in places, and the roof beams were filled with grey cobwebs. At the back of the room, like two huge gaping toothless mouths, the dark arches of the cold empty bread ovens stood open and cold.

Bennett's broad shoulders, probably once heavily muscled, now supported a frame of rounded fat with a small head that sat like a boulder on top of a set of bulging and creased chins. Bennett was seated at a table on a wainscot chair that was deeply out of place with the setting; heavily carved, the arms ending with clawed feet. Behind Bennett, the back rose, and wedged between two curling finials was the lion's head. Once richly covered in red velvet, the plush material was soiled and threadbare, dark tufts of wool padding bursting from beneath Bennett's elbows where they rested on the chair. It was not just Devereux who liked to hold court, and had the situation been different Matthew might have laughed at the man seated before him.

There was a vacant chair opposite Bennett; Matthew ignored it, his thumbs finding his belt he looked down at the seated man.

Leaning back against the aged upholstery, Bennett said simply. "Sir, it is good to meet you."

"Why the request for this meeting?" Matthew said bluntly.

"The word is that you have now taken control of Devereux's business," Bennett said; his voice held still a trace of the accent of his Scottish father, and it lent a gentleness to his speech. Matthew knew too much of Bennett to be taken in by the man's simple clothing, relaxed manner and amiable smile.

Matthew cast a gaze around the remains of the disused bakery before his eyes came to rest upon the man opposite him. "You've heard right."

Bennett's eyes were open wide. "Matthew, may I call you that?

Matthew nodded in ascent.

"Matthew, I am a simple man. My businesses, and those that were Devereux's, are now yours, are very different. There is room for both of us in London. Do you not agree?"

"That might be the case," Matthew said, his voice non-committal.

"Exactly, and if we start from the right place, and if you were prepared to set to right a few wrongs Devereux made against my poor self as an expression of your goodwill, then I see no reason why we both cannot continue to work and live side by side in the city," Bennett said smiling warmly at Matthew.

Matthew's eyes narrowed. "And what wrongs would those be?"

"I think you know what they are, Matthew," Bennett said, a cold edge sliding into his voice, his thick pink hands tightening on the lion's feet of the chair arms.

"I'm not sure I do," Matthew said, his brows furrowed in confusion.

Bennett drummed a meaty forefinger on one of the lion's exposed claws. "Do I need to remind you? You have been at your master's right hand for years; you know his business as well as he did, if not better."

"Maybe so," Matthew said.

Bennett leant forward and glared at Matthew – the placid brown eyes, no longer friendly, had darkened. His voice had a grating edge when he spoke, and the volume was raised. "The Kings Arms belongs to me, and I intend to take possession. There are two ways this can happen, and it would be easier for you, a lot easier if we did it my way."

Bennett stood, facing Matthew, his arms folded, resting on the mound of his belly.

"You'll understand that I'm just getting myself acquainted with his business," Matthew said simply.

"There is another way that this could go," Bennett said suddenly, his voice friendly once more.

"What's that, then?" asked Matthew.

"Perhaps you don't want to run your master's business, it would be an onerous task, I have no doubt, one fraught with problems. It might be that a man like yourself would be in favour of making a quicker profit," Bennett said bluntly.

"A quicker profit?" Matthew repeated Bennett's words slowly.

"Indeed. I would be prepared to take over your master's business, and I could provide you with a not inconsiderable amount in return," Bennett then shrugged, "And you, quite a lot the richer, would be free to leave London."

Matthew took in a long breath, his eyes, for a moment, resting on the dirty floor. Looking up, he met Bennett's enquiring gaze and asked. "How much, exactly, would a not inconsiderable amount be?"

Bennett smiled, revealing a mouth filled with a chipped line of top teeth. A leather purse was on a table to the right-hand side of the monstrous chair. In a smooth movement, Bennett upended it, shaking the leather bag until all the gold coins leaked, chinking, onto the table. Casting the purse aside, he looked towards Matthew.

Matthew didn't meet his gaze. His eyes were fastened on the pile of gold coins.

CHAPTER NINETEEN

It had been planned for months, and Matthew didn't consider cancelling it. It was good for trade, and would mean the White Hart would be busy all weekend. The travelling band of players were already setting their staging up in the yard at the back of the tavern.

They came yearly to the inn, always with a new play, and it was a popular weekend. During the day, they performed farce, juggling, feats of strength, and conjuring tricks. The backroom of the tavern became a cardroom, the kitchens, filled with extra staff, worked round the clock preparing a constant supply of food and the White Hart, well stocked for the event, provided jugs of quality ale for its regular clientele and a watery version for visiting customers.

It was too lucrative to cancel, and why would he? Myles might be missing, but it needed to be business as usual, especially with Bennett prowling around the edges of his territory. The last thing he wanted Bennett to see was a chink in his armour. He didn't want to give the slightest hint that he was not entirely in control.

Where Myles was, he didn't know. He'd had men make discrete enquiries, but that amounted to nothing, and Daytrew's men had been present regularly looking for him. He'd also heard the news that the printer had turned up dead with his brains leaking out, buried in a midden. This was also being viewed as the work of Myles Devereux. The rumours were too quick on the heels of the incident, and Matthew was fairly sure Bennett was behind them. Everyone was talking about the three murders, and in the same breath, the name Devereux was linked with them, along with something far worse – the Protestant Heresy that had been nailed around London was also seen as his doing.

Myles stopped dead, then retreated back into the shadows of the alley. The man who had just dismounted in the yard of the White Hart, surrounded by his men, was Garrison Bennett.

Any plans he had to walk unnoticed into the yard of the White Hart, hidden by the crowd of revellers waiting for the play to begin, evaporated. He'd hoped Matthew would let the event go ahead. It would provide the perfect cover for his return to the White Hart; the Inn would be packed, the streets around it busy, and Daytrew's men would not be able to look into the faces of all the revellers. It was nearly two days since he had left the White Hart to visit the Sheriff, two days of biding his time in London's dark alleys and the lanes waiting for tonight. Waiting to return to the White Hart and pondering over and over why this had happened to him.

From the dark confines of the alley, he watched as Matthew emerged from the back of the tavern and appeared to greet Bennett. After a few moments, both men disappeared inside, Bennett's men remaining in the yard, watched, he noted, with suspicion by his own.

On the stage, before the main performance, was a man taking the part of a milkmaid singing a bawdy song, the audience joining in the chorus, and he was accompanied by a flute player. He finished the song amid cheers from the audience and refused to provide them with another until they threw him a coin. A man Devereux recognised as Martin Sinton, a clog maker from the next street along, provided the coin, flipping it up the be caught by the milkmaid who made a pretence of storing it between her false breasts before embarking on another musical tale of sin and debauchery.

Movement from the first floor drew his gaze. It was the shutters to his own room being opened. Myles' whole body stiffened as he realised that Matthew had opened them to afford himself and his guest a better view of the entertainment below. And the guest standing next to Matthew was Bennett.

Devereux fell back against the wall breathing hard. Myles felt as if he had been physically thumped in the stomach. Bennett, in his own room? Was there any coming back from this? The damage was complete. The news would be spread far and wide that Devereux was gone and that Bennett was now in control. How could Matthew have been so stupid as to allow this to happen?

Myles prowled the narrowest streets and alleyways, the cloak cowling his face. It had been a long time since he had been alone outside the walls of the White Hart, and the feeling was disconcerting. Eventually, he found what he wanted. At the back of Shaw Row, a line of drying laundry hung; he unclipped what he wanted and darted into the darkness of the next alley before anyone could see him.

The play had finished, and entertainment in the yard at the back of the White Hart had turned to different sorts designed to part men from their coin. A cockfighting ring had been set up to the left of the stage, men stood three deep around it, and many more had climbed on the stage to get a better view.

Ale was being served in the yard from barrels on trestles, their contents guarded by Devereux's men, who also kept a keen eye out to ensure no jugs were handed over before coins had been presented. An arrangement of three tall hogs head barrels topped with wooden planking was in use as a card stable, the players standing while they held their cards, and to the left of this dice, players sat in a ring on the floor of the yard and rattled bone dice into a broad wooden dish set between them.

Women, carrying platters, wove between them, selling cooked game, fish, cheese, bread and griddle cakes. Behind each, one of Devereux's men, ensuring no straying hands helped themselves without paying.

It was a lucrative evening. With money being made from ale, gaming and food. A woman dressed in plain wool with a cloak around her head made her way through the yard. She kicked away a dirty hairy hand from one of the seated dice players as he sought to find a naked leg beneath her skirts.

Undeterred, he seized a handful of her skirt and pulled her to a halt. "Come on, lassy, come and sit with me. I could use some good luck."

"It's not luck he's after lass! Dan, let her go, otherwise, Devereux's men'll be down on us if she so much as yelps!" The man seated next to him said.

The girl's nails had found the man's hand and dug hard into the flesh.

"Hey! There's no need for that," Dan said, using his other hand to prise the girls from his. "Come 'an sit on my knee."

"Dan, bloody stop it. You've had too much ale," his friend advised, jabbing Dan hard with an elbow.

A man opposite said. "If you want her, go an' take her somewhere else; we don't want to be involved again. Remember what happened at the May Fayre?"

"Come on, that wasn't my fault. She was willing, how was I supposed to know she was the landlord's daughter?" Dan protested, then yanking harder on the dress, he unbalanced the girl who, arms flailing, sat down heavily on the ground. Dan wrapped his arms around her and hauled her onto his lap. "There you go. Now come an' keep me warm, and I'll share some ale wi' ye'."

"Dan, let her go. Or there's going to be trouble," the man to his left said through gritted teeth.

Dan pulled the struggling woman closer, clamping her tightly, her arms pinned to her sides beneath his. "Come on lassy, give Dan a kiss."

Dan leered at the girl, his invitation a row of exposed broken and blackened teeth. The girl didn't meet his eyes, twisting her head away from him.

"Dan," one of the other men warned.

Dan loosened one arm from around her and used a strong grip to turn the girl's head towards him.

"Just one kiss, lass, and I'll let you go." With an arm around her neck and the other around her body, he hauled her head towards his, his mouth seeking hers, the girl continued to silently struggle, but the grip he held her in was too firm for her to break. Suddenly she stopped struggling, muscles relaxing, and her face, beneath the hood, met Dan's.

A gurgle of delight escaped Dan's lips before he pressed his foul mouth against the girls.

There was a moment of silence. Dan's hand dropped from her waist and took a tight hold of the girl's rear, squeezing it hard.

A harsh, shrill squeal, like a pig under the butcher's blade, erupted.

"Let her go Dan!"

At the same time, Dan flung himself back away from the girl, releasing her. Both his hands flew to his mouth.

"What the!" the man to his right said.

The girl was on her feet in an instant; a second later, she'd taken three quick steps away from the dice players, ducked beneath a tray held aloft by a serving woman, and disappeared.

"Dan, what's the matter. Dan?" the man to his right laid a hand on Dan's shoulder where he lay on his side, knees drawn up to his chest, hands clamped tightly to his face, eyes screwed shut, moaning.

The door opened at the top of the stairs, and a man stepped through. "Sir, I know it's late, but there's a woman wishing to see you."

"Send her away; I'm not interested in listening to bloody petitions at this time of night," Matthew growled, turning away from the messenger.

"Sir, I would have done; only the name she gave me was one I thought you would be interested in?" the messenger persisted. "She's asking for you, not the Master, and her name is Mistress Fitzwarren."

Matthew turned back towards the man and fixed him with a stare. "Fitzwarren?"

"Aye, and I know that the Master always wants to know when Fitzwarren is here, so I thought it might be the same for a woman with that name. Best to check anyways, I thought," the man said.

"Quite right, send her up," Matthew said, crossing to the door and holding it open. Watching the man descend the stairs towards a simply dressed woman.

Matthew stepped back from the door as she arrived at the top of the steps and crossed the threshold. Before he could close the door, the woman's hand was on it, slamming it shut.

"What the hell," Matthew spluttered.

"What the hell, indeed," Myles Devereux said, dropping the hood from his head.

Matthew's eyes widened even further.

"What happened? You're covered in blood?" Matthew said.

"Don't make me think about it!" Myles was already on his way to his room; opening the door, he went straight to the table where wine and glasses were kept, hastily slopped wine into one of them, a good quantity spilling over the rim, he drank quickly, rinsing his mouth, he spat the wine on the floor.

"What are you doing," Matthew said, his voice worried.

Myles didn't reply. Instead he filled his mouth with more wine, sluiced it around and spat again on the floor. Wiping the back of his mouth with his hand, he raised his eyes and met Matthew's. "I am trying to get rid of the taste of Dan Wingnot."

"Wignot the tanner?" Matthew said, still utterly confused.

"The very same," Myles said, filling his glass and, this time, sending the wine down his throat rather than to the floor.

"Tell me what's happened; where have you been?" Matthew said.

Myles, another full glass of wine in his hand, hitched himself up onto the end of his desk. "Why don't we start with why Garrison Bennett was here tonight?"

Matthew flung his arms up in the air. "I had no choice. Bennett must have ears at the Sheriff's office, and he got to know pretty soon afterwards what had happened. No one expects to see you back; they are blaming you for all three murders."

"Three murders?" Myles said, putting the wine glass down unevenly, liquid spilling over the glass top to the desk.

"Preston was found with his brains panned in," Matthew replied.

"Are you sure," Myles' replied quickly.

"Of course, I'm sure. Preston was found half buried in the midden, been dead a few days, they think. I guess he was probably already dead when we went to the print shop and was missing, allegedly visiting his client," Matthew said.

Myles stalked across the room. "I thought Preston was the key, Matthew, if we found him I'd know why all this has happened and I could dump him at Daytew's door."

"I know. I went to see Bennett because I thought I might be able to find out if he was behind this," Matthew said, following Myles across the room.

Myles turned to face him suddenly. "And is he?"

Matthew shook his head slowly. "I think he's profiting from it, he's certainly helping to spread rumours across London that the murders are attributed to you, but I don't think he was behind it."

"And why was the shit here?" Myles spat.

"I haven't a lot of choices, have I? I'm trying to find out what I can, to protect your business, and I don't have time to fight a war with Garrison Bennett. He thinks I am considering selling out to him, and while he thinks he might buy your business from me, he's not going to make any moves to destroy it. I was playing for time," Matthew explained.

"Are you sure that's what you were doing?" Myles said his tone acid.

"For God's sake, Myles, what other choice do I have?" Matthew replied.

There was a moments silence between the two men. Myles broke it, "So what have you found out?"

"I had thought, like you, that it was Preston. It seemed likely he had produced those sheets and was behind having them nailed up around London. For some reason, he was involved with Galveston. We know Galveston was stealing money, perhaps to pay for this scheme, or he was indebted somehow to Preston, and Anne Hesketh was killed because she knew who her son Danny had been working for. But now I am at a dead end. There's another man, or men, involved in this, and they were manipulating Galveston and Preston," Matthew finished.

"And they killed Galveston, torturing him first, to find something out. Like, who else knew who Danny Hesketh was working for?" Myles replied slowly.

Mathew nodded. "That does make sense. Danny has disappeared, there's no reason to suppose he'll not turn up dead, and if his mother knew who he was working for, then if they killed her as well, they'd be safe."

"The missing page from the ledger had her name on it. That's why they took it." Myles said slowly.

"My God!" Matthew replied.

"Stuffing the page in her mouth after they'd hanged her was just a nice way of sending the dogs in my direction. There was nothing to link me to Galveston's murder, but there is to link me with Anne Hesketh's, and as there is a connection between her, Galveston and Preston, then I get blamed for all three murders," Myles said, shaking his head.

"It's not good," Matthew said. "And if Anne's son, Danny, is dead as well, and I think he will be, then that makes four murders to account for."

"Thank you for pointing that out," Myles said sarcastically. "So, this other man, what have you found out?"

"I'm thinking it has to do with this," Matthew raised the creased protestant sheet from Myles' desk.

"I think you are right. We find the man who wrote this, and we find the murderer," Myles said, taking the sheet from Matthew's hand.

"That's not going to help. Galveston Ad-Hyce is dead. It's his name on the bottom," Matthew said unhelpfully.

Myles flapped the sheet in the air. "We don't know for certain that Galveston wrote this, they could have just used his name, or there is more than one Ad-Hyce in London."

Matthew inclined his head in acceptance of his words. "There's a couple of taverns that have a reputation for being sympathetic to the Protestant cause; I can have some questions asked."

Myles flung the page on his desk. "Someone has to know who is behind them. Any man who writes something like this is not a man who wishes for anonymity in the shadows. He will have been active; he will be a man rallying support for the Protestant cause. We've been looking in the wrong place. Galveston and Preston were not behind this at all. We've been fooled."

Matthew's eyes rested for a moment on Myle's blood-stained face. "Are you going to tell me what happened with Dan Wignot?"

Myles fixed Matthew with a cold stare. "Never ever, mention that man's name in my presence again."

Within an hour, there was a heavy guard in the tavern; nobody would be able to break through it quickly to get to Devereux. And it was natural to have such a presence of armed men when the tavern was hosting the players and all the trouble such an event would bring with it. Food and more wine had been provided, and Myles, in bed, the platter next to him, the covers warming his cold body, listened to the business of the White Hart being carried out loudly in the yard below. It was good to be back, it was good to be warm and to have banished the feeling of hunger. Although he dare not be seen in public, at least from here he could direct this investigation, find out what news there was quickly, and hopefully, very shortly find out what bastard was behind it.

And then he could deal with Bennett.

CHAPTER TWENTY

Matthew didn't knock. He flung the door open to Myles' room shouting loudly. "Get up, now! You can't stop here!"

Myles, hauled from sleep, sat bolt upright in the bed, startled, heart pounding, unaware for a moment of where he was.

Matthew scooped the dress from the floor where Myles had discarded it the night before and flung it on the bed. "Get this on. I've got to get you out of here. Now."

Myles didn't move. "What's happened?"

"There's no time," Matthew hauled the covers from the bed, "Up now, get dressed. The White Hart is plastered with Heresy. Someone has nailed those sheets up on every wall.

"The one Preston printed?" Myles said, ejecting himself from the bed.

"The same, I've had them taken down, but you can be sure it will have been reported to the Sheriff," Matthew said, holding out the dress for Myles to take.

"You want me to put that back on?" Myles said, not taking the offered garment.

"How else am I going to get you out of here? Put it on, come on, there's no time to waste," Matthew shoved the dress in Myles' face.

Myles, cursing, snatched the wool garment and began to feed it over his head. "I can't believe this is happening. Are they like the ones on the press we found at Preston's shop or the one that Fitzwarren brought?"

"I didn't stop to check. Does it matter?" Matthew shot back. "I've had them taken down and burnt."

"Yes, it does; go, get one before they torch them all," when Matthew didn't move, Myles extended an arm and pushed him towards the door.

Myles wriggled into the dress; the front was still wet with blood, and the musty smell of the heavy fabric wrinkled his nose. He cursed as he was forced to breathe the acrid aroma before his head emerged from the top. In the daylight, the blood on the front was apparent, a wide wet stain spreading across the neck of the dress.

Matthew returned, a partly burnt sheet in his hand. Myles reached for it, but Matthew moved it out of his reach. "You can look at it later. We need to go."

Matthew was also looking at the blood on the dress. "You can't leave here looking like that. Even the cloak won't cover it."

Matthew had his knife in his hand, hauling the covers from the bed and taking it to one of the sheets, splitting it. He balled the white linen strip, rubbed it in the ashes in the grate, shook away the worst, and handed it to Myles. "Wrap that round, and put the cloak over the top."

Matthew at the front, with Devereux behind, descended the stairs into the tavern below. It was quiet, a few slumbering bodies were at the far end, but none raised their heads to view the men's passage. The guards Matthew had posted nodded to him as they passed them and entered the yard at the back. Smoke rose from a brazier where the paper had been burnt, and around it were two men warming themselves from the last of the heat. The yard was littered with the evidence of the previous night's entertainment, broken ale cups, a smashed jug; the board on top of the barrels was providing a bed for two of the revellers. More were asleep on the edge of the stage, the smell of the previous night's ale and food lingered still, but now with a cold and sour edge.

"Come on," Matthew hissed, taking Myle's elbow and steering him out into the street, across it and into a dark alleyway that led to another road some distance from the tavern.

Matthew spoke as he walked quickly. "I've paid two of the lads to give a false tale when Daytrew's men arrive that should send them across the city in the wrong direction. I'll take you to Harringdon, and I'll come back later with clothes."

"Harringdon?" Myles said, stumbling after Matthew, the dress was too long, and both his hands held it up so he didn't trip.

"It's as good a place as any; there'll be beggars aplenty there by now looking for a day's work; one more isn't going to be noticed. Just wait there until I come back," Matthew said over his shoulder.

Myles couldn't argue with Matthew. It was a reasonable idea. Myles had other taverns he controlled apart from the White Hart, but they were all known to belong to Devereux. If Daytrew's men were searching for him, they would check any locations around the city known to be connected to him. So the beggar's market was as good a place as any. Here, men, women and children gathered early in the day, hoping for work. The pay would be poor, the hours long, but it was better than starving to death. Men needing labourers would arrive and choose from the assembled crowd those they deemed fit enough to work; the rest were left to melt back into the fabric of London to try and survive until the next day when they may be fortunate enough to earn a meal. In his tattered dress, Myles was not likely to raise comment amongst the similarly dressed starving Londoners.

Myles attached himself to the back of the main press of those wanting to be hired, adopting a pronounced limp and crooked back to make himself as unattractive an employment prospect as possible. At the front were three men on horseback picking labourers from amongst the rabble. Two men on foot made sure those they selected were the ones who came forward, battering back with sticks any who sought to take their places.

It was an ugly scene. Desperation made men brave, or perhaps it was something beyond that; maybe it was madness, Myles thought. A man who had been thrust back, a stick pressing him back into the arms of the crowd, began an impassioned plea with his aggressor. Showing him wasted muscles, making promises his emaciated body had no hope of keeping. Tears accompanied his words; he caught hold of the man's sleeve, pulling him to a stop with a surprising strength for a walking corpse. It did him no good, his action was rewarded with a punch in the face that split a lip, blood pouring from it in a stream down his naked chest. Still, he persisted in making his case until the flat of the stick hit him firmly in the chest and sent him sprawling to the ground.

Suddenly one of the mounted men pointed in his direction, Myles dropped his gaze to the floor. It wasn't enough; the press of hopeful workers was brutally parted by one of the men approaching him.

"You woman! Get to the front," he forced his way towards Myles, viciously using his stick and elbows to clear those from before him.

For a moment, Myles thought he was saved. "I'm here, master, I'm here," a voice shouted.

A woman, half the height of Myles, leapt before him and flung herself towards the approaching man.

"For God's sake, woman, how many beatings does it take! My master doesn't want you, now or ever – do you hear?" She was pushed hard to one side.

Myles pulled the filthy linen around his face. Breathing through the fabric, he inhaled a mouthful of ash, the fine dust caught in the back of his throat and he coughed loudly, his hand to his face holding the material in place.

The man stopped in his tracks.

Realising what had stopped the man's advance, Myles issued a series of loud, barking, spluttering coughs.

Backing away from Myles, the man called over his shoulder to his master. "She's pox ridden."

It created before Myles a space, and in an instant, it was filled with a press of willing men and women. "Take me, master .... I'm clean of the pox .... Strong as an ox, sir .... I'll do the work of two men, master ...."

And so it went on.

Myles was once again at the back of the eager workers; for the moment, he was safe. They'd only approach him once.

Where the hell was Matthew? The remaining throng of disappointed men and women was beginning to break up, those who had been lucky enough to gain work had left, and the men, their task completed, had turned their horses and were riding from Haddington Square.

Myles kept himself close to a small group that seemed to be drifting toward the river. It was either that or stand exposed in the emptying square. Myles realised too late where they were heading. Three armed men were near the exit from the square to Mill Street, and they were evidently looking for someone. The starving streamed towards the men; any attention was welcome.

"Have pity, master …."

"Alms for the poor, sir …."

"May God's blessing be upon you …. Alms for the needy …."

The men were pushing through the vocal crowd, grasping at them and staring into each hunger-pinched face before discarding it and moving to the next. "Out of my way. You! Come 'ere."

Myles cursed, pulling the linen tighter around his face. The woman beside him had dropped to her haunches and was picking spilt grain kernels from between the cobbles. Myles dropped down and joined her.

"Ger off! These a' mine," a thin hand tried to push Myles away.

"I'll help you, here," Myles, meeting her sunken angry glare, deftly picked half a dozen grains and dropped them into her hand. He kept picking wheat from the floor all the time, keeping his eyes on the men walking along the crowd's edges. As long as they didn't press through them, there was a chance they'd not see him.

One of the armed men stopped. Through three pairs of legs, Myles could see his boots, clean brown leather, rising to his knees and then black hose; the rest of him was out of sight. He took two steps to his right and then stopped.

Myles held his breath.

Eyes fixed on the boots. The boots took half an uncertain step to the right, then stopped again. Their owner's voice he heard over the tops of the heads of the beggars between them. "This is pointless, Tom; there's no one here but filthy beggars, and I've no mind to be mired with their stench for the rest of the day."

"Just check them, Garth, will you," Tom's voice replied from the left, the tone annoyed.

"I 'ave!" Garth replied, then "You, get out of my way."

The man with the boots had pushed one of those before him; losing his balance, he staggered back into the arms of the crowd, and the whole three-deep row stumbled backwards. A leg banged into Myles, the owner tumbling over him, yelping, flattening Myles against the wet cobbles. Another fell on top; the woman to his right was similarly smothered in bodies, grains spilling from her opened hand, and a shrill shriek of despair ripped past her broken lips. Someone trod hard on his left hand as they struggled to right themselves, and the stinking weighted rags across his back squirmed.

Myles pulled his hands beneath him and braced his body against the blows from above him. The weight forced his face hard against the ground. Another must have landed on the top of the pile. Myles felt his ribs compressing; the weight above him was too much. With every muscle tensed he fought to free himself, but he was trapped. He let his breath go and in an instant of panic, realised he couldn't take another. His mouth, open wide, tried to capture the air, but he couldn't draw it in. Myles tried again, the strength of desperation upon him, not to free himself but to lift himself from the ground just enough to breathe.

His body was locked solid to the cobbles. Nails clawed at the ground, the only part of his body he could move. Feeling his vision blurring, the heels of his palms hard on the stones, he tried again to push himself up; his strength was going, and his vision ....

"Ger' off 'im," he heard the words; they seemed to come from a distance, then again. "Ger' off."

There was a slight release of the pressure on his back, enough for his shaking arms to lift him enough to try and take a breath. His crushed chest didn't respond; the air choked in his throat. Panic raged through his mind, shaking arms released his weight, and he dropped down again on the cobbles, saliva running from his mouth.

The pressure was suddenly gone; Myles was unaware of the trampling feet and boots battering him as they righted themselves. Then a hammering on his back began. Rhythmic and constant.

"Yer winded, that's all, come on," It was the crone's voice close to his ear, and she delivered a series of solid thumps to his back. Suddenly, as if a blockage had been removed, the restriction in his throat disappeared. His first breath was shallow, halting, insufficient for his starved lungs; the second shaky still was like nectar.

"Up ye get, lad," the woman had hooked an arm around his and was tugging at it.

Myles raised a hand towards her and tried to speak, but words were beyond him. He needed more time.

She seemed to recognise this, and the tugging stopped, a hand gentle on the side of his face stroked his cheek. Myles closed his eyes; he felt the panic begin to recede, and in its wake, a sudden shaking took hold, sending tremors to his arms and legs.

"Yer all right, lad. Susie's 'ere," the woman cooed softly.

She gave him a little more time, then looping a bony arm under his, she tugged again. "Come on, lad. We can't stop here, ain't safe."

Myles raised his head. The crowd had thinned, and there was no sight of the brown boots through the legs, and the soldiers' voices were absent. Slowly he made it to his knees; the material of the skirt caught around his legs, making the struggle difficult, his body still weak and shaking. Hands on his knees, he pushed himself upright, swayed, and found himself stopped from falling by the woman's arm around his waist.

"Come 'wi me. I know a place," Susie said, slowly guiding him from Haddington.

Myles' heart continued to hammer in his battered chest. He was sure they had been looking for him. But who would know he was there? Myles stumbled suddenly on shaking legs, coming to a halt. Taking a long, steadying breath, he felt the old woman adjust her hold, and they continued their slow shamble across the cobbles.

Exhausted, they stopped when they reached a narrow alleyway from the square. Releasing her hold, the woman sat down, and slithering down the wall, he joined her. There was sweat on his forehead, he wiped it away with the linen around his neck, drying his face. It was the cold sweat of fear. The woman next to him didn't move, her eyes were closed, and she was breathing heavily, exhausted.

Knowing he wasn't observed, he pulled the burnt sheet Matthew had retrieved from inside the dress. HIs hands shook too much, and he couldn't focus on the print.

Myles rested back against the wall; when he felt his strength returning, he left the woman and went back as far along the narrow alley as he dared, he had a view of part of Haddington, and from there, he kept a watch for Matthew.

CHAPTER TWENTY-ONE

Myles waited, and still no sign of Matthew. The bells across the city had rung for sext, and it began to rain. He waited, soaked to the skin, the cold penetrating every fibre of his clothes. Where else could he go? What had happened to stop Matthew from coming back? When the bells struck for vespers, the thought in his head was, would he ever return?

Had he been left here, stripped of everything? Clothes, money, food .... he had nothing. Money, why didn't he have any? Why had he allowed himself to be bundled from the room in such haste that he didn't have a purse with him? Why had Matthew not checked?

Myles hugged his knees closer, the cloak wrapped tightly around him to ward off the cold of the coming night. His mind was back in his book-keepers office, looking down at the cold corpse nailed to the floor with a poniard. He was missing something; he was sure of that. There was a connection with the printer, Preston, who was now dead, that was clear. Galveston had carried out work for Preston, the bills the boy had prepared were missing, and there was the shared name on the bottom of the printed sheets that Myles now knew had originated in Preston's workshop.

Had Galveston been involved with some Protestant plot? Myles had never considered Galveston as possessing any religious fervour, but then you could never really know what was hiding within a man's soul. He could have fallen foul of some religious group or …. or whoever shared his surname could have, and somehow Galveston had become implicated.

And if it was Bennett.

Bennett.

It didn't seem like Bennett's work, but then perhaps Bennett has some help? Maybe someone was working with him to find a way to permanently rid London of Myles Devereux. If they tied him to a Protestant plot, then the Queen's men would be hunting for him, and if they found him, it would not be long before he would be following in his brother's footsteps and finding himself tied to a stake above a smouldering pile of faggots.

Myles swallowed hard and tried to banish the image of his brother from his mind. And for once, he succeeded. If he was caught, he would not be tried for crimes against the city, his business dealings would not be questioned, and he would not be called to account for work he carried out for the Parishes. The matter would be a simple one of Heresy.

The more Myles thought about it, the more that this seemed likely. He would be removed, and using the religious charge would prevent a trial that could embarrass many men in the city. He had dealings with people who would not want their business or connections with Myles Devereux aired publicly.

If this was the case, then who was helping Bennett? Someone who did not want their connections with Myles known? Someone who would benefit from Myles' death?

But who?

Myles had many debtors and was quite aware that many of them would dearly wish him dead, but that was a long way from taking action to secure it. And this plan, if it was one, was elaborate. It had taken time and planning to tie him to this Protestant Heresy. Had Galveston been forced to be a part of it, and when his role was fulfilled, he was murdered?

Myles cursed, his breath billowing in the cold air. Pondering the problem was getting him no further forward. The more he thought about it, the more questions he came up with. Myles withdrew the partly burnt sheet, the light of the day was nearly gone now, and he couldn't read the words on the page.

He needed to talk to Matthew.

Myles knew he couldn't stop where he was indefinity; already, he was attracting strange looks from those who had passed him and then found him and the old woman still in the alley when they returned. Resolving to wait one more hour, he went back to where the woman was and seated himself on the ground; a little less rain fell here, an overhang from a roof above stopping some of the downpour.

She moved sideways. "Come 'ere lad, there's space for us both."

Myles joined her. He wrapped his cloak around them both, covering their heads and stopping the worst of the rain.

"I 'ad a son like you, once?" Susie said, her head close to his.

Myles managed half a smile. "Did he wear a dress as well?"

The woman elbowed him, laughing. He realised she wasn't as old as he'd first thought, her face bone thin, with hollowed cheeks and eyes that seemed to have retreated into her face. But not a crone, probably more his own age. One of her hands emerged from her ragged plumage, and when it opened, he saw the handful of grains that she'd not dropped when the crowd had fallen over them. She offered them towards him. She shrugged when he shook his head and put one in her mouth.

Catching his eye, she said. "Rain's made 'em soft."

Myles refused the offering again, despite her reassurances that they wouldn't break his teeth.

"When the cloth fell from ye face, I cud see's you were no lassie," the woman went on, popping another grain into her mouth, then added. "there's plenty out there hide behind woman's skirts, what is it that you've done?"

Myles didn't answer. What had he done to end up soaked, penniless and wearing a poor woman's stolen clothes in a London gutter?

"Ye can tell me, I'm not goin' to get you into trouble, am I?" Susie continued, her eyes on the remaining few grains she added sadly, "Not much o' a meal!"

"An angry master, is all," Myles replied, knowing he needed to say something, and it seemed to satisfy the woman, who went back to slowly eating the remaining grains and lamenting how few she'd managed to save. If Matthew returned, he'd have the sense to check the adjacent streets; he'd not expect Myles to be stood in the middle of Haddington Square alone in a rainstorm. Myles drew his knees closer, pulled the cloak tighter around them, and tried to conserve his body's warmth. It had been a long time since he had felt this cold.

"Is that you?" a voice he recognised called through the rain.

"Who the hell do you think it's going to be?" Myles hissed back.

Myles carefully unwound himself from the floor, his muscles cold and resisting. Slowly, he pushed himself to his feet. "Where've you been?"

"Daytrew arrived with men; he was at the White Hart for over two hours. Everyone was questioned. Had they seen you? Did they know where you might be? When was the last time you'd been there? It was bloody endless," Matthew complained.

"Did he learn anything?" Myles asked ugently.

Matthew laughed. "Plenty, I would imagine, but nothing that's going to serve him well. He's despatched men on a chase across London in the wrong direction, and I've more men posted to keep the trail alive. He's going to spend all night chasing a ghost and feeling he's getting closer. So he'll not be bothering us for a while."

Matthew had a bag slung over one shoulder. "What did you bring."

"Clothes, money and I've a room at the Buck Inn rented with an entrance through the stable yard," Matthew said, already turning to leave the alley.

"A purse, quickly," Myles said, his hand extended.

Matthew's brow furrowed. "What for?"

"Just give me it," Myles demanded through chattering teeth.

Matthew, cursing silently, unhitched the bag from his shoulder, fished inside and retrieved a leather purse. "Here, we've not the time for this."

Myles took it, pulled the strings apart with shaking fingers, removed two coins and retreated down the alley.

"What the hell are you doing now?" Matthew hissed after him.

Myles turned over Susie's hand, met her watery gaze and pressed the two coins into it.

"For God's sake, come on," Matthew said a little louder.

Ten minutes later, they had made it through the stable yard at the back of the Buck Inn, up a set of wooden open stairs to a balcony; from there, they could access a narrow passageway to the room Matthew had rented.

"This should be safe. I got Marlow to hire the room; his horse is in the stable at the back; there's no reason for anyone to suspect he's not here. And he'll be back later to take a meal downstairs as well," Matthew reassured, closing the door; Marlow was one of Matthew's most reliable men.

"Get that fire lit, man," Myles said, taking the bag from Matthew and shaking the contents out on the bed. It didn't look good, "What have you brought me?"

"Apprentices' clothes, money, and food," Matthew said bluntly from where he was kneeling on the floor near the fire. "And bad news. Danny Hesketh has been found with his brains dashed out on the river bank; probably been dead a while as well, so I've heard. So we can't even argue that he killed his mother."

Slopping the soaked skirts and linen shift to the floor, Myles pulled a dry, coarse blanket from the pallet and began to use it to dry himself. The rough open weave raked his skin, bringing blood back to the surface and reviving the feeling in his numbed limbs.

"Shit!" Myles, swathed in the blanket, began to search among the soaked cloth on the floor; he'd forgotten about the folded sheet Matthew had given him; he'd had it against his skin beneath the linen held in place by the belt of the skirt.

Unfolding it, he breathed a sigh of relief; the rain had not completely ruined it, although the ink along the bottom edge had run, blurring the words. All that was left was the lower third; the rest had been turned to ash in a brazier in the yard at the back of the White Hart. But it was enough. Even with this small piece, it was sufficient to know that it was different from the one Fitzwarren had given him and different from the one set in the press at Preston's.

The lines were spaced wider, the font size was larger, and at the bottom, it bore no name, just now some blurred initials. It was just a call to arms to the Protestant faithful to rise against their Catholic masters. The only thing it had in common with the other two was that it was still Heresy. Matthew said they were nailed to the walls of the White Hart? The question was, had they appeared anywhere else in London last night?

"Did they find these anywhere else?" Myles asked, waving the sheet in the air.

Matthew sat back on his heels in front of the fire that was beginning to create a thickening line of smoke from the smouldering kindling. "There were a few in the surrounding streets, but not many; most of them were nailed to the White Hart's walls. Unfortunately one of them reached Daytrew."

Myles returned his eyes to the paper. "This is different to the other two."

Matthew blew on the embers and sat back again. "I saw that when I pulled some down. The one

Fitzwarren gave you, and the one on Preston's press filled the page. Not a line wasted, not a space that was not used. That one has maybe a third of what the others contained."

"I agree. And it doesn't make much sense either, not from what I have here anyway. Listen to this

"He that setteth foot on the path of the Popery will commeth up against the wrath of the Lord and the evil of the Books of Solomon."

"What on earth is that supposed to mean, and here, further on ..... 'the Lord gives good barrels of ale for the feast of the evils of the Mass.' This is senseless," Myles finished.

Matthew finishing with the fire stood. "Senseless or not, it's Heresy and treason."

"Treason?" Myles looked up.

"The top part stated there would be a pension in heaven should a man bring himself to kill the Queen," Matthew provided, "Nailing that lot to White Hart means they don't need to try you for murder now, do they, not when they can hunt you down for Heresy and Treason."

Myles stared at Matthew. "This wasn't my doing?"

"Who is going to think that? No one," Matthew's thumbs had found his belt, and he stared down at Myles. "How we are going to keep you safe, keep Bennett off our backs and find a way out of this. I honestly don't know."

Myles said. "There's nothing to link these to me apart from them being nailed to the tavern. Come on, these things appear all over London every few months."

Matthew leaned over Myles. "That might be the case, but these have your name on, near enough."

"What do you mean," Myles whipped the page back off the bed, and stood next to Matthew, his eyes scanning the text. "Where?"

"There, where the ink has run," Matthew stabbed the bottom of the paper. "M.D. Those two letters will tie this right back to you, and you fled from the Sheriff's office, which is an admission of guilt as far as Daytrew is concerned."

"M.D," Myles said quietly, his eyes on the blurred print. Now he had been told what the letters were, he could see their form within the ink that the rain and spread across the sheet. M.D. would be seen as none other than Myles Devereux; the paper dropped from his slack hand to the floor, his vision for the second time that day failed him and before Matthew could catch him, Myles descended into an untidy pile at his feet.

When Myles opened his eyes for a long moment, he had no idea where he was. The ceiling, cobwebbed, beamed, and smoke-stained, was alien. Swivelling his head sideways, he found Matthew kneeling next to him.

"Here, lad, do you want a drink? You scared the wits out of me," Matthew said, holding a cup out unsteadily.

Myles stared at him, his mind spinning like a dervish, wouldn't tell him what he needed to know; he searched wildly for what had happened, for the why? Then, like a massive gate slamming open in a storm, the facts, the reality, hit him like a blow. Myles convulsed once, Matthew twisting away, managed to miss the vomit aimed at him. Myles' stomach continued to force its contents out until, eventually, the spasms produced nothing more than gas and saliva.

After a moment, Matthew held the cup towards Myles again, who took it into a shaking hand, spilling beer over the wooden rim as he sought to set it to his lips.

"I thought you must have looked at it already, lad. I thought you'd known they'd added your name to the bottom of it, or at least enough to make it seem like they were your doing," Matthew said quietly, accepting the cup back and refilling it from a jug on the floor.

Myles, his face pale, looked up at Matthew. "Someone wants me dead, don't they?"

Matthew dropped to the floor, sitting cross-legged and regarded Myles with a clear gaze. "It does seem to be that way. Many would wish it upon you, but no one before has launched such a scheme at you as this. You've no choice left but to leave London."

"Leave London," Myles repeated weakly.

"France maybe or Ireland, and don't forget we have trading contacts in Bruges," Matthew said. "There's the money we made from the deal with Brinswold and the gold at the White Hart. We can take all of that with us."

"Leave," Myles said again quietly.

Matthew leaned over and clapped him on the arm. "Yes, leave as soon as we can."

Myles stared at the floor.

"Come on, we can start again. There is too much here to fight against. You can see that, can't you?" Matthew said. "If I thought otherwise, you know I would tell you."

Numb, and not from cold, Myles nodded.

Matthew placed his hand on his shoulder. "Stay here; Marlow will be here as well. There's no-one knows where you are; you'll be safe until I get back."

"How long?" Myles managed.

Matthew shook his head. "An hour, maybe two, but no more. We get out of the city, and then we can decide where we are going. Be ready. Get dressed, and give me that paper for the fire, we could do without being caught possessing it."

Myles looked around; it didn't come to hand, he had no idea where he'd dropped it.

"When you find it, throw it straight in there, do you hear?" Matthew said, pointing towards the flames.

CHAPTER TWENTY-TWO

Myles, dry now, slowly put on the clothes Matthew had brought. Plain, simple, worn and not his usual attire, but he barely noticed. The sudden sickening shock was gone, replaced with the simple reality that he had lost the game.

The Heresy that had been nailed to the White Hart, his tavern, had sealed his fate. Before that, he might have been able to find the murderer, but it wasn't a murderer that the Sheriff wanted now; it was a Protestant rebel who was also wanted for Treason. There were no higher crimes.

Treason.

Matthew was right. Escaping the city was the best course of action. To be caught now was to die a slow, public and cruel death. Better to live a little poorer than he had been than to die a rich man. Most of his wealth was in buildings like the White Hart, and there would be no time to do anything with those; he could take only what he could carry. There was enough money at the White Hart collected over the years to still make him a rich man, and it seemed he would have to content himself with that.

Greed could be his undoing.

He'd seen men do it before. Rush into flames in burning houses to save possessions, never to emerge again and be found smouldering amongst the ashes of their wealth the following day. There was a point to say enough was enough, and he knew he was there now. Be content, walk away, or ....

Die.

Not much of a choice.

Myles slewed on a doublet and began to fasten the simple wooden toggles at the front. Matthew hadn't brought boots, and he'd tried his best to dry the ones he had been wearing before the fire.

The clock struck for compline. Not long now. Matthew had been gone nearly an hour. The paper Matthew had given him was still on the floor next to the simple pallet bed; Myles scooped it up and looked bitterly at the two blurred impressions of an M and D. He was about to drop it into the fire when he stopped. Was it actually MD? Angling it towards the flames, he tried to throw more light on the sheet, but the page was creased, and the illuminating flames just cast wavering unhelpful shadows across the indistinct letters. Rather than burning it, he folded it and slid it inside the doublet.

Agitated, Myles paced from one end of the small room to the other. Then stopped himself. The floor was uneven, the boards loose on the rafters, whoever was below could hear his passage across them, and it was better to draw as little attention to his presence as possible. Marlow, who had supposedly rented the room, could be below taking a meal, and it might raise questions if someone were heard in his room. So instead, Myles forced himself to lie still on the pallet, the coarse blanket over him, listening for the sound of Matthew returning.

He heard the promising tread of heavy steps up the stairs at the back of the Buck Inn once and sat up, flinging the blanket aside and reaching for his boots. But it wasn't Matthew. The footsteps passed his room, and he heard another door open, and a woman's voice called a greeting.

He pulled his still-wet boots on anyway, better to be ready. Matthew couldn't be much longer. He'd said an hour, maybe two. It was a ten-minute walk, no more from the Buck to the White Heart; Matthew knew where the money was in a coffer in his room. Up the stairs, unlock the coffer with Matthew's key, take out the money, and put it in the bag. That should take minutes only. Then send the men to lay another false trail for Daytrew might take a little while, but not long, fifteen minutes maybe, but no more. He'd only need to send two or three out across London, with a few coins to place some bribes, and that would be enough.

He should have been back by now.

He should have been back a long time ago.

The bell struck again.

Three hours.

Fear, sudden and irrational, choked in his throat. Myles was on his feet in an instant. Something was wrong, and sitting here was like being a fly caught in a web, and somewhere a spider was coming for him, he was sure.

Throwing the dark, still sodden cloak around his shoulders and collecting the purse of money, Myles stepped outside the door of the rented room onto the balcony. It was dark, and it was still raining. He had little idea of what he was doing but knew he wasn't waiting in the room any longer. Marlow had his horse in the stable, Matthew had said. Myles knew it well, a black mare with a white star chest. The stables were on the opposite side to the balcony, he could wait in there, and when Matthew arrived, he'd see him take the steps to the first-floor room.

Crossing the yard silently, Myles found the horse he was looking for in the fourth stable; lifting the kick bolt, he let himself in, smoothed a hand down the mare's neck and closed the door quietly. Standing next to the animal, hidden by the shadows, he watched.

Myles had been in the stable only long enough for the panic to drain from him, it was replaced by the feeling of cold air that crept through the thin and poorly fitting clothes. As he stepped this way and then that to avoid the worst of the drops from the leaking stable roof, the question had already formed in his mind of whether this had been a foolish idea when he heard them. A sudden stampede of a dozen pairs of feet at least heralded the entrance into the yard of Daytrew's men.

Myles slunk back into the darkness. His heart was pounding.

"On my order. You four take the taproom, you six take the rooms up there, and you two check the stables. And remember, the Sheriff wants him alive, so no mistakes this time," the leader, standing not far before the stables, issued quick instructions.

Myles heard the shuffle of boots as men positioned themselves as directed, followed by a moment's silence.

"Go!" The leader ordered.

Myles jumped.

Sliding around to the darkest side of the horse, where little light from the yard fell, Myles dropped to the floor and pulled the straw over his body.

He heard a man in the stable next to him, speaking quietly to a startled horse, then the sound of the door closing and the kick bolt spinning home.

"What have we here?" the man said.

Myles could see his pale hands on the top of the stable door through the straw. He'd seen the unlatched kick bolt. They could only be fastened from the outside.

"Steady there, lassie," the door creaked open, and the man was in the stable with him. He could hear the man's hand patting the horse's neck and his rustling footsteps as he circled the stable.

Myles took a long quiet breath in and held it. The man was moving back towards the horse's head, about to duck beneath her neck and inspect the other, darker side of the stable, the man was no fool, and the moonlight from the yard flashed along the length of a poniard.

Myles closed his eyes. Listening to the light footfalls as they came closer, two more steps and the man would stand on him. Myles braced himself.

"He's fled, he was in that room there, but he's gone, sir," a man shouted, accompanied by the noise of heavy footsteps on the wooden stairs to the balcony.

"For God's sake, Alwyn shut up; he could still be hereabouts," the man who had issued the orders hissed under his breath.

"Sorry, sir," Alwyn replied, sounding crestfallen.

The man in the stables cursed. "Alwyn, you're a bloody idiot."

Myles heard the man step back towards the stable door, patting the mare's neck before opening the door. Myles exhaled through the straw when he heard the noise of the kick bolt slap back into place.

Myles stayed where he was listening; the last thing he wanted to do was startle the horse. They'd not recheck the stables, and outside, he could hear the men regrouping, feet clattering back into the yard of the Buck Inn.

"Where next, sir?" it sounded like the man who had been in the stable with him who spoke.

"A few more questions for Devereux's man, Matthew, I think. Find out what else he knows," the officer replied before the group of reassembled men left the Inn yard.

What had Matthew told them? Had he sent the Queen's men straight to him? Why? Myles tried to ignore that thought and concentrate on the more pressing issue of getting out of the Buck Inn without being seen. Marlow's horse was still here, so either he was in the tavern or would be back at some point. But could he trust Marlow?

Who could he trust …. ?

CHAPTER TWENTY-THREE

Myles found one of his men loitering at the front door of the merchant's house. He'd provided them to Fitzwarren in return for silver. Why he was guarding a merchant's house, he didn't know or particularly care to know, but Fitzwarren might be here.

It was a gamble, but he was short on options.

Myles walked directly up to the man, flipped his hood back, and demanded. "Get Fitzwarren here, now."

Obviously not expecting to see his master, the man hesitated.

"Are you deaf?" Myles said, glaring at him.

"Sorry, master. I'll get him right away," the man turned, held the door open for Myles, then followed him in, stepping quickly along a dark corridor.

Fitzwarren was here!

That, at least, was something, and he'd not given himself away for nothing. Further, inside the house, he heard a rapid knock on a door, a quick exchange of voices, and footsteps returning to him. Fitzwarren, with a mildly puzzled expression, wearing white linen and an unbuttoned doublet, emerged from the gloom.

"I've a matter to discuss," Myles said before the other man could speak.

"Of course, follow me," Fitzwarren turned, retracing his steps to the room he had just left. Myles turned to his man – "You, wait here."

As soon as the door closed, he said, "The man outside. Have you the means to keep him from leaving or speaking to anyone?"

Fitzwarren said nothing, Devereux's tone and appearance lent enough gravity to his request, and he left.

Myles surveyed the room. The remains of a meal were on the table. Empty glasses and crumbs. Lifting a linen cloth, Myles found some bread, cheese and ham beneath it on a wooden platter. A silver salt pot, a mustard pot, and two gilt candle holders holding double-wicked candles casting an even light across the table.

Fitzwarren returned; closing the door behind him, he leaned against it and asked. "What has happened?"

"I'm in a trap, Fitzwarren, and I can't get out," Myles stated bluntly.

"One of your own making?" Fitzwarren asked, pushing himself away from the door.

"No. It's the book-keeper and everything that has happened afterwards, and I am now wanted for Treason and Heresy," Myles dropped heavily into one of the chairs at the table.

Fitzwarren laughed bitterly and lay a hand on Myles' shoulder momentarily. "Then you are at least in good company, and we finally have something in common."

"It's not funny, Fitzwarren," Myles' said, pulling from the touch.

"I didn't say it was. The thought of being hanged, revived and then watching my innards sizzle on a brazier has also darkened a few of my nights," Fitzwarren pulled a chair out and sat down next to Myles. "You've been linked to those printed sheets, I assume."

"There's more. Hesketh, the woman I told you had been murdered, I was summoned to the Sheriff's office, and he produced the missing page from my ledger …. It was in her mouth," Myles said dryly.

Fitzwarren sat back in his chair, folding his arms. "Go on."

"I left via an open window and made it back later to the White Hart. Bennett was there, trying to secure a deal with Matthew for my business. I spoke to Matthew after he'd got rid of Bennett; in the morning, there were more sheets, different ones though, and they were nailed mainly to the White Hart. Matthew had most of them burnt," Myles reached inside his doublet and pulled out the burnt and stained sheet, laying it on the table and slid it towards Fitzwarren.

"I met up with Matthew later. He told me Hesketh's son had been found dead, so there was no way we could accuse him of being the murderer, and he told me that charges of Treason and Heresy were being brought against me. He secured me a room at the Buck Inn, went to get the money, and didn't return. The Queen's men arrived, and I got out just in time. And here I am, traitor to the crown and God," Myles finished morosely.

Fitzwarren was quiet for a moment, examining the paper; putting it down he reached over and selected a handful of abandoned cutlery and began to lay knives and forks end to end in a line across the table.

"What are you doing, Fitzwarren?" Myles said in dismay.

Fitzwarren raised his hand. "Just listen. It's a puzzle, that's all. We just need to look at it from a different angle to solve it."

Fitzwarren reached across the table, selecting the salt and mustard pots, a wine glass, a small serving dish and a candle holder.

Picking up the salt pot, he fixed Myles with a stare. "That line represents truth. What we know goes below it, and what we don't goes above it. This is Galveston, and we don't know why he was murdered? Agreed?"

"Fitzwarren, games are not going to ...."

"It's not a game. Do you agree we don't know why Galveston was murdered?" Fitzwarren said forcefully, still holding up the salt pot.

"I agree," Myles said half-heartedly.

"Good," Fitzwarren put the salt pot down above the line of silverware, then fished inside his doublet for a small purse. Producing a coin, he held it up. "But, we do know he was stealing from you, agreed?"

Myles nodded and watched Fitzwarren put the coin on the table with an audible click below the forks. "Anne Hesketh was killed. Why?"

Myles shrugged. "Matthew found out her son had been the one who nailed up the sheets that you brought me. We are guessing, but it seems likely she was killed and her son was because they knew who it was. Although that doesn't explain why my ledger ended up in her mouth."

"It's a good reason why they are both dead, so let's put them together here," Fitzwarren put down the mustard pot and a small serving dish next to the coin.

"Now, Preston," Fitzwarren said, holding up a wine glass.

"He knew more than he was telling me. He should have identified the watermark as a spoked wheel;

there was more of that paper in his shop when I went back, so he knew where they had come from, whether it was his shop or another," Myles said, his brow creased with thought.

"Alright. So he was murdered then to prevent him from telling anyone about the Heresy, so let's put him next to the unfortunate Hesketh's. He, too, knew who had printed them," Fitzwarren set the wine glass down.

"Is this helping," Myles asked impatiently.

"Yes, quite a lot," Fitzwarren regarded the arrangement over steepled fingers, then asked. "You've not missed anyone else out, have you?"

"No," Myles shot back. "Why?"

"What about Matthew? Where shall we put him, and where shall we put Bennett, I wonder," Fitzwarren said, selecting a silver coin and a worn penny from the purse. "What's Bennett's involvement here?"

"He's just trying to take advantage of the situation. Galveston's murder wasn't his style," Myles said.

"I agree. But something is bothering me. Anne Hesketh, we agree, was killed to stop her from telling anyone who her son was working for," Fitzwarren said thoughtfully.

"That makes sense, so why the ledger?" Myles said.

"Why the ledger, indeed? Someone wanted her dead and her son to stop them from talking; I suspect someone else used Anne's death to point a finger in your direction. That had nothing to do with why she died, it was just convenient," Fitzwarren said, tapping the penny on the table.

"Bennett?" Myles said.

"Possibly, whoever wanted Galveston dead didn't want to inflict the fatal blows, and he used the same people to dispatch Anne and her son. If he'd employed Bennett, then perhaps your rival could not resist taking advantage of the situation," Fitzwarren held up the penny and then placed it down below the line of cutlery and picked up the paper Myles had brought, "And this is the hasty work of a fool. I would wager they tampered with a page that had already been set and changed a few words to create an illusion of a religious ramble in a hurry."

"Bennett!" Myles said.

"Exactly," Fitzwarren slid the paper beneath the penny and picked up the silver coin. "Leaving Matthew, where do you want to place him?"

"I can't believe he would be behind this," Myles said, then a memory of the soldier's words in the yard drifted into his mind. How had they known he was there? And they were going back to ask him some more questions.

Fitzwarren saw the confused look on Myles' face and asked. "Are you doubting him, or are you being made to doubt him?"

Myles reached forward, took the coin from Fitzwarren's hand, and set it down on the table, firmly below the line. "Matthew isn't a traitor."

Fitzwarren picked up the penny. "I would wager Bennett knows who is behind all of this. Our only unknown is who murdered your book-keeper; what happened afterwards we can account for."

Myles looked at the arrangement of pieces of crockery, glasses and coins on the table. "It's the only one that sits above the line."

"Exactly that. We can tie all these together, but not that one," Fitzwarren tapped a finger on the salt pot, raising his eyes to Myles' gaze, "Bennett is your key."

"I need Bennett to name the man who killed Galveston; he's the heretic," Myles said, pointing towards the penny.

Fitzwarren inclined his head on one side. "That would indeed be a solution. If you could find the source of the original prints and Galveston's murderer, everything else would link to him, I agree."

"First I need to find out why Matthew didn't come back. He should have been no more than an hour, and then we were going to leave the city," Myles said.

"You were actually going to leave London?" Fitzwarren asked, sounding surprised.

"I was, but not now. The only reason Matthew didn't come back is because someone wouldn't let him," Myles replied, his eyes fixed on Fitzwarren.

"Very well, I'll find out, wait here. It'll take me about an hour to get to the White Hart and back," Fitzwarren replied, beginning to fasten his doublet.

Fitzwarren returned sooner than Myles had expected, a grim look on his face when he opened the door.

"What's happened?" Myles said, a sudden fear clamping an icy hand around his throat.

"Matthew is not at the White Hart. He didn't return either and the Queen's men are also looking for him," Fitzwarren replied.

"Bennett! That shit has Matthew, doesn't he?" Myles' voice grated with anger. "He wouldn't have left me. He told me Bennett had already offered him money to hand my business over to him."

"I would say so," Fitzwarren replied, "If he believes you've been disposed of, and a warrant for an arrest for Heresy would, generally, remove a man permanently, then it would be wise for him to lay a claim to your business before someone else does."

"How am I going to do this? I've no men at my disposal anymore? How!" Myles rose from his seat and paced around the room.

Fitzwarren's grey eyes watched his passage. "Myles, you possess more cunning and imagination than any man I've ever met, now is the time to put it to some use."

Myles stopped and drummed his fingers on the table.

CHAPTER TWENTY-FOUR

Garrison Bennett's shop was relatively quiet, the hour was early, and as yet, London was still beginning her new day, the cold making the start sluggish. A man with a dozen horse bridles looped over one arm was transferring them to nails hammered into the roof beams. Two poor-looking customers were examining the animal cages on the floor and exchanging quiet words, and, at the back of the shop, a muscled man, bare-armed and with two broad knives at his belt, leaned against the door frame to Bennett's private rooms, watching them closely. His attention changed immediately when the door to the street opened, and two men entered, one hooded, the cowl shadowing his face, the other behind him, taller, well dressed, pushing him forward. Taking a firm hold on the arm of the hooded man, he stepped towards the door to Bennett's office.

"I've business with Bennett," the newcomer announced, the delivery making the words a command.

The man hanging the bridles stopped, eyes fastened on the strangers. Bennett's man straightened, taking a step away from the door. His face impassive, he said. "An who might you be?"

"Who I am is not important. That I have business with your master, is all you need to know," came the calm reply.

Bennett's man folded his arms, a confident smile on his face. "That's not how it works. Name?"

The man didn't reply. Instead, he raised his hand and whipped the hood back from the smaller man standing in front of him.

Bennett's man gawped. "Stay there."

A moment later, he had disappeared through the door.

Admittance to Bennett's presence didn't take long. The old bakery smelt of dust and damp; Bennett, legs crossed, an elbow on the sprouting stuffing of one arm of his throne-like chair, regarded the entrants with unconcealed curiosity.

"'An I thought I was too old for surprises," Bennett said, his soft Scottish accent rounding the words.

The man who had been in Bennett's shop leaned against the door, and two other solid-looking men stood behind Bennett, both armed and both with their eyes fixed on Myles Devereux.

"Sin sorpresas, aunque sean disagredables, nadie estaria dispuesto a vivir. Not all surprises are pleasant," Myles Devereux announced smiling.

"Enough," the man to Devereux's left cuffed him hard across the back of the head. "Master Bennett, I would speak with you alone, I have a proposal that I believe you'd rather hear that way."

Bennett licked his lips, his eyes fixed on Myles. "You're about to be traded, Devereux. How does it feel?"

Myles, with an insolent expression, returned Bennett's gaze and said. "It is nice to have a value."

The smile dropped from Bennett's face, and the words earned Myles another hard slap that made him stagger sideways. His cloak swung apart, revealing bound wrists; unable to save himself, Myles careered into a wooden coffer set next to the door.

Bennett laughed. "Trussed like a foul!"

Myles regaining his balance, stayed where he was, hitching himself up awkwardly onto the end of the coffer, the wooden box creaking as he did so.

Bennett waved his hand in the air. "Give your blade to Pete and that poniard as well."

Richard Fitzwarren hesitated momentarily before smoothly unbuckling the sword belt and handing it to Bennett's man along with the poniard.

"Any more?" Bennett asked. "If you want to deal with me, we need a certain level of honesty first."

Fitzwarren smiled. Reaching down, he pulled a knife from his boot and one from a guard hidden beneath a sleeve. Handing them over, he said. "Don't lose them."

Satisfied, Bennett waved a hand in the air. "Go on, lads, wait outside. You'll hear me if I want you."

Fitzwarren stepped to one side, allowing Bennett's men to exit the room; the man Pete closed the door.

"We are alone, as you requested," Bennett said, settling back in his chair. "So tell me, why have you brought me this wretch."

"I believe he has a value to you," Fitzwarren said simply.

Bennett's hand thumped hard on the chair arm, and he laughed loudly. "He is wanted for Treason and Heresy, sir. Myles Devereux has value now only as candle tallow – he'll burn in this world before he burns in Hell."

"That might be the case, however, I believe that you might have had difficulty recovering the location of his wealth from Matthew, am I right?" Fitzwarren said evenly. Crossing the room, he stood next to Myles. Myles moved quickly to the other end of the coffer, his bound hands on the edge, and he tried to use it to ram it into Fitzwarren.

Fitzwarren, laughing, sidestepped the sliding coffer. "You think bruising my knees might be an advantage to you?"

Myles cursed, giving the coffer another angry push before rising and standing with his back to the wall.

"Still has quite a temper," Fitzwarren remarked. "You have Matthew, am I right?"

Bennett inclined his head but said instead, "How would he persuade him to tell me. Surely Devereux can tell me himself?"

Fitzwarren shook his head. "If only it was that simple. Even Myles Devereux doesn't know where his wealth is; the only man who does is Matthew."

Bennett leaned forward in his chair, his eyes fixed on Devereux's face enjoying the look of pure anger he was bestowing on Fitzwarren. "Is this true?"

Myles ignored the question.

"It is, and if you bring Matthew here, I can get him to tell you where Devereux's money is," Fitzwarren said evenly.

"How?" Bennett demanded, his right hand tightening on the top of a carved lion's foot.

"I'd have nothing left to trade if I told you that," Fitzwarren said, "Just bring him here, and I will prove the truth of my words very quickly."

"And what do you want?" Bennett demanded.

"A portion of the money, what else?" Fitzwarren said. "I have Devereux, but he's only the lock; you have Matthew, who is the key. A certain amount of unwelcome cooperation is required."

"I have them both; if you'd not noticed, you are trapped here with my men outside. So I have both the lock and the key in my possession," Bennett said slyly.

"But you need to know how to apply the key to the lock, and that information is in here," Fitzwarren tapped his head. "I warrant that you've failed so far to have Matthew tell you where to find Devereux's money, you need this small piece of the puzzle to get Matthew to tell you. And he will tell you, if you bring him here, it will not take long."

"Very well," Bennett hefted his bulky body from the chair. Crossing the room, he opened the door and exchanged quick words with one of his men on the other side before returning to his chair.

"Could it be that you are a puppet?" Bennett said to Myles, a meaty finger tapping his chin.

Myles, fury still burning in his eyes, glared back at Bennett.

Bennett laughed. "Oh, so that is the truth of it. Matthew's the master, and he'd let you burn for him."

Myles cursed under his breath, dropping his eyes to the floor.

There was the briefest of knocks at the door, then it opened, and Matthew, bound at the wrists, battered and with dried blood caking one side of his face, was pushed through the door. Bennett waved the man who had brought him away, and the door closed, leaving the four of them alone.

"Well then, you have the lock and the key; show me how they work," Bennett said, his voice low, the threat obvious.

"First, we need to agree on a price?" Fitzwarren said, amiably.

"A price!" Bennett spluttered.

Myles picked that moment to dive for the door hammering twice on it with his bound fists before Fitzwarren pulled him away. The door burst open, and three of Bennett's men fell into the room.

"Lads, it's alright; that fool Devereux thought he could escape. Leave us," Bennett said, waving the men away again.

Matthew was staring between Myles and Fitzwarren through his one good eye, the other closed and swollen.

"My price is twenty pounds," Fitzwarren stated simply.

"Twenty pounds!" Bennett repeated disbelief in his voice, his eyes wide.

"It is only a small portion of his wealth," Fitzwarren pointed towards Matthew.

Bennett's fingers drummed on the lion's claw for a moment. "Alright, laddie, then I agree. Twenty pounds when, and only when, I have all of the money."

"Of course," Fitzwarren said, smiling.

"Get on with it, then," Bennett said gruffly, sitting back in his chair.

Fitzwarren rounded the end of the coffer where Myles still stood, his back against the wall. "Are you ready for this?" Fitzwarren asked.

The bonds dropped from Myles' wrists, and in his right hand was a blade that he passed to Fitzwarren. Before Bennett could rise, it was levelled at his chest, and Myles, his hands against the coffer, slid it across the doorway. When it was in place, he pushed Matthew onto it, and began to cut the rope from his wrists.

"You bastard, you'll not get out of here alive!" Bennett cursed his hands, white-knuckled, grasped at the lion's feet.

"It's been said before," Fitzwarren replied. "Now, out of that chair and against that wall. I'd wager you've a blade or worse in there somewhere."

The colour rose to Bennett's cheeks.

"Move!" Fitzwarren said, nothing of pleasantness in his voice.

Matthew and Myles had pulled another coffer across the floor to bolster the first.

"That's not going to stop my lads," growled Bennett making his way towards the wall.

"It won't have to in a minute," Myles said. Matthew rocked Bennett's chair back, and Myles, leaning down, pulled out two poniards, handing one to Matthew.

"Do you recall what I said about surprises?" Myles said, standing in front of Bennett.

"You came back for him?" Bennett said, gesturing towards Matthew.

"No, I came back to find out who murdered my book-keeper," Myles said, the blade flashing in his hand.

Bennett laughed. "You think that will save you from the flames?"

"Talk with him later! We are leaving," Fitzwarren pushed Bennett towards the back of the old bakery. Behind them, they could hear a sudden commotion and shouts from the front of Bennett's shop.

"Go, now!" Fitzwarren then ordered Matthew, "There's a door between the two ovens to the yard; it won't be guarded anymore, but that'll not be the case for long."

The passage between the two bread ovens was narrow, and Bennett feigning an inability to fit, stopped. "I canna' you idiot!"

"Oh, you can! Breathe in, Master Bennett," Myles advised, pressing the cold point of a knife into one of Bennett's rounded buttocks. There was a yelp, and then Bennett moved quickly along the passage. The door at the end, unlocked, led to a small yard, and the gate to that was open and beyond that freedom. Bennett found himself quickly bundled into the back of a waiting wagon as smoke rolled over the top of the bakery filling the yard. Shouts from the street at the front of the bakery and voices raised in panic could be heard.

The bakery was on fire.

"Surprise!" Myles Devereux said, sitting down next to Bennett, the knife still in his hand and a broad grin on his face.

CHAPTER TWENTY-FIVE

The journey was short, and Bennett had no idea where he was. A grain sack was dropped over his head as he was pulled from the wagon and thrust through a door. When it was whipped from his head, he found himself facing Myles Devereux in a small non-descript room; the only other man present was Matthew.

"You will note, Master Bennett, that your hands are not tied," Myles Devereux said without humour.

"Hah! Are you trying to tell me I am free to leave?" Garrison Bennett shot back, dusting flour from the sack from his doublet front.

"Of course, after our negotiations are complete, you can leave. Indeed I will make sure you are delivered safely into the arms of your concerned men," Myles said, "I have already asked the question I want the answer to – who killed my book-keeper and why?"

"Well, then. Tha's two questions, not just the one, isn't it?" Bennett snarled back, coughing as he ran his hands over his head and dislodged more of the finely ground wheat.

Myles folded his arms. "I'm not averse to making you look the same way Matthew does. It's a simple enough question, and in return, you gain your liberty."

"You expect me to believe that?" Bennett snapped, dusting his shoulders and sneezing loudly.

"Oh yes, because as much as it pains me to admit it, I am going to need you," Myles replied, his long fingers twisting the blade. "I do not have a liking for having my heels torched, and I wish to deliver to Justice Daytrew the man responsible for murdering my book-keeper and papering London with his Protestant slander."

Bennett's eyes narrowed. "An' how would I help wi' tha'?"

"Very simply. I would imagine that you know who he is, and you provided men to aid him for a fee. I'm not asking for you to tie yourself to the murders, just to say that this man asked you, and being a good citizen, you didn't want to be involved in this foul plot, and so you turned him down. As simple as that. I'm asking you only to identify Ad-Hyce," Myles explained patiently.

"An' you think I would do tha'?" Bennett spat back; any softness the Scots lilt had once added to his words was gone, his voice raised now, bore the threat of the Highlander.

Myles slid his hand inside his doublet and pulled out the burnt-stained sheet. "This was your doing, and I've found men who would confirm that. Now surely you wouldn't want that becoming common knowledge?"

Bennett glared at the paper. Myles, smiling, folded it back up and tucked it away again. "So there is the bargain. Liberty for lies and silence."

"How do I know you won't use that anyway?" Bennett said.

Myles shrugged. "You don't. But you could rescind your testimony and that would make life difficult for me."

"You've just torched my shop; I'll like to make your life more than difficult; I'm goin' to make it bloody short," Bennett growled back.

Myles smiled maliciously. "Singed perhaps, but not burnt down, nothing a decent thatcher can't fix. So, do we have a deal?"

"Do I have a choice?" Bennett growled, like a trapped animal, his eyes roved around the room, seeking any escape.

"A very final one, yes," Myles said, the blade in his hand. "And there are three men outside that door, including Matthew, who I have no doubt has a score to settle. Well?"

Bennett glared at Myles. "You're awash with sin, Devereux, even if I do as you ask, there's a fair chance I'll get to see them strap faggots around yer legs. Quite an entertainment now tha' they'll no longer put a powder bag around yer neck to finish yer off."

Myles let out a long breath. "If I fail, then you will get your entertainment, and if you think that is the way it will go, you've very little to lose by telling me who killed Galveston and why."

Bennett seemed to consider this for a moment. "An' what's to say another tattle-tale won't lead them back to ye?"

"If I hear that tattling voice is linked to you, then your production of that Heresy will become known, and I shall leave that information safe with my lawyer …."

Bennett cut Myles off, laughing. "Yer lawyer! I can see how much yer think of yerself."

"Come now, Bennett, they are a business necessity in our current world and don't forget you have your own. What's his name? Ah yes, I remember Clement, a lawyer by name but not, it has to be said, by reputation," Myles said, grinning, then his voice cold, he demanded. "Do we have an agreement?"

Bennett scowled at him, and folded his arms across the top of his stomach, regarding Devereux with a cold expression. "Your book-keeper was the brother of Hester Ad-Hyce, a bloody foolish preacher bent on trying to uproot the Catholic church from England. Galveston was fed up of being forced to fund his idiot brother's schemes, and when he refused to give him any more money, then Hester had to do something else. He knew who Galveston worked for, and when he found out he couldn't get his hands on your gold in any great quantity, he forced Galveston to tell him how he could profit from the situation. Galveston, unfortunately, told his brother that I'd be the one man in London who would be happy to see the back of you."

"So your men did kill Galveston and the Hesketh's?" Myles said.

"No, I think we'll say that once your book-keeper had been forced to tell his brother how he could profit from you, he killed him. He could hardly leave him alive to warn his master, could he?" Bennett said he'd dropped his arms from his stomach and linked them behind him, stepping slowly across the back of the small room as he spoke. "The fool brought me a page from your ledger to prove he had connections with you and that his brother had given him the idea of a scheme that would rid London of you."

"A scheme? What was it?" Myles pressed.

"Bloody simple," Bennett continued to roam across the small room as he spoke. "There were people in his way, and Galveston had told him how to tie the murders to you, all I had to do was pay him."

"The Hesketh's?" Myles said bitterly.

Bennett shook his head. "Not my doing, although I was being kept appraised of what was happening, and there was a possibility to place the blame for the murders at your door; how could I resist. He'd shown me the sheet he had from your ledger and told me he'd leave a portion of it with each of the bodies. It would look like you'd killed them for a debt. All he wanted was gold."

"He placed the ledger sheet in her mouth," Myles asked.

"I had a man there to ensure he kept his side of the bargain. Half was in her mouth, the rest was in her son's, but that seems to have been washed away, at least it wasn't found with his body," Bennett said, stopping his traverse in the middle of the room, and facing Devereux. "So it looked as if you'd killed all three. Very satisfying."

"You couldn't leave it there, though, could you," Myles said, a degree of bitterness had crept into his voice.

"I wouldn't have wanted to leave it to chance, and, as I said, the river stole one of the clues he left for Daytrew," Bennett finished. "If I'm honest, I got the idea from Hester, I knew Preston the printer was dead, and you had been foolish enough to visit him before his death, so by chance, you tied yourself to his murder as well. Hester didn't want his scheme stopped, with a charge for Heresy being brought against him, so he had to get rid of the printer. After you were linked to Preston's death, I had the idea to do a little printing of my own."

"And you added treason to my list of crimes!" Myles said bitterly.

Bennett laughed, throwing his arms wide and stepping towards Devereux. "Treason and Heresy. My old da' always said if you are going to do a job, do it right. Come on, Daytrew was being too slow; this was a surer way of clearing the shit out of my path. The Queen has a particular reputation for dealing with such sinners. How did you find out?"

"I have my ways?" Myles replied carefully, not about to be drawn into a conversation on the topic; it had, after all, been based on a guess. A good one, but a guess nonetheless.

"I would bet your source is that nobleman who dragged you into my presence, who has now conveniently disappeared. He's in your pocket, isn't he?. How much does he owe you?" Bennett said nastily, his meaty hands, balled in fists, were on his hips, and he leaned slightly towards Devereux.

"He hasn't disappeared. He's outside. And not everything in my life revolves around bribery," Myles replied coldly.

"I would very much doubt that. Who is he? You might as well tell me; I will find out," Bennett said, "I, too, have ma' ways."

"I'll leave you to find out, I think. Back to business, do we have a deal?" Myles said, changing the subject to the matter he wanted to discuss. "I will have a hold over you as you will over me. And .... you leave with your life. Just agree and tell me where I can find Hester Ad-Hyce?"

"Not very much of a choice, is it?" Bennett said, his voice had lost its edge of temper, and there was a sudden note of defeat in his tone; he flung his arms wide and took a shuffling step closer to Devereux.

Myles leaning backward, banged on the door behind him twice. It opened immediately, and Matthew and Fitzwarren entered.

"Still fancy your chances against me?" Myles said, aware of what had been going through Bennett's mind. He was by far the bigger man, and a life of violence would have given him plenty of tricks to disarm Devereux, that, and he was desperate.

"Fair play isn't in your blood, is it?" Bennett spat, stepping backwards.

"Fair play," Myles exploded. "You've branded me with two murders, probably three, and tarred me with treason and heresy. Where, exactly, is your sense of fair play?"

"The bloody Kings Arms, you've moved into my streets, tried to take my business ....."

Fitzwarren stepped between them. "Gentlemen, you digress. Bennett, does Devereux have a deal .... or not? I don't care either way, and I have other business that claims my time, so a swift answer would, on this occasion, be appreciated."

Bennett's furious eyes locked with Fitzwarren's cold stare. "I'll find you ...."

"Yes .... yes .... and have me torn limb from limb, fed to the dogs, etcetera. Contain your fury, Bennett. Does Devereux have a deal?" there was a short double-edged blade in Fitzwarren's hand. "Yes .... or no?"

Bennett's eyes flicked between the blade and Fitzwarren's hard indifferent grey eyes. "You leave me little choice."

The knife didn't move, Fitzwarren said simply. "Answer my question? Yes or no."

There was a moment's silence. Bennett's eyes never left Fitzwarren's. Then he nodded slightly before he spoke. "Yes, you have a deal. Ad-Hyce is lodging at The Bell Tavern last I heard."

Fitzwarren's face broke into a broad smile, and he clapped Bennett on the arm. "Well, done. A good choice well made." The knife, Myles noted, had not disappeared. "Devereux, can you arrange for Master Bennett to be reunited with his fellows after we have proved the validity of his words."

"I can indeed," Myles said with some satisfaction.

"You're going to leave me 'ere? I thought we had a deal?" Bennett growled, anger replaced caution and he stepped towards Fitzwarren and felt the sudden prick of the blade through his shirt.

"Don't!" Fitzwarren warned.

"Heed his advice, Bennett, he's a bloody nasty cur when he wants to be," Myles said, clearly enjoying this final twist in the negotiations.

"You will gain your freedom when we've tracked down Ad-Hyce, and not before," Fitzwarren said, forcing Bennett to the back of the room before they left, closing and bolting the door behind them.

CHAPTER TWENTY-SIX

"I'm going to cut that bastard's throat," Matthew growled, underlining his sentence with a fist, pounding on the table. Myles, along with Fitzwarren and Matthew, were seated around a table at the merchant's house where he'd found Fitzwarren.

"Matthew, there's not a lot of time. We can ponder Bennett's demise at our leisure later. The Bell Tavern isn't far from St Bride's in Fleet Street, which fits in well with our friends printing pastime. Fitzwarren, you have a dozen of my men here. To your knowledge, have any of them left this house?" Myles said, laying a calming hand on Matthew's arm.

Fitzwarren shook his head. "They're keeping a twenty-four hour guard on the house, working in four shifts. When not on duty, they are available should they be needed. I have a good man in charge of them."

Myles nodded. "I hope you are right. That should mean, if they have been here for the last week at least, they won't know that there is a warrant for my arrest."

"True. But, Devereux, you can't take them. I need this house under guard. I'll lend you what help I can, but this house and its occupants are my priority," Fitzwarren said firmly, his eyes as hard as flint.

"I don't want them all. Two should be enough to sniff out Ad-Hyce at the Bell. What do you think?" Myles suggested, elbows on the table leaning towards Fitzwarren. "We find him and deliver him to Daytrew, and Bennett confirms his involvement with the murders."

"As ever, Devereux, you have an ability to make it sound so very simple," Fitzwarren said, rising.

Myles grinned. "Let's hope it is."

"I will make some arrangements and get two of your men. It has been a long day already. Perhaps a meal at the Bell is in order," Fitzwarren said a little wearily.

"I'm not staying," Myles said, standing quickly and making the chair rock behind him. "I'm sorry, Matthew, you'll have to stop here. Even with your face looking like that, you are too well-known around the city."

"And you aren't?" Matthew said, rising as well. "There are men across London looking for you. You can't go?"

"I'm going. Matthew, this man holds my life in his hands; I am not stopping here and trusting the venture to others," Myles said, his eyes alight with anger.

"Your confidence, as ever, in my abilities heartens me," Fitzwarren's words were laden with sarcasm.

"I trust you. But I'll not stop here and wait while my fate is decided," Myles said vehemently.

Fitzwarren clapped Myles on the shoulder. "Well then, we had better perform another deception."

The Bell Tavern was opposite St Bride's church on Fleet Street, a haven for the printing apprentices, their masters and clients alike. A busy tavern that served food from the start to the end of the day.

"You hate this, don't you?" Myles whispered into Fitzwarren's ear as they approached the tavern.

Fitzwarren sighed. "Not at all, Mistress. Your charms are beyond compare."

Richard Fitzwarren, with Myles Devereux on his arm, wearing one of Anne Carter's best dresses, entered the Bell Tavern where ahead of them, already eating a meal, were two of Myles' men. Stepping through the doorway, they halted; an attentive innkeeper instantly assessing the cost of their apparel banged his hip against a table end in his haste to reach them before they changed their minds and left.

"Sir, welcome to the humble Bell Tavern. I'm Jake Denton, landlord, and can I suggest the table near the fire? 'Tis cold outside, and the lady might appreciate the warmth," Jake Denton said, swinging an arm towards the fire and a table.

"Indeed, that would be appreciated," Fitzwarren replied. "Lead the way."

Jake scuttled across the tavern before them, extracting a cloth from his apron front, he attempted to remove the worst of the previous occupant's meal from the table, pulled out the chairs, and Fitzwarren and Myles pretended not to notice the detritus of crumbs, crusts and ale stains on the oak table.

"Right then, sir, what can I be getting you an' the lady," Jake said, feeding some additional logs onto the dwindling fire.

"What would you recommend?" Fitzwarren asked.

Myles wasn't listening; his eyes were roving around the room. At the opposite end, he found his two men seated together, alert and paying more attention to the inn than the pies and ale set before them. Three grey-haired men, their heads topped with expensive plumed bonnets, sat around a table; before them was a printed sheet that was the subject of the discussion. Two young boys entered and went straight towards a serving woman they evidently knew. She smiled at them, ruffling the hair on the head of one of the lads; she disappeared and reappeared a moment later with two wrapped bundles. The boys, it seemed, had been sent to collect lunch for their masters.

".... the pies are excellent, and the pheasant .... " Jake was saying to Fitzwarren.

Two younger men, their meal finished, the trenchers pushed to one side, were engaged in a dice game. The bone cubes rattled on the table between them. The man on the right laughed painfully loudly when he won, the sound in the small room making Devereux wince. Christ, was there any need? The look on the other man's face told him he was in agreement with Myles.

".... I shall take the pheasant and the game pie for my wife .... You like a pie don't you my sweet ..." Fitzwarren said, elbowing his wife and winking at Jake as he slipped a coin into his hand.

Myles attempted not to scowl at him and almost managed, and tucking his cloth into his apron, Jake grinned back at Fitzwarren. "I'll get them brought out right away."

"Was there any need?" Myles said under his breath as Jake headed back across the bar.

Fitzwarren, ignoring Myles, called across the room towards Jake. "And whatever you have to drink that you can recommend."

Jake turned and bowed clumsily in their direction and asked hopefully. "Wine?"

"The bottle!" Fitzwarren shot back, smiling.

"You can pay for this travesty, do you hear me?" Myles said through gritted teeth.

"Oh, shush, just remember I am helping you," Fitzwarren said, obviously enjoying the situation, "Oh, watch out, my sweet, Jake's back!"

"I'm sure you'll enjoy this," Jake set down two dented pewter goblets and poured wine reverently into each one. "It's a fine tipple."

Fitzwarren picked up the wine, sipped, and nodded in appreciation, smacking his lips. Satisfied, Jake put the bottle down and retreated towards the kitchen.

Myles picked up his cup, his eyes watching the inn room carefully over the rim and tipped the liquid into his mouth. His eyes widened, he gagged, and the wine shot from between his lips.

"Oh, my dear! You're choking," Fitzwarren said, rising from his chair and taking the clumsy goblet from Myles' hand, he thumped him hard on the back. "There, is that better?"

Myles glared at Fitzwarren. "How did you drink that shit?"

Fitzwarren grinned. "I didn't."

As Myles watched, Fitzwarren emptied the battered goblet on the floor before refilling it, "Come on, I need to empty this bottle."

Myles, scowling, picked up his over-filled drink, a quantity slopping over the rim, drew it towards himself and dumped the contents on the filthy, matted floor rushes.

"Jake? Jake?" Fitzwarren called across the tavern to attract the landlord's attention; raising the empty bottle in the air, he waggled it.

Jake, understanding the gesture, a pleased expression on his face, disappeared to get another, arriving back at their table.

"Thank you, I always apprethiate a good wine," Fitzwarren said, slurring his words slightly and taking the bottle.

The meals arrived soon. Devereux picked at his plate, redistributing the contents but eating nothing.

"Not hungry?" Fitzwarren asked, grinning.

"My current woes are sufficient. I don't feel the need to add a bad stomach to them," Myles replied, pushing the crust of a broken pie across the wooden trencher. A slight smile lit his face. Taking a piece of the pastry in his right hand, he lowered it beneath the table and whistled; the tasty morsel was spotted by a terrier that wound its way between the stool and table legs at speed. Making sure no one was looking, he tipped the trencher, sending the rest of the pie to the floor; the fatty lumps of meat and pastry were gone in five rapid gulps.

Fitzwarren shook his head, sending his own plateful to the floor. "Poor animal."

Jake, looking pleased, arrived a few minutes later to collect the empty trenchers. "I knew you'd enjoy them, sir."

"Indeed, exthelent fayre, another bottle if you could," Fitzwarren slurred, patting his stomach.

Jake arrived back and began to fill Fitwarren's pewter goblet.

"You mighth be able to help me with something, actually," Fitzwarren said, watching the wine pour from the bottle, an oily film swirling on the top.

"If I can, sir, I gladly would," Jake replied.

"My wife's couthin workth in a printers hereabouts. I wondered if I could slip a coin to one of the ladth to find him rather than us tramp the streets," Fitzwarren said, pulling the wine towards him.

"I know most of the print shops in the Fleet and around 'ere; it might be that I could tell you myself," Jake said helpfully.

"Well, we would be most grateful. Wath was his surname, sweetheart, it'th a damnable mouthful I never remember it," Fitzwarren asked across the table.

"Ad-Hyce, it's Welsh, I believe," Myles replied, his voice sickly sweet.

"Thatth it, Adth-Hath," Fitzwarren said, punctuating his sentence with a loud hiccup.

Jake shook his head, his expression showing genuine sadness. "An unusual name, one I've not heard before."

"Wath was his first name, darling?" Fitzwarren said quickly.

"Hester," Myles replied.

"Hether Adth-Hath, that's right," Fitzwarren said happily.

"We have a Hester lodging here, I'm not sure which printer he works for, and I not know him as a Welshman though," Jake said, his voice hopeful.

"Hith family are from Walth, but he'th never lived there, so I doubt he doesn't have the lilt of the Welsh," Fitzwarren slurred. "What's he look like?"

Jake shrugged, his face creased as he tried to think of something to say, then it brightened. "About your age, sir, but not as tall, brown hair and always very neat. He's a hardworking man, sir, and was very upset by what happened to his employer. Master

Preston, did you hear about it? He's been in here a time or two in the past?"

"Do tell, what happened?" Fitzwarren asked, leaning across the table towards Jake.

"Poor man was found dead with his brains leaking out. Poor Hester had to find another master, he was very upset by the news. I'd seen Master Preston a few times in here with Hester, lovely man. Who would do such a thing?"

"That'th awful, poor man," Fitzwarren lamented.

"I know, sir. The streets are not as safe as they once were. When I was a lad were all our doors were unlocked, and our neighbours were our friends, but now .... well .... you just don't know," Jake said, shaking his head sadly.

"Indeed. I think your Hethter is our man, I can recall my wife mentioning he worked for a man called Presthton, isn't that right my sweet," Fitzwarren said, leaning across the table and taking one of Devereux's hands in his.

Myles just nodded, and tried not to pull his hand from Fitzwarren's hold.

"Is he here now?" Fitzwarren asked.

"Usually comes back around six. Shall I tell Hester you were looking for him? What name should I give?" Jack offered helpfully.

"No need. We'd like to surprise him. Reserve me this table for tonight, and we'll come back at sixth," Fitzwarren fished in his purse and handed the coins to Jake.

Jake looked at the silver coins, delight plain on his face. "Of course, sir. I'll keep this table free and have a good fire for when you return."

When they returned, Jake approached them across the tavern. "I'm sorry, sir. Hester returned early tonight and wanted to take a meal in his room. I knew of your intentions and tried to dissuade him; I didn't give you away, but I said he might enjoy a pleasant surprise if he took his meal by the fire tonight."

"Where did he go," Fitzwarren said, his voice steel-like, held not a trace of the drunk of a few hours ago, and behind him, two of Myle's men loitered a few steps away.

"To his room, he was not happy; I'm sorry, sir," Jake said, his brow creased, realising he was unlikely to profit for more overpriced wine and food.

"Which room is it?" Fitzwarren, his arm hooked through Jake's, was leading him towards the stairs at the back of the tavern.

A flicker of doubt clouded Jake's face.

"Which room?" Fitzwarren demanded again.

Jake swallowed hard and said, "At the end of the passage, on your right, the last door."

"You with me. You stop with Devereux," Fitzwarren issued orders to Myles' men.

Myles, furious, stepped forwards. "I'll be damned if I will."

The four men, one holding his skirts high, tramped up the steps. The corridor was only wide enough for one man. Fitzwarren hammered on the door at the end of the passage.

No answer.

His fist hammered on the door a second time.

"Break it in," Myles shouted from the rear.

Fitzwarren, kicked it hard and took an immediate step back, having no intention of meeting a blade on the other side. No weapon offered a greeting, only an empty room, cold, the grate a mess of ashes, the bed empty and the windows shuttered against the London weather.

Myles was trying to push by his men from the rear when he heard Fitzwarren say. "We've been duped; this room's not in use."

Myles stopped. His fury that had been directed towards the room swung around a hundred and eighty degrees and hauled him in a blind run back towards the innkeeper, Jake. A man emerging from a room on the right blocked his passage.

"Out of my way," Myles growled, extending an arm to shove the man aside. His hand connected with the man's shoulder, pushing him back; Myles turned sideways to pass him and looked directly into his eyes, one of which was crested by a severed brow.

Myles' mouth formed the word, "You!" as the man dived for the stairs.

Devereux flung himself after him, taking two steps that got him to the top of the stairs, the third should have landed on the top step caught in the folders of Anne Carter's best dress, and Myles, arms flung out before him, flew down the stairs head first.

When Myles came to, he was propped against a wall in the taproom of the Bell, and Richard Fitzwarren was leaning over him. "Can you stand, sweetheart, or should I carry you?"

Myles, a hand on the wall, tried to push himself upright. Fitzwarren caught his wrist and pulled him up. "Daytrew has been summoned. Take one of your men and get out of here."

"What about Ad-Hyce?" Myles said, trying to find him in the room

"He's there," Fitzwarren stepped sideways and behind him, seated on a chair with a knife levelled at his chest by one of his men, was Hester Ad-Hyce. He was as white as river ice, his brow bore a sheen of sweat, and tears had run down his face. "You've knocked his shoulder from its socket, and he's in a lot of pain, one I can sympathise with as it happens."

"I need him …. he needs to tell …. I can't …." Myles tried to start the sentence three times and failed.

"Don't worry. I accidentally trod on Ad-Hyce's shoulder, and he's told everyone in here about his printing schemes and how he killed Preston with a lever from his press. Go, your presence would only …. complicate things," Fitzwarren said and gestured to one of Myles' men. As Myles walked on unsteady feet up the street away from The Bell, he was passed by Daytrew's creaking litter, held between four sweating men and on its way to the tavern.

Myles, back at the White Hart, secure in his room, with a sizeable guard deployed by Matthew, waited. All the pieces of the puzzle were laid at Daytrew's door, but the question was would he order them correctly. Or would the fool ignore what was before him and still hunt for Devereux. Was the evidence against him too convenient to overlook? Would they believe Bennett? What if they didn't question him?

Myles was unable to sit still, he roved around the room, he had once loved the sanctuary of it, and now it felt like a prison. The huge bed in the middle getting in his way as he wandered from one end to the other. The shutters were open, and he could see into the yard below, hear if anyone arrived. Would it be Daytrew with his men again? Should he have gone elsewhere and waited for the outcome? It might have been safer.

The gates to the White Hart that normally stood open, had been closed, and Myles heard the noise of them opening. Returning to the window, hands on the sill, his breath held, Myles gazed down into the yard.

It was Fitzwarren.

Myles, unable to wait, met him on the stairs.

Fitzwarren smiled as he took the steps two at a time. "You have the luck of Odysseus, it seems. Hester, realising he was fast in a trap, had little choice but to twist what he had left for his cause."

Myles frowned, he was backing up the stairs towards the empty outer room, pushing the door open for them both. "What do you mean?"

"I told you before, the fault of the radical is they need to pin their names to their actions. Ad-Hyce had put his name to his declarations against the church, not to throw the hounds a false trail and lead them to his brother, but to tell the world he was God's messenger on earth," Fitzwarren said, entering the room and closing the door behind him.

"Did Daytrew believe him?" Myles asked, quickly, relief plain on his face.

Fitzwarren nodded, and put a hand on Myles' shoulder. "Hester Ad-Hyce has already adopted the role of martyr."

"What did he say?" Myles asked.

"Interestingly, he had taken the bills that your clerk wrote out for Preston, he didn't want a link discovering between Galveston and the printer at that point. If he had not been discovered, he would have helped to dispose of you, and with Bennett's gold he could have continued to work at the printers and produce his declarations against the church. He didn't want to limit himself to spreading his message around a small portion of London. His plan had been to use the money to produce hundreds of these and then to take them to other cities," Fitzwarren explained.

"So that's where they went," Myles said.

"They didn't actually go anywhere, he burnt them in the fire at Galveston's," Fitzwarren said, then added, "And your money, Ad-Hyce called every Sunday, and took the half-crown from Galveston."

"That's why he bought two pies from the Havelock, the poor bastard even bought his murderous brother a meal every week!" Myles said, genuine shock in his voice.

"It seems so. The money he used to buy paper, but it wasn't enough. Hester knew it would take years to accumulate enough to buy the paper he needed to print enough sheets to widely distribute his message. He knew Galveston worked for you, and had access to your money, but when he found out Galveston couldn't steal him enough, he forced him to tell him how he could profit from you. All Galveston could think of was to produce a scheme to dispose of you and he knew Bennett would pay for that," Fitzwarren said.

"And then he killed him, his own brother, who had been helping him?" Myles said, disbelief in his voice.

"I don't think Galveston was a willing participant in the scheme, I would guess he was terrified of his brother, and with good reason." Fitzwarren said.

Myles' brow furrowed for a moment. "He was more worried about what his brother would do to him than what I would do to him if his deception had been discovered?"

Fitzwarren laughed. "I know it's a disappointment, but unfortunately it's true. It seems he'd already resolved to dispose of Danny Hesketh, the fool had overcharged him to nail his messages up, and it also seems he'd carried out less than half of their bargain. I suspect Danny nailed a few up and then burnt the rest."

"And his mother knew about them and Hester?" Myles asked.

"He wasn't sure, but suspected there was a good chance Danny had confided in his mother, he'd told the butcher so he probably had, and it was a chance Hester couldn't take. Not if he was going to launch his scheme across the whole of England," Fitzwarren said.

"That was his plan?" Myles said.

Fitzwarren nodded. "It seems so. He was going to print hundreds, then take them himself across England and make sure they appeared in every city."

"And Bennett? Did Daytrew go to see him?" Myles asked.

"He did, but if I am honest, his testimony isn't really that crucial. Hester wants to die a martyr and he would not wish his actions to be attributed to another."

"Even murder?" Myles said, his voice incredulous.

"Even murder. God, he feels, will forgive him, and ensure the safe passage through heaven of the souls of those whose lives were sacrificed for the true word of God," Fitzwarren said.

"Well, God might forgive him, but I bloody won't," Myles said, annoyance in his voice.

"I'll take my leave, I don't think the Sheriff will be interested in you any longer," Fitzwarren said, turning towards the door.

"Are you going to tell me why my men are providing a guard on a merchants house, or is that going to remain a mystery?" Myles asked.

"I thought you knew me better than to ask that question again," Fitzwarren said, a slight smile twisting one corner of his mouth.

"A mystery then!" Myles replied wearily.

Fitzwarren stepped towards the door then paused. "Your brother was a man I was lucky enough to count amongst my friends, for him, I will always help you. I hold my friends close, and you should as well, Christian Carter is one of those, and my actions have brought trouble to his door."

"Trouble follows you, Fitzwarren," Myles needing to say something, said, a little too flippantly.

"I think, you'll find, it steps in both our shadows," Fitzwarren said, turning and opening the door.

CHAPTER TWENTY-SEVEN

Three days later, Myles, accompanied by a full complement of his men, arrived outside the Sheriff's office. Dismounting, he discarded the reins and made his way up the steps and ignored the clerk seated at the desk. The clerk watched, open-mouthed, as Devereux banged three times on the Sheriff's door with the polished silver handle of his riding whip.

Myles smiled at the clerk briefly and returned his attention to the door as he heard a voice cursing on the other side.

The door whipped open. "I told you I was not to be .... Master Devereux!"

"The same!" Myles said, stepping inside the office.

"I am returning this," Myles dumped a cloak into the Sheriff's arms. I believe the issue of Anne Hesketh's murder has been resolved?"

"Err .... Indeed. Justice Daytrew apprehended the man responsible for her murder and several other .... crimes," the Sheriff replied haltingly, disposing of the cloak onto the end of his desk.

"And would it have not been polite to have at the very least informed me of this?" Myles spoke loudly near the open door for not only the benefit of the Sheriff but also for those listening in the office outside.

"I would have thought the news would have reached you soon enough," the Sheriff said, attempting to regain control of the hopeless situation.

"Well, it didn't, and I shall not readily forget," Myles Devereux said, slamming the door in the face of the Sheriff before striding through the outer office to reclaim his horse.

Myles' bed felt comfortable again now that the hounds had found a different scent. The shutters were open on the London night, a sky, pricked with stars and a waning moon filled the window. The cold of the night was banished from the room by the blaze in the hearth, cut logs crackled and orange flames danced along their lengths.

Myles closed his eyes. His breathing was steady and even. Sleep not far away.

A yowl, sudden, piercing and urgent yanked him away from the oblivion of slumber. Propping himself up on his elbows he scanned the room.

Nothing.

Had he imagined it?

The only noise came from the busy flames as they caressed the wood. Dropping back into the embrace of his bed Myles closed his eyes again.

The yowl was repeated again.

More awake this time, he had a sense that it was coming from outside the window and he knew the cause of it. Pressing his head into the pillow, Myles ignored the now persistent caterwaul.

Myles gave in before the cat did.

Cursing, he slid from the bed and advanced towards the open shutters. The rooms dim orange light from the fire was caught in the wide eyes of a feline sitting on the sill. It's sleek black fur was wet and straggly, droplets of water drooped its whiskers and dripped from its nose.

Myles glowered at the cat. Reaching for the shutters he began to close them on the animal.

Yowl.

Myles stopped. His eyes locked with those of the cat. Cursing, he pushed the shutters back.

"If you scratch me, I'll throw you in to the yard!" Myles scooped the cat up and dropped it on the rug in front of the fire before sliding back into his bed.

In the morning, dry, content and purring on the pillow next him, Myles found that he was sharing his bed with the cat.

Want More?
Follow the adventures of Richard Fitzwarren in the
Mercenary For Hire Series
By Sam Burnell

Sam Burnell

If you enjoyed this book why not help other readers out and share your thoughts with them so they can find a good historical fiction read.

The End

Printed in Great Britain
by Amazon